THE VICTORY CLUB

A CELEBRATION OF FRIENDSHIP, SECRETS AND
SECOND CHANCES

BUFFY ANDREWS

The Victory Club

A Celebration of Friendship, Secrets and Second Chances

© 2025 Buffy Andrews

All rights reserved.

Published by Andrews Creative Concepts

York, Pennsylvania 17404

Print ISBN: 979-8-9926396-2-9

Ebook ISBN: 979-8-9926396-3-6

~

To my mother—
whose love steadied me through every storm,
whose quiet strength shaped the core of who I am,
and whose spirit lingers in every line I write—
this is the echo of your laughter,
the warmth of your hand in mine,
the legacy you left in my heart.
Love you bunches and bunches, forever and always.

ALSO BY BUFFY ANDREWS

Psychological Thrillers

Samuel's Secret

The Perfect Husband

Women's Fiction

The Moment Keeper

The Memories We Keep

The Stone Giver

A Year of Second Chances

Our Fragile Hearts

Then Came Hope

Contemporary Romance

It's in the Stars

Class Acts: Gina and Mike

Class Acts: Sue and Tom

Class Acts: Tess and Jeremy

Young Adult

Ella's Rain

The Lion Awakens

Middle Grade

Freaky Frank

High Street Dares

Will, Middle Name Trouble

Picture Book

One Frog, Two Frogs, Three Frogs, Four

Coming Soon

THE SILENCE PROTOCOLS

A gripping psychological techno-thriller series tracing the cost of control—and the women who won't be written out.

PROLOGUE
1944 • HIGH & COOPER STREETS

The kitten shot out from under the porch like a drop of spilled milk, tail straight as a matchstick, paws skittering over the hard-packed dirt between High and Cooper. It darted past a stack of ration crates and a bicycle with a cardboard "V" whispering in its spokes.

Evie Gross saw it first, a white blur, a dare. She dropped her jump rope and ran.

At the far end of the alley, Dot Carter heard the yowl and followed, cautious at first, then fast. Her braids slapped her shoulders. Her father's lunch pail knocked her knee with every stride.

Maggie Thompson came in from the side yard, skirting the rows of beans in her mother's Victory Garden. The dirt was warm and crumbly between her toes. She'd lost one sandal by the lilacs and didn't have time to go back.

On the Thompson porch, the radio clicked and hummed, voices rising and fading with troop movements, then a pause, then hope. Every window was open to coax a breeze, and the air smelled of hot tar, sliced tomatoes, and the sharp bite of laundry soap.

"Left!" Evie shouted.

Dot cut across the packed earth and blocked the alley's mouth with her small body and the lunch pail like a shield. Maggie crouched low, hands open, voice soft, using the sounds meant for the shy and the scared.

The kitten hesitated, its nicked ear tilted, one paw lifted as if the smallest movement could hold back time.

"Easy," Maggie whispered.

Somewhere down the block, a screen door snapped. The radio found its voice again and began to read the names slowly and carefully. The girls didn't look up. Not yet. The kitten trembled, then leapt toward the waiting hands that didn't close, only waited.

Later, they would argue about who saw it first, who saved it, who named it. For now, they breathed in the same quick rhythm and listened as the radio spoke a name they knew, learning without yet realizing it the art of holding what trembled.

1

VICTORY CLUB, RENEWED

PRESENT • MANCHESTER MEADOWS

Manchester Meadows smelled of lemon polish and steamed carrots that morning, scents that clung to the halls as stubbornly as memory. Outside, maples traded patches of light with the glass panes, dappling the floor in shifting amber. The corridor hummed with the low murmur of voices, the squeak of rubber soles, and the steady roll of cart wheels carrying towels, pill cups, and routine.

Maggie Thompson sat near the edge of the common room, one heel hooked under the strap of her sensible shoe so it wouldn't slip free. She told herself, as she often did, that this arrangement was only temporary, just until the girls stopped worrying, just until her hip remembered its job again. A nurse passed with a bundle of towels, peppermint trailing in her wake, and Maggie pretended she didn't see the sympathetic glance.

Then it happened, a sound that broke through the quiet hum. A laugh. Clear, certain, and impossible to mistake.

Maggie startled, standing too quickly and catching herself on the back of the chair. Her hip complained, but she hardly noticed. The laugh came again, rising from the doorway like a bell rung in another lifetime. And there she was, Dot Carter, smaller than Maggie remembered but standing with the same unyielding tilt to her chin, like a question finally answered after too many years of silence.

"Dot?" Maggie whispered, as if the name itself might scatter the vision.

Dot's head tilted, eyes still sharp despite the years, and her hand flew to her chest. "Maggie Thompson. For heaven's sake."

They met in the middle of the rug, gripping one another's forearms the way church ladies did when they wanted to cry but refused to let tears undo them. Up close, Dot smelled faintly of lavender soap and the dry paper of books left too long on a shelf, like a library just before closing.

"What are you doing here?" Dot asked, her voice softening on the last word.

"Fell on the back steps in March. The girls won't let it go," Maggie admitted. "You?"

"My choice," Dot said, lifting her chin in that familiar old way. "Got tired of people fussing over my stairs."

They sat together, and though the room around them kept moving, carts rattling, aides coaxing patients, televisions buzzing faintly, something inside Maggie finally settled. It felt as if a missing chair had been slid back under her table.

A flutter at the courtyard window caught their eyes. A woman in a lavender cardigan bent toward the screen, speaking softly to a squirrel as though addressing a skittish child. She laughed, a quick, bright note, and the squirrel flicked its tail in response, as if the conversation made perfect sense.

Dot's fingers pressed into Maggie's sleeve. "Evie?"

The aide by the window turned, smiling in surprise. "You know Ms. Gross?"

"Since we were nine," Maggie said, already pushing herself to her feet. "Bring her in, please."

Moments later, Evie Gross appeared in the doorway, sunlight woven into her hair, eyes still the same fierce blue under the winter pale. She squinted at them for an instant, and then the years peeled away so quickly Maggie could almost feel the rush of it in her bones.

"Well, I'll be," Evie said, and her smile was the exact one from a thousand summer afternoons. It hovered, searching, then landed. "You two look like trouble."

"You took your time," Dot teased.

"I didn't know you were here." Evie's voice thinned for a beat. She glanced at the aide's badge, nodding as if to anchor the information somewhere it wouldn't slip away. "I didn't know where anyone was."

"We didn't either," Maggie said gently, taking Evie's hand. It was cooler than she expected but strong. "Seems we all drifted into the same harbor."

The three of them claimed a round table by the window. Light fell across their hands like a benediction. At first they spoke in the practical shorthand of age—knees, daughters, roofs, restless sleep—but gradually the words thinned, leaving room for the old shape of them to emerge.

Dot pointed at the activity board on the wall. "Look, Sock Hop Singalong: Songs of the '50s. Apparently we're living in poodle skirts this week."

Evie grinned. "Fitting. Some of our best bad ideas started then."

Maggie felt something click inside her, small and certain, like a drawer sliding home. "We should meet," she said, surprised by the firmness in her own voice. "Regularly. Tell it all before we forget the good parts and the hard ones run away with the story."

"All?" Evie asked, eyebrow lifting.

"Not just the cat," Dot replied, her smile softening. "Though Victory will require a proper memorial."

"Tomorrow," Maggie said. "After lunch. We'll start with the fifties. Evie first, Barnard and bylines wait for no one."

Evie's laugh sparked, putting ten years back into her face. "Bossy," she said. "I missed that."

"Organized," Dot corrected. "Also, wise."

Maggie reached for the small spiral notebook her grandson had given her for crosswords. She set it on the table with a little thump, uncapped a pen, and wrote carefully on the first page in tidy hand:

Victory Club — Meetings

After lunch. Window table.

Order: Evie → Dot → Maggie.

Don't skip the parts that cost.

She underlined the words a second time and closed the notebook with a quiet snap, as if sealing a promise.

The three of them lingered in the hush by the window, the kind that comes after long winters when the first birds test their voices again. Outside, the courtyard squirrel darted across the grass, its tail high, and Evie laughed, so bright that an aide passing the doorway paused to listen.

For a moment, Maggie saw them not as they were now but as they had been, three girls in cotton dresses on a splintered bench, knees knocking, arms flung tight, the world waiting to be broken open. She felt that summer's laughter slip through the years and land here, in this bright square of afternoon.

Her throat tightened, but it wasn't sorrow. It was recognition.

They had found one another again.

2

LEMONADE FOR VICTORY

1944 • EVIE

Evie Gross was nine and already in a hurry.

The war lived in the house the way steam lived in the kitchen, clinging to the walls and curling into corners. Ration points clipped from the book and tucked into her mother's apron. Sugar measured down to the spoon, butter scraped thin as paper.

Three doors down, the Taylors' Blue Star service flag hung in the window, its single star bright against the fabric. On the corner, Mr. Han kept his radio low on the porch, the announcer's voice solemn, reading names in a steady cadence. Sometimes, Evie held her breath through the names as if her silence might somehow keep them safe.

That afternoon, the alley baked in July heat. Cicadas rasped in the trees, and the air shimmered above the tar. The kitten—Victory, they'd decided after three minutes and three arguments—slept in a flour-sack bed under the porch steps, one ear nicked like a torn stamp. Evie checked once, twice, three times. Still breathing. Still theirs.

She darted to the Lantz yard, where the great oak cast a round puddle of shade across the grass. Dot Carter was already there with a tin can whose lid had a slit cut into it, "V" penciled bold on the side. War Savings Stamps. Maggie Thompson stood beside her, clutching a hand-lettered sign she'd made from the inside back of a cornflakes box:

V-STAMPS FUND • 5¢ LEMONADE • HELP THE BOYS

"Ready?" Evie asked, the word bouncing inside her chest.

"Ready," Dot said, tapping the tin like a drum. "If we sell sixty cups, that's a whole page of stamps."

Maggie lifted the sign a little higher, shy but certain. "Mrs. Lantz said we can borrow her card table if we don't block the walk."

Evie grinned. "We'll put it by the mailboxes. People are already stopping there."

They set to work the way they always did: Evie charging ahead with ideas, Dot sorting those ideas into steps, and Maggie smoothing the edges so nobody got poked. The three of them hauled the wobbly card table to the corner and covered it with a white cloth that used to be a bed sheet. Evie squeezed lemons with both hands until her forearms ached, juice stinging the small scrape on her knuckle. Maggie measured sugar with careful precision—her mother had insisted on accuracy. Dot lined up nickels in tidy rows and double-counted each one before dropping it into the tin.

Across the street, the Taylors' Blue Star winked from the window. Mr. Han adjusted his radio dial, a hair this way, then a hair more, as if careful turning might coax the static into a safe ending.

Their first customer was Mrs. Rossi in her worn house dress. She pressed a nickel into Dot's tin. "For the boys," she said, her accent wrapping the words. Then, glancing toward the porch steps, she added, "And for that little cat of yours. A house needs something soft."

Evie poured carefully, trying not to slosh. The lemonade was a little too tart, which made it perfect.

Next came a man from Maple Street with his ration book already half-out of his pocket. "Can you take points?" he asked, embarrassed, thumb worrying the edge of the paper.

"Wish we could," Dot said, gentle but firm. "Cash only for lemonade today."

He nodded, fished a nickel from his pocket, and tucked the ration book away like something breakable.

By the second pitcher, the air smelled of citrus and warm dust. A breeze stirred their cardboard sign, and the penciled letters seemed to lift and march across the box. When the sun slid an inch lower, the shade shifted off their feet and onto the table, making the jar of sliced lemons glow like coins.

"How many so far?" Evie asked, bouncing on her toes.

Dot counted the nickels. "One dollar, fifty. If we keep going, we'll have enough for a book by Friday."

"Two," Evie insisted. "We can do two."

Maggie set down the sign and nodded toward the porch steps. "Victory needs water."

Evie went quickly, saucer in hand. The kitten lifted its head, blinking, its whiskers trembling. She set down the dish and watched its pink tongue lap the surface like it was tasting moonlight. "You're good," she whispered. "You're ours."

When she came back, Mr. Han stood across from the stand, holding out two paper cups. His smile was kind, but it bent at the edges like paper folded too often.

"Two," he said. "One for me. One for the radio."

They laughed, the way children laugh when they're trying to be brave beside grown-ups who are trying even harder.

By late afternoon, the tin was heavy. Dot gave it a tiny shake and looked startled, as if the sound itself might spill their luck. Maggie steadied her hand. "Careful," she murmured.

From the porch, the announcer's voice slipped into its solemn register, listing towns no one on the block had ever visited, strung together like beads on a cord. Evie didn't listen closely—not today. She lined up three paper cups and poured even when no one stood in front of her, just to keep her hands moving, to stay ahead of the silence pressing in between the words.

"Evie?" Dot asked gently.

"I'm fine," Evie said, and she almost meant it. "We're going to fill a whole page."

A car rattled past and the cardboard "V" taped to Mrs. Lantz's bicycle fluttered like a real flag. The kitten slept, the lemonade sweated, the girls counted. The coins chimed and clinked like a kind of music.

When the shadows stretched long, they folded the cloth, counted the money again just to be sure, and promised Mr. Han they'd meet him at the post office in the morning. Evie hefted the tin, feeling its good weight tug at her arms. It was the weight of promise, of something larger than the three of them, and it was enough.

"Tomorrow," she said.

And they believed her.

3

DON'T SKIP THE PARTS THAT COST
PRESENT • MANCHESTER MEADOWS

Manchester Meadows kept afternoon time by sound, wheels on linoleum, a cart clinking spoons. Sun pooled on the window table where the scrapbook lay open. A pressed violet had left its ghost on the facing page.

Evie's finger rested in the margin beside a photograph of three girls on a bench—knees touching, arms flung tight, all certainty and summer. The bench boards ran in neat slats, paint flaking like confetti. One girl's shoelace trailed, a white ribbon against dust. Two soda bottles sweated rings onto a newspaper that bragged about record peaches.

Dot tipped her head toward the picture. "We were small."

Evie's mouth lifted. "Loud. And sure."

Maggie flipped open her little spiral notebook and wrote at the top in tidy script:

Victory Club — Session 1: The 1950s

Order: Evie → Dot → Maggie

Don't skip the parts that cost.

She underlined once and looked up. "Ready?"

Evie drummed two fingers, a grin threatening. "Petticoats and lead type. I'd start with the day Mrs. Henderson slid a stack of headlines across the desk and told me to cut them by half without losing the point."

"Then me," Dot said. "The bus to Washington. The first time my feet felt exactly where they should be."

"And I'll close the decade," Maggie answered. "A ring sooner than expected, a kitchen that never cooled, babies who didn't read clocks."

From the television lounge down the hall, a thread of doo-wop drifted in—*In the Still of the Night*. For a breath the room tilted, present to past and back. A floor fan clicked through its rotations like a metronome for memory.

"Tea?" Maggie asked. "If we're opening a decade, I could use a cup."

"Black," Evie said, holding up two fingers. "No sugar."

"Peppermint," Dot added. "Teacher's orders."

Maggie rose carefully, smoothing her skirt with the back of her wrist where the veins made a soft blue map. She brought back three ceramic cups and set them down. Steam stitched the air between them, bright and clean. On the bulletin board, the Sock Hop flyer was turned on its pin, arrowing toward their table as if it approved. Someone had drawn a small musical note in the corner; the ink winked.

They drank and fell into an easy, planning silence—the kind that had words in it even when no one spoke. Outside the window, a squirrel inspected the bird feeder, tail knitting punctuation in the air. Farther off, a mower coughed and thought better of it.

Evie sketched in the air as she thought. "Homeroom to print shop to the little side door at the paper. I could still feel the metal stairs under my shoes. You remember the ones? Narrow as a secret."

Dot answered with sidewalks and grocery-store corkboards. "Clipboards," she said. "Always clipboards. And a hat when the sun didn't care that we were righteous. We learned to pass water jugs hand to hand with the caps tied on so they wouldn't spill in the street."

Maggie listened and remembered she was the one who kept the kettle filled and the hems straight. "And I learned to set a table for five with two good plates and three that didn't match," she said. "You could feed more than you thought if you didn't apologize first. There was a trick to stretching stew—slice the carrots on a slant, make them look like more."

An aide in blue scrubs, Kris, her ponytail looped like a question mark, paused with a tray. "Milkshake day—vanilla?"

Evie wrinkled her nose, amused. "A malt would've made it authentic."

Dot accepted a cup and closed her eyes. "If I concentrate, there's a jukebox in this."

Maggie took a spoonful. It tasted like summer light softened in a blender. She saw crepe-paper swags in a gym and a boy waiting for the slow song, eyes on his shoes until the first notes told him to be brave. The memory lifted and settled gently, like a bird changing branches.

Kris leaned on the cart's handle, friendly. "Y'all need anything else? I can tilt the blinds if the sun's in your eyes."

"We need the sun," Dot said, opening her eyes. "It remembered us."

Kris blushed at being included in the decade that had happened before she was born. "I'll leave you to your club, then." She tapped the corner of the Sock Hop flyer as she left, straightening it without thinking.

"We won't skip the parts that cost," Maggie said, more to herself than to them. The words she'd written made a little door inside her that would need opening. She could already feel the hinge.

"No," Evie agreed. "But we'll tell the joy first where we can." She tilted the scrapbook toward the light, careful of the violet's brittle stem. "You knew it was a good summer when we stopped writing our names on things. We were so sure we'd know them again."

Dot smiled at that. "And then life taught us about lost and found."

They laughed softly, the kind of laugh grown women gave each other when they'd crossed fire together and remembered the pattern of the flames. The fan clicked. The doo-wop faded into an advertisement about dental implants, then returned as if it, too, preferred 1956.

On the next page a news clipping had been glued at a shy angle. Someone—Maggie, long ago—had circled a tiny photograph of three teenagers at a county fair booth, their hair set in cones of lacquer, their faces washed white by the flash, all faith and nerve. Behind them hung paper V's cut from grocery bags. A penciled arrow read *We made $7.42.*

"We charged a nickel for the penny toss," Evie said, reading her own handwriting as if another girl had written it. "The trick was to act like our game was the sure thing. Boys loved the word *sure*."

"And we loved the word *ours*," Dot said. "We kept a tin with the money in it and wrote every penny down. Funny how you think a notebook can hold a life steady."

Maggie's eyes went to the pressed violet again. "That came from Mrs. Lantz's yard. She let us pick one each if we carried her groceries in. And we dried our skirts on her railing after we got caught in the sprinkler at Feinberg's—the one that spun slow and threw glittering arcs of water across the lawn."

"Speak for yourself," Evie said, mock-prim. "I never got caught."

"You got forgiven," Dot replied, and they grinned like girls who'd learned to translate mercy.

Evie reached for the pen and Maggie let her, knowing the pen steadied certain hands. Evie wrote below the meeting rules:
Session notes:

- Name the joy before the cost.
- Tell one thing you didn't tell at the time.
- Whoever needs a break says "pause," and we all pause.
- If we cry, we pass the tissue box clockwise so nobody has to decide first.

Dot watched the words bloom and nodded approval. "Add one more: We correct the record when memory gets bossy."

"You would," Evie murmured, writing it anyway.

"Memory got me through lesson plans," Dot said. "But I didn't marry it."

Maggie turned the pen end over end, thinking of all the times she'd bitten the cap of a pen and kept lists in the margin when the days felt monstrously long and ordinary. "I'll hold the time," she said. "Not strictly. Kindly."

"That was always your specialty," Evie said, and now the grin was unmasked.

A resident drifted past their table, slippered feet whispering at the threshold. Mr. Delaney, who always wore the same wool vest no matter the weather, paused to consider the photograph. "Pretty girls," he said, a little confused by how time made people into matryoshka dolls—one young face inside another. "Going somewhere nice?"

"Everywhere," Dot told him gently. "Eventually."

He nodded as if that solved something he'd been working at and continued down the hall toward the lounge, following the song like a string tied to his wrist.

When the room quieted again, Evie closed the scrapbook carefully and rested her palm on the cover as if to borrow a little of its weight. "We were nine and thought we'd be young forever," she said. "Turns out we were right about the forever part, just wrong about the kind."

"We stayed us," Dot said. "We didn't keep all the same pieces, but we stayed us."

A breeze found its way through the screen and lifted the edge of a paper napkin. The maples whispered against the roof. *We started with a V and a kitten,* Maggie thought. *We could start again.* Starting didn't have to mean pretending nothing had happened; it could mean saying yes anyway.

Maggie drew a line under the rules and, because it comforted her to make things official, numbered a blank page for notes. She wrote the date. She wrote the time—2:17—and beside it, *Sun on the table.* She would want to remember the light later, the way it kept its promise to come back.

Evie's hand hovered above the scrapbook as if testing the temperature of a pool. "I had a cardigan with pearl buttons," she said, voice taking on the warmed-through tone it used when she slipped from now to then. "Mrs. Henderson always wore shoes you could hear before you saw her. That day in the print shop, she paired us off and gave me headlines to cut. I loved the sound of the paper knife through newsprint. Every slice was a decision."

Dot's eyes softened. "Decisions were our first grown-up thing. Not secrets, not boys—decisions."

Maggie let herself picture it—the print shop smell, the ink that never fully washed off, Evie with a pencil behind one ear and a hunger for the right word. It comforted her to know that the girl at the bench and the woman at this table were made of the same fiber.

"Tell the part you didn't tell at the time," Dot prompted, tapping the rule with her fingernail.

Evie's mouth worked, not quite a smile. "That I was scared I'd cut too much and be left with nothing that mattered." She looked up. "It would become a theme."

"No spoilers," Maggie said, and they all laughed.

Kris reappeared, sliding a small box of tissues to the center of the table as if she, too, respected rules. "In case," she said, and ducked away.

Dot turned her tea in its circle, watching the light make an amber window across the cup. "My part I didn't tell then," she said quietly, "was that the first time the bus pulled away, I thought of turning back. Not because I doubted the march. Because I doubted myself. Then a woman I didn't know squeezed my hand and said, 'We learned to be brave together.' And I believed her."

Maggie's secret for the decade tested the door in her chest. She placed her palm there, the way Evie had on the scrapbook. "Mine was how quiet the house got at three in the morning," she said, and the words came like a small, well-mannered animal finally trusting your hand. "How I'd stand in the kitchen and make a sandwich I didn't want, just to feel like I was feeding someone. I didn't tell anyone about the sandwich."

Evie reached over and bumped Maggie's wrist with her knuckles, the friend's blessing that meant *I see you*. Dot set her peppermint tea down like an amen.

An orderly rolled past pushing a cart of folded towels, crisp squares stacked like pages. The laundry smell—cotton, sun, a hint of soap—rose and threaded the room. It reminded Maggie of clotheslines and clothespins in her teeth, of the way sheets made soft tunnels for children to run through.

"Alright," Evie said, brisk out of tenderness, and tapped the notebook spine with her forefinger. "We had our preamble, our rules, our milkshakes. Any objections to proceeding?"

"Only one," Dot said. "If you get to Barnard and you start grandstanding, Maggie and I are allowed to heckle."

"Friendly heckling," Maggie added. "We are a civilized club."

Evie lifted her chin. "I've never grand-stood. I have occasionally stood."

"On soapboxes," Dot murmured.

"That is a trope and you know it." Evie lined the scrapbook square to the table's edge as if accuracy might escort courage to its seat. "We're not doing nostalgia," she said, and her voice steadied. "We're doing witness."

Maggie felt the word go through her like a small bell. *Witness.* To witness meant to hold without owning, to honor without embalming. It meant there was still a live wire running from then to now.

She slid the notebook closer to Evie. "Begin when you're ready."

Evie set her cup aside, laid both hands flat on the table as if swearing in, and gave them the kind of look that had once quieted a pressroom. Her eyes were still storm-clear when she meant business. The fan clicked. Somewhere, a phone rang, was answered, hushed. The room waited with them.

"Alright then, Barnard."

4

CHASING THE BYLINE

1952 • EVIE

Evie stood at the bottom of the porch steps with her suitcase and felt the house trying to keep her. Painted shutters, straight white pickets, the bed of marigolds her mother coaxed into bloom every June; everything leaned toward her as if to say *stay*.

"You were my whole miracle," her mother said, not dramatic, just true. "They told me there wouldn't be another."

Evie hadn't known that. The words settled behind her ribs like a second spine. It explained the porch light left on, the first-day photographs taken with hands that wouldn't quite let go, the extra hug at camp drop-offs.

Her mother took Evie's hand as if checking a pulse. "Are you sure?"

"Yes." Evie made her voice steady. "If I don't go now, I'll talk myself out of it."

She'd spent spring reading headlines in the post office line and wanting to be under them. Murky reports from Korea, Ike versus Stevenson chatter, a solemn young queen pictured on the front page with a crown not yet set on her head. She wanted the hum of the place where news began, the city where words were made and cut and printed.

"It's far," her mother said, eyes on the road as if Manhattan might already be visible there.

"It's a train ride," Evie answered. "And I'll come home on holidays."

The screen door whispered open. Her father stepped onto the porch, heavy in his work boots. He kept his hands in his pockets like he was holding himself together. "You make sure they hear you, kid," he said, words shaped as if he'd chosen them last night.

"I will," Evie said.

He gave one short nod and let the door ease shut again.

Mrs. Lantz from next door called good luck across the hedge. The kitten they'd named Victory, no longer a kitten, stalked a moth under the porch and flashed her tail like a flag. Evie looked at the garden, the porch swing, the crooked stepping stones to the gate, and put each one in a careful mental drawer. She would need to take them out later.

Her mother smoothed Evie's collar, then, because she couldn't help it, smoothed it again. "Write if you can't sleep," she said. "Write if you can."

"I will." Evie lifted the suitcase.

At the station she hugged her parents once more, longer. Her mother slipped a folded paper bag into her coat pocket, cookies, napkins, two dollar bills, and a safety pin "just in case." Her father pressed a fountain pen into her palm. "A reporter's tool," he said, as if it were a wrench or a level. The conductor called *All aboard* with a voice that didn't invite discussion.

On the train, fields unrolled into mills and smokestacks, then steeples, then factories with their brick shoulders against the sky. Evie sat with the *Herald Tribune* folded on her lap and the faint grit of coal dust in the air, a second-hand perfume that meant forward. Across the aisle, a woman in a neat felt hat read quietly and ate an apple to the core. When the train curved, Evie saw the woman's reflection in the window and her own layered on top of it, small, determined, a ghost guarding a braver self.

Manhattan rose like a metal thicket. Grand Central made a cathedral of departure. She followed the river of people past the constellations on the smoke-dimmed ceiling, mind snagging on every sound, heels ticking, taxi whistles, a newsboy calling "Late final!" as if the day could be persuaded to make one last version of itself.

Barnard's brick looked warm in late August, even with the city heat pressing its cheek to everything. The dorm smelled like floor polish and toast. Her room had creaky floors, two narrow beds, a tall window with a sliver of Claremont Avenue, and a radiator that hissed like a person with opinions.

Her roommate, Liz from Cleveland, owned three sweater sets and a laugh that took up a whole corner of the room. She unpacked family photographs and a tiny clock with luminous hands. "I type fifty words a minute," Liz said, proud as showing a medal. "What can you do?"

"Chase things," Evie said. "And cut."

Liz pinned a college pennant above her bed. Evie set her typewriter on the desk and the fountain pen beside it. From the window she could see the edge of Riverside Church's tower, an arrow pointing up.

It wasn't Manchester. It was better.

She learned the campus fast: Milbank steps for watching, Lehman stacks for hiding, the newsstand on Broadway that stacked the *Times* and the *Herald Tribune* in precise, promising towers. Mr. Stavros ran the stand and knew everyone by what they bought. "You're a headline girl," he told Evie after a week, setting aside a paper before she even asked. "I can tell by the way your eyes count."

Across at Columbia, city noise tucked itself around Morningside Heights and made room for argument, students talking with their hands, professors walking fast with papers clamped under their arms, bells stitching the hours from Riverside's tower. The air tasted faintly of ink and pretzel salt.

Barnard didn't have a journalism major, but Evie found the rooms where people argued about sentences. She registered for political science and constitutional law and whatever else sharpened edges, then answered a flyer tacked near Milbank: *The Barnard Bulletin—contributors welcome.*

That wasn't enough. *The Bulletin* met on campus; the reporting didn't stop there. *The Columbia Daily Spectator* accepted contributors from Barnard and Evie crossed Broadway with her name already written on the sign-up sheet in her head.

The *Spectator* office smelled like ink and carbon paper and something electric. A copy editor with ink on his knuckles waved her toward the assignment board. "If you're here to look around, look fast."

She looked fast. She signed up faster.

The office crackled with the energy of a beehive. A fan clicked in the corner, keeping time for urgency. Words she didn't know yet but would lived here: *hed, dek, graf, nut, TK.* She watched how the older writers tucked a pencil behind one ear and listened with their whole faces. She liked the way the pages came back bleeding red and meant improvement, not failure, the way a coach's whistle meant *keep running.*

She learned the campus by its paperwork too, forms to sign, lines to stand in, cards to keep in your wallet like talismans: library, dining hall, student ID. For money she shelved books in Lehman after dinner. The circulation desk woman, Mrs. Kline, wore a string of pearls every day and greeted everyone like they were a chapter she looked forward to. "Writers start as readers," she told Evie, tapping a stack of returns. "Be greedy."

Nights, the city made its own lullaby—sirens, a radio behind a neighbor's thin wall, the bell that tolled the hour with a polite pause you could count. On Fridays, Liz pulled Evie downtown to an automat where the glass cases winked and you could buy a slice of pie with nickels and a smile from the woman refilling coffee cups.

On Sundays, Evie walked along Riverside Drive and let the river underline the skyline. She mailed letters home with small, true news: *I found the library. I found a newsstand that smells like warm paper. I found that the subway platform is the hottest place on earth, and when the train arrives, it's like grace.*

In constitutional law, Professor Ellison chalked *Marbury v. Madison* on the board and said, "Power isn't only words on paper; it's how those words live." Evie underlined *live* twice. In political theory, a graduate assistant raised his eyebrows when she argued back; afterward he said, surprised, "You're quick." She filed the compliment in the drawer labeled *Use later.*

Her first *Bulletin* brief came back with *CUT BY HALF* penciled across the top. She took a breath and cut. The headline ran smaller than she imagined and larger than she feared. She kept the paper on her desk and pretended not to.

She learned names the way she learned streets, by walking them. Call the dean's secretary before the dean. Learn the janitor's schedule; he knows which doors are stuck and which classrooms open sooner than the clock says. Wait by the newsroom phone until it becomes yours for a minute, then make the call that needs making. Hold the receiver the way you hold a nervous hand, steady, patient, ready to listen past the first no.

On a Wednesday in October, the phone rang for her.

"Evelyn?" her father said, using the full name he saved for bank forms and big news. "It's Grandma."

"What about Grandma?"

"She's at the hospital." He cleared his throat. "You should come."

The train home felt longer than the train out. Hospital air made everything smell like linen and lemon. Grandma Gross looked smaller against the white, but her voice had the same iron braid under the kindness. Her hands, always busy, now rested on a crocheted blanket someone from church had made, soft blue squares joined with care.

"You're where you're supposed to be," she told Evie, as if she could read doubt like a headline. "Don't let anybody teach you small. They'll try to fold you down to fit their world. Don't you bend."

Evie pressed her cheek to Grandma's hand and promised. In the corridor she leaned against the cool wall and stared at a bulletin board full of notices, donor lists, blood drives, a schedule of visiting hours, and thought how much the world ran on women's quiet organizing, the way they pinned days together like laundry on a line.

After the funeral, carnations and strong coffee in the red-brick Lutheran church, she sat in the car and watched Main Street move at its small-town pace. Mrs. Lantz in her house dress, the postmaster setting out the flag, the druggist pulling the blind to cut the glare.

Back at school on Sunday night, she opened her notebook and wrote three sentences about casseroles and backbone and the quiet work of women who keep things from falling apart with Tupperware and prayer lists. No one had assigned it. She wrote it anyway. Grief, she decided, was logistics as much as hymns.

October slid toward cold. Evie made herself a rule: one piece a week for the *Bulletin,* one for the *Spectator* when she could wedge it in. Financial-aid lines. The library's new-books cart and the strange democracy of what people took first. A profile of the woman who sorted the campus mail, who knew everybody by their handwriting.

She learned to wait by the copy desk with a polite expression until a harried editor scribbled, *Fine, kid, run it.* She carried change for the subway and the pay phone and ate when someone put food in front of her because she might not sit down again for a while.

Mr. Stavros began keeping two papers aside for her without asking. "You'll want both takes," he said as the Eisenhower signs multiplied in shop windows. "A reporter needs two eyes."

On the newsstands, Eisenhower began to eclipse Stevenson. Evie copied ledes longhand and crossed out every word she could live without. She taped the best ones inside her closet where nobody would see. She kept Grandma's funeral program in her wallet until the edges went soft.

There were small lessons, too. The professor who remembered her name but looked over her shoulder when she spoke. The photographer who called her *sweetheart* and then, when she stared at him, switched to *ma'am.* The night an editor sent two boys to a late lecture because "it might run long," and Evie took her own notebook anyway and stood in the aisle. Later, the editor read her copy and said, "Huh," as if bumping into competence in a dark hallway.

Election night turned the *Spectator* office into a hive. Coffee rings on every surface, ashtrays filling like hourglasses. A radio on the filing cabinet crackled counties and precincts, the returns stacking like bricks. Evie stood at the city desk, fingers cold from trips to the pay phone, then warm again from the crowd of bodies around the map. Somebody shouted, "Ike takes Ohio!" and someone else threw a pencil up like a firework and immediately swore when it came down.

"Copy!" an editor yelled, and a runner took the pages from Evie's hand. She watched them go with the same breath-held feeling as watching a paper boat enter a current. The printer in the basement coughed and rattled. When the first edition slid out, smudged and perfect, the whole staff let out a sound that was half cheer, half prayer.

She walked home at two in the morning with Liz, their coats unbuttoned because adrenaline wore like a second sweater. The city had that strange late-night kindness, as if it were willing to carry you a little. They split a bagel from a cart, the sesame seeds sticking to their fingers like confetti. "You looked like you belonged," Liz said.

"I did," Evie answered, hearing certainty and recognizing it as hers.

Classes kept their grip. In Ellison's course, she wrote a paper about rights that lived or died in the choosing. In seminar, a boy asked if she was really going into news, and when she said yes, he nodded as if he'd been testing a wire and found it live. She took notes on yellow paper she could see in dim light, and she lined her pencils up like soldiers before every exam as if tidy could make genius.

Money ran thinner by Thanksgiving, so she took an extra shift in the library and learned the smell of wet coats steaming dry in the cloakroom. She made a friend at the circulation desk, Ruthie from the Bronx, who wore red lipstick and had four brothers. Ruthie taught her how to stand in a subway car and never fall, even when the tracks curved like a question. "Hip to the pole, kid. Let your knees do the work."

On a gray afternoon, Evie carried her laundry to the basement and found a scrap of newspaper under the washer, an old headline about a coal strike, already outlived by the next day's worries. She folded it into a small bird and set it on the windowsill, a superstition she didn't quite believe. When she came back an hour later, the paper bird was gone. She let that count as luck.

Some nights, she missed the porch and the quiet creak of her mother's rocker, the sound of her father's boots on the back step. On those nights she let the city hold her—bell tower, siren, radio behind a neighbor's thin wall—and reminded herself this was not leaving; it was arriving.

She didn't become a byline in a day. There were pieces that died in the slush pile and pieces an editor rewrote into an unrecognizable cousin and pieces that made it to the page wearing her words like a borrowed dress. She learned the gentle cruelty of the spike and the harder kindness of a colleague who put a cup of coffee near her elbow without saying anything. She learned to keep a dime in the small pocket of her skirt, always.

Then came a Thursday. An editor barked, "We need someone at the lecture. Now," and the boy next to her said, "She's fast," and Evie was already on her feet with her notebook, checking that she had a dime for the subway and a dime for the phone. The lecture hall smelled like chalk and wool. She stood in the back, spine against the cool plaster, and wrote down every verb the speaker favored. On the way out she called the desk, breathing steam into the mouthpiece. "Got it," she said, "Give me twenty minutes."

The story ran the next morning on page two above the fold with her name spelled right, steady as type. She took two copies from the student lounge rack—creased , already thumbed—and later showed one to Mr. Stavros at his stand. He saluted with the corner of a paper like a flag. She kept one tucked beneath her notebook like a secret talisman and slid the other between the closet wall and her dresses where she could touch it before bed without anybody seeing.

She wrote home: *I'm eating. I'm safe. I love you. P.S. They heard me.*

Liz stuck her head around the door and said, "You look taller."

"Maybe I am," Evie said.

That night, she taped Grandma's funeral program a little more securely into her wallet and used her father's pen until the ink ran thin. She fell asleep to the radiator's mutter and a radio somewhere far off playing a song that sounded like both a train whistle and a lullaby.

Tiny things grow, Grandma had written.

Evie turned out the lamp and believed it.

5

THE ROAD TO HOWARD

1952 • DOT

The applause had already moved on to the next name when Dot Carter sat down with her diploma and a heartbeat that would not lift.

Valedictorian. The principal's smile, the choir behind her, the wooden folding chairs that complained every time someone shifted. She had imagined this night since she learned to diagram a sentence. It should have felt like arrival. Instead, the honor lay across her lap like something heavy and a little unreal.

She found her parents in the front row. Her father in his best gray suit, back straight as the piano. Her mother with a lace handkerchief, eyes shining so bright Dot had to look away before she started. Pastor Jones and half of York Baptist sat just behind them, nodding like they had helped carry her to the stage.

Page six would run a grainy photo with the caption *Bright Future for Local Girl.* No mention that she was first in her class. No mention that she was the first Black student to earn that honor. She heard the whispers and comments anyway—the pie-case murmurs at the diner, the hardware-store comment said loud enough for her to hear. "Political gesture," as if you could politick your way through Latin verbs and lab reports.

The ceremony ended with a hymn sung too fast. Outside, the June air wrapped everyone in warm arms. Girls in white dresses squinted against the last light for pictures. Boys loosened ties like they had earned the right. Dot smiled when asked and let herself be pulled from one embrace to the next. Mrs. Lantz pressed cool cheeks to hers, Coach shook her hand like she had just hit a home run, the seventh-grade teacher cried before she could manage words. It felt like standing in a river and letting other people move the water.

At home, the house breathed cinnamon and cheese and peach syrup. Church ladies took over the kitchen the way they did when joy or grief required a crowd. Pans arrived with foil notes: *Love you, baby. We're proud. Warm at 325 degrees.* Uncles unfolded lawn chairs and argued baseball and the election and whether the latest Senate hearings were sense or show. A baby slept in a laundry basket, and nobody saw any reason to move him.

Dot moved room to room, receiving the guests. Yes, ma'am, thank you. No, sir, haven't picked a school yet. She didn't say the part where the envelopes had come thin and polite:

We regret to inform you
While your accomplishments are impressive
Due to limited space

Not closed doors, exactly. Just doors not meant to open for her.

In the kitchen, her mother had turned her headscarf into an apron and was laughing with Sister Mae about somebody's potato-salad sins. She caught Dot's eye and the laugh gentled into a look that said, *Eat a roll while nobody is watching.* Dot obeyed, and the butter tasted like a small rescue.

"Speech was fine as rain," Mrs. Wheeler told her, patting her arm. "You took your time and didn't let the silence bully you."

"Thank you," Dot said. The compliment slid into the part of her chest that was still learning to believe praise without flinching.

Later, when the house quieted to the soft clatter of women washing borrowed dishes, Dot climbed the stairs. In her room the window was open to June and crickets. The quilt her mother had made, a Log Cabin with confident reds and blues, glowed in the lamplight like a map of choices. She reached beneath the bed and drew out the only envelope that felt different when she touched it.

Howard University. Warm ink, invitation, scholarship that wasn't everything but said clearly: *We see you. Come.*

A knock. "Dot?"

"Come in."

Her father eased onto the edge of the bed in his shirtsleeves, hat in his lap. "I think about why we came here," he said. "From the city. You were five. You probably remember the candy store and not much else."

"A little."

"In the city, you would've had separate schools." His voice stayed level. "Separate and less. I didn't want that for you. I wanted you to sit beside the same children who'd be in front of the class someday and know you belonged there, too."

"It's not easy here," she said. Small and true.

"No." He looked at his hands, the grease lines from the shop that never entirely washed away. "I picked hard now for easier later. That was the bargain I tried to make."

Roots, not comfort, settled. He turned to her, and the tired left his face. "I see you, Dot," he said with the weight of a vow. "Even when they don't. And one day they will. Just keep stepping."

"I wanted them to want me," she admitted. It felt like placing a fragile thing between them and seeing that it didn't break.

"Howard is a good school." When she hesitated, he added, "Sometimes the place that wants you back is the one God aimed you toward."

She slid the letter into his hands. His smile broke easy and wide. "Well now," he said, and she finally heard the celebration she hadn't let herself feel all night.

They talked practical. Suitcase or trunk. Shoes that could take a campus hill. A train that left before daylight. "I'll get you to that platform," he promised, rubbing the knee that would argue about it later. "Your mother will pack enough to feed the car."

"She will," Dot said, already smiling at the picture.

Before bed, her mother pressed a cool palm to Dot's forehead as if feeling for fever and future at once. "You'll need safety pins, bobby pins, and a way to remember who you are when you get tired," she said.

Then, softer: "When you don't know, pray. When you do know, still pray."

The train south carried a low, steady note. Daybreak put a pale gold edge on everything. Her mother had packed too much—boiled eggs, sweet rolls, a jar of lemonade wrapped in a towel to keep it cool, napkins tucked with a grace folded into them. At the station, her father adjusted the strap on her suitcase and said, "You call us collect if you have to. We'll pick up." His voice was light, but his eyes kept a ledger of her face as if to save it.

Dot found her seat in the car everyone slid into once the Mason–Dixon passed, no sign needed, just the practiced shuffle of custom. The fan turned lazy circles. The upholstery was tired at the edges. The window smudged the fields into watercolor. She kept her back straight and her hat pinned just so and balanced celebration and caution on the same breath, the way you do when both are true.

An older woman across the aisle nodded and lifted a paper bag. "Grape soda? Lord, August's got no manners this year."

"Yes, ma'am. Thank you." The first sip fizzed like permission.

A porter stopped by, smile tucked in like a secret. "You heading to school, miss?"

"Howard University."

"Good hill to climb," he said, pride warming the words. "World looks different from up there."

They fell into the rhythm of rails. Dot read for a while, Du Bois in a borrowed paperback, the edges already thumbed soft, then switched to watching. Tobacco sheds, a white horse in a dark field, a laundry line doing semaphore in the wind. She unfolded one of her mother's napkins and wrote three words on the corner in pencil: *Keep. Stepping. Anyway.*

Washington was a shoulder of buildings and a thicket of monuments when the train slid in. The platform met her with heat and a shout of city, the whistle call of taxis, the sing-song of vendors, a soldier's laugh that sounded like relief. She felt that old two-beat in her chest, *You do not belong* and *You belong,* and decided the second voice would get the microphone.

Howard sat on its hill like a promise someone had kept. Red brick, white columns, trees shouldering shade onto paths edged with chatter. Students crossed in bright bunches, brown faces in all the beautiful variations she'd seen only in the mirror and at church, not in classrooms. Nobody stared. No one asked *Why are you here?* The question dissolved at the gate.

The air felt charged, band practice somewhere, a debate underway beneath a tree, hands describing ideas so large they needed a sky. A group of girls walked ahead, arms linked. One wore saddle shoes, one carried a chemistry text like it was a love letter, one sang under her breath and didn't mind who heard. Dot wanted to fall in step and found she already had.

Orientation took place under a striped tent that snapped like flags. A dean with spectacles and command welcomed them, then a woman from the English department followed with a voice that made you sit taller. "You are the story and the storytellers," she said. "You will not ask permission to be brilliant." Applause rose like weather.

Slowe Hall smelled like floor wax, hair pomade and something good someone had smuggled from home. On the bulletin board by the stairs: choir auditions Tuesday, work-study sign-ups, young women's prayer circle Wednesday at seven. Her room held two narrow beds, a window with a slice of campus, a desk with a drawer that stuck and then gave.

"You must be Dot. I'm Loretta. Chicago," her roommate said with a grin that started in her eyes. She wore lipstick the color of late cherries and a string of faux pearls like she'd been born with them.

"Dorothy," Dot said out of habit, then, "Dot." Her voice loosened when Loretta laughed.

"You'll like it," Loretta said, waving as if to include the whole campus. "Took me a day to find where to stand, and then I decided everywhere."

Dot unpacked the way her mother had taught her, books first, then dresses, then the quilt. She shook the Log Cabin spread onto the bed. Dark and light strips spiraled toward the red square at the center, hearth, her mother always said. Some folks said quilts like that once hung to whisper safe house to the right eyes. Maybe it was only a story. But Dot liked believing women had spoken to one another in cloth when words were too dangerous.

Loretta touched the border. "Your mama made this?"

"Every stitch." Dot smoothed a corner. "She says a home you can fold is still a home."

"That's a sermon," Loretta said, approving.

They walked the Yard at dusk, the grass taking the day's heat and giving it back softly. A boy balanced a basketball on his palm like a planet. Two girls argued Claude McKay versus Langston Hughes with the seriousness of surgeons. From the chapel steps a hymn drifted, low and steady, the kind that builds a backbone.

"U Street is a short walk down Georgia that way," Loretta said, pointing. "If you need new shoes, a good laugh, or a song that gets into your bones."

Dot smiled. "All three eventually."

Practical came next. The scholarship covered tuition, but books were on her. She signed the work-study sheet and, two days later, tied on a white apron in the dining hall. Miss Estelle ran the place with a spoon in one hand and mercy in the other. "We feed genius," she said. "Genius gets hungry just like everybody else. Don't be stingy with the beans."

In the slow minutes between breakfast and lunch, Miss Estelle trained Dot on the register and, also, life. "Smile, but not like you owe it," she said. "Stretch your back when nobody is watching. And when a boy says you're pretty, say 'I know' and ask if he's done his homework."

Afternoons, Dot found the library. Founders rose like a keeper of promises. The reading room smelled of paper and hope. She touched the banister as if it might speak. It did. Work hard. Ask better questions. She lost an hour in the stacks and found herself again at a table under a lamp, reading lines by Phillis Wheatley so carefully it felt like prayer.

Classes stacked up: political theory that walked her through the bones of power, American government that insisted words and how they lived were not the same thing, a survey that pressed Du Bois and Hughes and Wheatley into her hands and said read like your life depends on it. In a required science course, the professor drew the human heart on the board, valves like doors, and she thought about how some open with a push and some never have.

In freshman comp, Dr. Carter, no kin, circled a sentence in purple pencil. *Good. Strong spine.* "Do not be afraid to write in the voice God issued you," she said, eyes kind and unsparing both. "People will try to loan you new ones. Decline politely."

Evenings, conversations spilled onto the grass, someone's cousin organizing a voter drive back home, a pre-med explaining how a heart-beat looks on paper, a future teacher arguing that the truest revolution is a well-run classroom. A law student came to the dining hall for late coffee and talked about arguments headed to the Supreme Court, schools, separate and not equal, he said, eyes bright like a man holding the edge of a new country. "Mr. Marshall came by the law school last week," he added as if sharing weather. "He said, 'Make your case so clean it shines.'"

Dot carried trays past tables of talk and felt a door open somewhere she couldn't see yet. She tucked the law student's sentence into her pocket.

Papers came back with pencil lines and *Good. Push farther.* Dot learned to raise her hand first and not apologize. She learned which dining-hall table became a study group after dessert. She learned the route from Slowe to Founders you could walk without breaking a sweat, and the one that would. Belonging loosened her shoulders and dropped her voice half an octave she hadn't known she had.

Some nights, the upstairs-room ache returned, the diner whispers, the hardware-store shake of a head meant for her to hear. On those nights, she sat on the floor with her back against the bed and traced the quilt seams. Under her thumb the seam felt like a quiet yes. *We weren't meant to fit, we were meant to make,* the stitching seemed to say.

On Sundays, she visited a church off Georgia Avenue where the choir climbed a scale like a ladder to air. The pastor's sermon landed steady: *Do not despise the day of small beginnings.* Afterward, mothers with hats like gardens pressed food into her hands and advice into her pockets, carry a scarf, keep a dime for the phone, say no like a full sentence.

She called home from the vestibule, the pay-phone cord warm with a hundred other voices. Her father reported on the Buick's stubborn carburetor and her mother asked if the bed was comfortable and whether she'd found a place for her sweaters. Dot answered yes to every-thing and meant it mostly.

Loretta dragged her to U Street one Friday, hand-me-down shops with treasure disguised as coats, a lunch counter where the jukebox stacked Dinah Washington and Billie Holiday, a bookstore that smelled like dust and miracle. They tried on hats and opinions, paid twenty-five cents to see a movie and nearly missed the last bus back up the hill.

In October, the heat broke and the air turned clear enough to keep. The Yard traded cicadas for crunching leaves. Midterms arrived wearing serious shoes. Dot studied in a cluster on the floor with Loretta and two girls from across the hall, Ruth who solved math like untangling necklaces, and Anna who believed in flashcards the way some people believed in saints. They took breaks by standing, stretching, naming three things they loved out loud. "My mother's hands," Dot said once, surprising herself. "The way she turns dough and fixes hair and smooths a collar and somehow it's the same motion every time."

She wrote home twice a week. Not all of it would fit in letters, so she kept a notebook for the rest, the things that didn't have a place yet.

Words I learned today: interlocutor, precinct, injunction.

What I want to be besides right: useful.

What I keep remembering: Daddy's bargain. Mama's hands. Sister Mae's potato-salad rules.

Money ran thin near Thanksgiving, so she took an extra shift in the dining hall and pressed her laundry flat with the iron her mother had tucked in the bottom of the trunk. Miss Estelle slid an extra roll into her pocket with a look that said do not argue. The RA posted a note about a campus drive for coats; Dot mended the lining of hers and donated a scarf she loved anyway.

One rainy afternoon, she wandered into Andrew Rankin Chapel and found a handful of students in the pews, their notebooks open like prayer books. A visiting speaker stood at the pulpit, a woman with soft gray hair and a voice that sounded like a road being laid, the kind of voice you walk on. "Lift as you climb," she said. "And if the ladder isn't there, you braid one." Dot wrote it down and felt the words take root.

The ache of home visited less and then surprised her all at once, smelling cinnamon in the stairwell and swearing she was back in her mother's kitchen, hearing a screen door slap somewhere down the block and thinking of the baby sleeping in the basket at her graduation party.

She did what her mother had told her: prayed when she didn't know, prayed when she did. Both worked about the same.

The night before finals, Loretta fell facedown on the bed and announced she was going to abandon academia for a singing career and a traveling wardrobe. Dot sat beside her and rubbed a circle between her shoulder blades the way her mother did for her when she had a stitch in her side after running. "We'll pass," she said. "And if we don't pass the way we wanted, we'll pass the way we needed."

Loretta lifted her face, mascara smudged into bravery. "You talk like a teacher."

"Maybe I am," Dot said, the first time she'd let the thought out where the air could touch it.

Some Saturdays, a group from campus took the bus to help register voters in a neighborhood across town. Dot wasn't old enough to cast a ballot yet, but she could steady a line and pass out forms and keep children busy with chalk flowers on the sidewalk. She watched the older women, how they handled a man's anger by handing him a chair, how they wrote names slow to avoid mistakes, how they kept a casserole warm on a hot plate in the corner so nobody fainted. *Revolution with a recipe card,* she wrote later, smiling.

Mid-December brought cold that pinched cheeks and made the quad ring like a bell. Final grades crept in on typed slips slid under doors. Dot held hers and let relief land, a good kind of tired settling behind her eyes. She took the paper to the chapel steps and read it again, the columns tilting into the blue.

Back in her room, she took out the small notebook she kept for words she didn't want to lose.

Dear Mama,

I think I felt it today, the thing you said I'd know when I knew. Breathing without waiting for permission. In class they call on me like it's normal. In the Yard no one watches to see if I sit in the right place. Howard feels like a room built with me in mind. It's not perfect, but it's ours.

P.S. Tell Pastor Jones I found the library right away. Tell Daddy his bargain is working. I think this might be the "easier" he hoped for me. I'm learning to be useful as well as right. And I can carry three plates in one hand now. Miss Estelle says that's a credential worth mentioning.

She propped the envelope by the lamp so she wouldn't forget to post it in the morning, then lay back and let the hum of campus braid into her pulse, drums in the distance, somebody laughing in the stairwell, the radiator's small opinion on weather. Belonging doesn't roar; it settles. It makes plans.

Dot turned off the light and traced one square of the quilt in the dark, thumb counting stitches the way some people count blessings. The future didn't rush her. It stepped forward, small and sure, and waited for her to meet it on the hill.

6

THE QUIET CHOICE
1952 • MAGGIE

O n the morning of her wedding, Maggie stood in the little room behind the Methodist sanctuary while Dot fastened the tiny satin buttons up her spine. The lace had yellowed just enough to show its age, and Maggie loved it more for that. Outside, the organ warmed its low notes, the ushers whispered, and somewhere a child was told not to touch the peonies.

"You sure?" Dot asked, fingers steady, voice low.

"As I'll ever be," Maggie said, meeting their eyes in the mirror. It came out calm, not giddy—like a yes you could build a house on.

Evie slipped in, cheeks pink from the August heat, her blue dress making her eyes too bright. She held out the bouquet, stems wrapped in ribbon from Maggie's mother's sewing box. "I tucked a bobby pin under the ribbon," Evie said. "For luck."

Maggie smiled. "I'll take all the luck."

Her mother followed with a soft knock, dove-gray dress, lily-of-the-valley pin catching the light. She pressed a handkerchief into Maggie's palm—new linen, initials and the date stitched neat and small. "Something new," she said, smoothing a loose curl. "The dress will do for old."

"Ma," Maggie breathed.

"Marriage isn't magic," her mother said, kind but plain. "It's work. It's listening when you'd rather be right. It's someone who knows how you take your tea. Save a piece of yourself—not to keep back, but to keep whole—even as you give."

"I will."

Evie pretended to cough. "And it's dancing in kitchens," she added, grinning. "Don't forget that part."

Dot's eyebrows lifted. "And paying bills on time."

"Romantics," Maggie said, and they all laughed quietly, which helped.

In the nave, the choir began *Come Thou Fount.* The sound found Maggie's ribs and settled there. The air smelled of beeswax, peonies, and the faint bite of Lysol the custodian preferred these days. A rumor of polio had closed the public pool again, but the pews filled anyway. People stayed home from many things. You still came for vows.

At the doors, her father offered his arm. "Ready, peanut?"

"Yes," she said, and the yes steadied them both. Down the aisle: her father's arm firm, a squeeze at the rail when the minister asked who gave this woman. "Her mother and I." Proud and bewildered in equal measure.

Charles waited at the front in a navy suit that pulled a little at the shoulders. Nervous, yes. Steady, more. When he took her hands, his palms were warm. The vows were the ones her mother had said and her grandmother before her—no surprises, only weight.

"To have and to hold."

She meant it. The handkerchief bit gently into her palm. She was grateful for the bite.

"You may kiss the bride." A shy kiss, simple as bread. The organ turned to *Blessed Be the Tie That Binds,* and blue and gold from the stained glass threw themselves across the aisle in blocks of light. Dust became glitter for a second. She felt suspended—one breath—between the girl she'd been and the woman walking toward the door.

The reception lived in the church basement: lace cloths on folding tables, lemonade in a punch bowl that had belonged to someone's aunt, pies all the way down—cherry, shoofly, custard—names tucked on index cards. Her mother's cake tilted a little, sugared violets hiding a thumbprint. Perfect.

Evie coaxed Dot into a hallway waltz to a cousin's piano plunk; they returned barefoot, breathless, pretending they hadn't. Children chased each other between chairs until the ushers threatened to confiscate the balloons. Mrs. Lantz from next door pinned an envelope inside Maggie's glove "so no one walks off with it." Pastor Garvin prayed the kind of blessing that sounded like good bread—simple, nourishing, enough for later.

Maggie's father tapped a spoon to glass. "I'm no speaker," he said, and then did just fine. "Choose each other on the easy days and the hard ones. That's the whole trick." He lifted lemonade. "To Maggie and Charles."

"To Maggie and Charles," the room answered, a warm roof of sound.

Dot squeezed Maggie's hand under the table. "You look settled," she said, meaning it as the highest praise.

Evie leaned in, eyes bright. "Write me about the curtains. I expect detail."

"Curtain detail," Maggie promised. "And cake recipes."

Later, Maggie found her parents by the piano, her mother's hand looped through her father's arm, rubbing an invisible crease from his jacket. "There's our girl," he said, voice thick. Her mother kissed Maggie's cheek and said only, "Love him good."

They spent two nights at a borrowed lakeside cabin that smelled like pine and old quilts. Ginger ale from glass bottles. Eggs on a camp stove. The lake warm as a held hand if you waded past the shock. A storm on the third night that drummed the tin roof while Charles said into her hair, "We'll make a good life, Mags. You'll see." She believed him.

On Sunday evening, they unlocked the small, rented house on High Street with gingerbread trim and a bay window that made a proper seat in the bedroom. The old outhouse in back became a tool shed and a story. Their landlady, Mrs. Han, who kept a radio on her porch turned to a sensible volume, brought over a jar of pickled beets and a length of clothesline. "Welcome," she said. "Holler if the faucet kicks."

They unpacked in slow circles, setting down pieces of a life and then moving them two inches to the left until the room felt right. Maggie painted the kitchen canary yellow and stitched red-and-white gingham curtains with ricrac while Charles teased that she'd measure twice to cut a thread. When she hung them, the room smiled back.

They learned the good creak on the stair and the one that meant someone would wake. They learned the neighborhood's weather—Mrs. Taylor sweeping her porch in long, even strokes; the paperboy who whistled the same tune at dawn; cars at midnight sounding like they were heading straight through the heart of the house but never did. On Fridays, they counted pay envelopes and on Sundays they counted blessings, and sometimes the numbers matched exactly.

By twenty-five, three small voices lived in the house and the calendar was crowded with pencil: checkups, casseroles, church nursery. The front bedroom became a cradle room, then a fort room, then a place to hide when certain people didn't want their hair brushed. Mornings started with the percolator's cheerful hiss and the little ones' feet thumping down the hall in rhythms you could tell apart with your eyes closed. Evenings, she rolled socks into pairs and tucked them away like tiny finished jobs. The air held lemon polish, bread cooling, lilacs through the open window when the bush cooperated.

There were hard days, the kind that echoed with need. Colic that ignored lullabies. Fevers that burned worry down to its wire. A month when the hardware store cut Charles's hours and the grocery lists shrank to the size of a palm. Charles came home smelling of sawdust and oil, kind and tired in equal measure. They passed like trains some nights, a hello in the doorway, a kiss that promised more time later. The promise counted.

Maggie found her small sovereignties: a pantry lined in neat jars, the darning that made socks last, a trick for getting rust out of the tub that her mother swore by and was right about. On Thursdays, she wrote the week's meals in soft pencil on a card tacked by the stove. Meatloaf Monday, casserole Tuesday, chili Wednesday, fried chicken Thursday, fish Friday, Saturday leftovers, Sunday roast. The order calmed her. It felt like setting a table one place short and still finding a way for everyone to fit.

The women at church—mothers and aunties whether they shared

blood—drew her into their weather. They traded coupons like baseball cards. They shared recipes and the kind of advice that sounded like gossip until you realized it was love. "Keep a coin in your apron for the ice-cream truck," Sister Mae said gravely. "That keeps the devil humble." They taught her how to carry a baby on one hip and a potluck casserole in the other and not spill either.

Sometimes, between coupons and the oven timer, the old stage pressed through—sixteen again, heat of the spotlights, her voice carrying Beatrice across the auditorium. Applause once lived in these ribs, she thought. The echo lingers. She told the girls the story at bath time, making voices, and they clapped with wet hands. "Do it again," they said, and she did, because doing it again was its own kind of applause.

Letters arrived from Evie, postmarked New York, typed in bursts between classes and the student paper. *Cut by half, Magpie,* Evie wrote once in the margin of a recipe Maggie had mailed, teasing. *But the sauce is perfect.* Dot's notes came in a tidy hand from the hill at Howard— library discoveries, a picture of her bed quilted in Log Cabin squares. *I'm learning how power works,* Dot underlined, *and how to carry it without dropping your manners.* Maggie lined the letters in her dresser like touchstones. Three paths, she thought, all real.

Mrs. Han made a point of leaving stray newspapers on her porch when she noticed Maggie peeking at the headlines on her way to the market. "You take," she'd say. "News is a neighbor, too." Maggie read during nap time, the paper spread like a picnic over the kitchen table. She cut out a photograph of a dress pattern she'd try to copy and a column about a teacher in another county who'd won a small fight for her students. She tucked both into the recipe box under Casseroles.

The Grange Hall's flyer for *Arsenic and Old Lace* fluttered on the bulletin board, its edges rippling like a hand raised. Maggie felt the invitation every time she passed. Tryouts Tuesday, 7 p.m. She imagined stepping into a role again, the way a life might fold itself open.

But at 7, the house needed her: baths steaming, homework half-finished, and the baby—recently promoted to a bed—roaming like a joyful fugitive.

Maggie smoothed the flyer's corner and kept walking. Quiet choice, she told herself—brave, not small—and tried to feel only pride.

Winter pressed in with draft snakes Maggie had sewn for the doors and soup often. Charles built a wooden sled with red rails, initials carved on the side, and the children, cheeks apple-bright, screamed joy down Cooper Street just like Maggie once had.

In the evenings, when the youngest fell asleep on her shoulder, Maggie read by lamplight—cookbooks with their calm instructions, a stack of library novels with women who did brave, ordinary things. She colored the edges of the weeks with small delights: cinnamon toast after church, a new bar of soap that smelled like oranges, hemming a dress in the quiet and wearing it to the Sunday potluck as if it had always belonged to her.

There were days she felt like a room everyone kept walking through. Those days the tug came—not pain, a pull. It didn't accuse; it asked. *Is there more of you somewhere you set aside?* When it asked, she looked around at the life she loved and answered, *Yes, and you're safe with me until I have two hands free.*

One afternoon, the house finally hushed—the baby down, the older two with blocks—and Maggie stood at the sink with her hands in warm suds, looking out at the cherry tree, the tricycle on its side, the laundry flapping in the breeze. The tug came, a thread catching on a nail she knew was there. Not unkind. Certain.

The back door eased open. "Hey, you," Charles said, leaning in the frame, sleeves rolled, a smudge of grease on his cheek. "Alright?"

"Just thinking." She dried her hands and turned. The kitchen looked like hers—yellow walls, gingham soft with washing, the meal plan tucked by the stove. She felt both full and a little breathless.

"What about?" He wasn't a man who filled silence with talk. He waited. She loved him for it.

"Everything's... settled." The words weren't unkind.

He nodded. "It's a good life." He stepped close, warm palm at the small of her back. "I'm proud of it. Proud of you."

She let her forehead rest on his shoulder for a second longer than she meant. "Sometimes I wonder if I'm meant for... more. Or different. I don't even know what that means."

He brushed a curl from her temple, thumb gentle. "Maybe. You're more already, you know. And there's time." The small smile that always steadied her. "Don't forget it."

"Time," she repeated, trying the word on. It fit like a dress a little big in the shoulders—room to move.

The baby called from the next room—half complaint, half song. The tug softened, not gone.

"I'll get her," Maggie said, kissing his cheek.

He caught her hand for a beat. "We'll make a good life," he said again, not as a promise this time but as a reminder they were already in the middle of it.

That night, after the house exhaled into sleep, Maggie took out a school notebook and wrote a list no one would see.

Things that pull me:

Sing in the church choir again.

Start a recipe club and trade the good ones.

Maybe a column for the church bulletin—Kitchen Table Notes—just once a month.

Fix the hem on Mrs. Han's coat like I said I would.

Teach the girls to scramble eggs.

Learn the names of the trees in town.

She closed the notebook and slid it under the flour canister. Not hiding. Keeping. *Small beginnings,* she thought. *Quiet doesn't mean invisible.*

Spring returned with mud and tulips and the sound of jump ropes slapping the alley. The Grange's playbill changed to a square dance poster; Maggie taught the children the steps in the kitchen while the sauce simmered, laughing when they spun too far and bumped the chairs. On Mother's Day, the girls gave her a card where the stick-figure mother had a triangle dress and hair like fireworks. "That's you," they said proudly. "Your dress is loud." Maggie laughed until she cried a little and tucked the card behind the metal clip inside the recipe-box lid, the loud dress keeping watch over *Casseroles.*

Evie visited in June, her city sharpness wrapped in affection. She sat at the bay window with a glass of lemonade and asked a hundred questions—about the children, the curtains, the price of eggs, the church gossip. When the girls performed their square-dance steps, Evie clapped like a person who had paid for tickets. Later, when the house quieted, she rested her head on Maggie's shoulder. "You look rooted," she said softly. "I'm always running. It's good to see someone arrive and keep choosing it."

"Sometimes I want to run," Maggie admitted.

"Then we'll trade for an hour." Evie grinned. "You take my notebook; I'll stir the soup." They did, and both laughed at how right and wrong it felt in equal measure.

Dot sent a photograph from D.C.—her standing on a campus hill with a book tucked against her ribs, a quilt square peeking from her dorm window. On the back she'd written, *Belonging doesn't roar; it settles. It makes plans.* Maggie pinned it on the kitchen corkboard and read it when the house was loud.

Summer heat laid a hand on everything. Charles brought home a fan from the hardware store and set it in the doorway so it could push the day out and pull the evening in. They ate tomatoes with salt standing over the sink and let the children sleep on a quilt on the floor when the bedrooms forgot how to breathe. On the Fourth, they spread a blanket under the elm behind the church and watched fireworks like flowers that didn't know how to land.

In September, the girls started school, tin lunchboxes and knees full of opinions. On the walk home, Maggie lingered a minute by the bulletin board outside the Grange. A new flyer: *Women's Club— Tuesday Evenings: Sewing Circle, Recipe Exchange, Newsletter Volunteers Needed.* She ran her finger over *Newsletter* until the paper went shiny. Tuesday evenings were still bath and bedtime, but bath and bedtime were smoother now, the girls counting to twenty with their eyes closed while the youngest splashed, the clock moving like it knew her name.

She took the corner of the flyer in her fingers, not to tear it—just to feel the edge.

That night, after the children were down and the house sat like a well-behaved dog, she told Charles about the newsletter, about the way the word made her stomach feel like it was saying hello.

"Try it," he said, without fanfare. "I'll be ringmaster on Tuesdays." He winked. "Bath time can handle a circus."

"Are you sure?"

"I'm as sure as I was in a navy suit," he said, and she knew exactly what he meant.

The first meeting smelled like coffee and starch and the kind of perfume that comes in small bottles kept for years. Women unfolded themselves around folding tables—teachers and clerks and mothers and a woman from the post office who could lift a mailbag like it was a loaf of bread. They talked recipes and school supplies and whose husband could fix a radio.

Then Mrs. Wheeler slid a stack of paper toward Maggie. "You've got neat handwriting," she said. "And a knack for saying something true without making folks mad. Would you take the notes and pull together a page for the church bulletin? Not every week. Just when there's news."

Maggie smoothed the top sheet. "I could do that."

Walking home, cool air at her throat, she felt the tug rethread itself into something steadier. Not a demand—a direction. The children were asleep when she came in, hair damp and sweet. Charles had left the percolator set and a note in his blocky hand: *Sing me what they said.* She laughed quietly and hummed the meeting's talk while she wrote the bulletin page out longhand at the kitchen table.

A week later, when the folded bulletins lay in a neat stack by the chapel door, Sister Mae paused with her hatpins bright as lanterns and said, "This reads like a neighbor stopping by."

Maggie felt heat rise in her cheeks.

"Good," Sister Mae said. "We need neighbors."

Maggie carried the words home like something warm in her hands.

The quiet choice held. It kept holding. And it didn't feel small.

There would be years ahead enough to decide what to do with the tug. For now, there was this: a soft head at her neck, the click of the percolator starting again, the clatter of spoons as the girls "helped" set the table, a man wiping grease from his hands and turning the plates without being asked. A list under the flour canister growing, not shrinking. A newsletter corner with room for recipes and notices and the occasional sentence that made someone feel seen.

Maggie crossed the yellow kitchen and lifted that warm, outraged little body from its nap. In the quiet between breaths she heard—maybe only inside herself—the hush before a line lands. She tucked the sound away beside coupons and hymn numbers and the smell of fresh bread.

She breathed, steady. The choice she'd made kept meeting her in the doorway and turning into a life. And every now and then, when the kettle sang or the children laughed or Charles reached for her hand in the dark, the echo from those long-ago spotlights answered back—not to call her away, but to show her that applause can sound like home. And sometimes, it did.

7

THE HINGE BEFORE THE DOOR
PRESENT • MANCHESTER MEADOWS • EVIE

Peppermint first, then paper napkins. That's the window table today.

Evie arrived two steps late, cardigan unbuttoned, breath bright like she'd outrun a thought. Dot had already set the shoebox down like something that remembered. The lid read, in pencil: *1963–64.*

Maggie, neat as ever, opened her spiral and wrote in teacher-clean letters Evie could hear as much as see:

Victory Club — Session 2: The 1960s

Order: Evie → Maggie → Dot

Start: Birmingham '63 → Suburbia '63 → Atlanta '64

Don't skip the parts that cost.

Evie reached toward the shoebox and stopped, a reflex learned in darkrooms and newsrooms: ask before you touch what carries a story.

"Go on," Dot said. "It doesn't bruise."

Evie lifted a straw hat with both hands. Narrow ribbon. Shade that still knew how to do its job. The hat held summer the way bowls hold peaches, a little sweetness left in the weave.

"August twenty-seventh?" she asked, half teasing, half testing herself.

"Twenty-eighth," Dot answered, soft as a hand on a shoulder. "We left before dawn."

"Twenty-eighth," Evie repeated, pinning the number to the air. "I'll keep it there."

Maggie drew a small arrow under *Start* and read aloud, because reading aloud steadied all of them. "Birmingham. Then home. Then Atlanta. Say the pieces out loud if it helps."

Dot slid tissue aside. A yellowed diner check, a bent safety pin, a narrow slip of ruled paper creased into certainty.

"What's written there?" Maggie asked, though she knew.

Dot smiled at the slip. "*Write your reason. Fold it. Keep it where your hand can find it,*" she said, quoting a woman from a church basement. "Mine says: *My students deserve to sit where they please.*"

Across the room, an activity cart rattled past with today's schedule. *Film at 3: The Dream.* Someone had drawn balloons in the corner. Evie hoped for the whole clip, not the summary.

Kris, today's aide in cherry-red sneakers, arrived with three steaming cups. "Peppermint, just like you asked," she said, setting saucers with a precision that would've pleased Maggie's mother. "I put a cookie on each. Quality control."

"We're very pro–quality-control," Evie said. Kris laughed and squeezed Dot's shoulder before rolling on.

"Peppermint all around?" Maggie asked, arranging the triangle and looking up at Evie. "What do you want said plain before we turn the page?"

"That we learned courage in groups," Evie said. "And that objects matter. Hats and safety pins. A pen you can trust. They keep the story from slipping."

Maggie wrote it down, *Don't gild; don't flatten,* her lips moving with the words. Dot's mouth tipped, pleased.

The garden beyond the window was doing its August best: zinnias like small fireworks, a monarch skimming the lavender, a robin bossing the birdbath. Inside, peppermint steam curled toward the glass, the radiator made a gentle clearing of its throat no one believed anymore, and the hallway clock, always three minutes fast, hustled the afternoon along.

Maggie touched the spiral. "We'll stay with the plan," she said. "You begin, Evie. Not the park—save that for the next chapter. Just bring us to the door."

Evie nodded. She set the hat on the table, fingers resting at the brim as if it were a compass she didn't need to look at to believe in.

"It started earlier," she said. "Earlier than the picture you've seen. With a phone call that didn't know it would change my legs. With a map and a borrowed camera strap that pinched if you wore it long. With the sound a bus makes when it decides it'll go, whether you're ready or not."

The room went still. Dot's eyes softened. "That's enough for now," she said, and Evie let the breath go she hadn't noticed she was holding.

Maggie added a line beneath *Birmingham '63*: *the bus, the map, the strap; the moment before.* Then she tapped the next heading. "Suburbia?"

"My kitchen," Maggie said, and the room settled the way rooms do when a familiar story hits its first note. "We'll keep it to the before too. The TV balanced on the stack of church cookbooks because the counter made the picture crawl. Walter Cronkite low, the girls negotiating crayons like diplomats, the baby issuing vetoes from the high chair."

"You were making scalloped potatoes," Evie said.

"They were making me earn the 'scalloped.'" Charles called to say he'd be late because the truck had opinions about second gear. I considered whether we could stretch Tuesday's casserole into Wednesday if I added peas." She sipped peppermint. "Then the phone rang, the one on the wall with the curly cord, and Mrs. Lantz said, *Are you seeing this?* She didn't say what *this* was, which is how you knew it was big. I turned up the volume one click, just one. I didn't see the park yet, just a crawl at the bottom of the screen, a word you don't want near children. I stood very still with the dish towel in my hand and decided to learn new verbs. *Call. Write. Send.* It took me until morning to pick the first one. I'd been living on the safe ones—*stir, wait, sigh.*"

She looked out at the garden. "We'll put the rest in the next chapter. Today's set-up. The potatoes submitted. The girls colored a dog green and insisted it was an artistic choice. The baby slept twenty-two minutes, which is a crime against mothers. I folded the towel and made a list on the back of a spelling test. That's where my part starts."

Maggie's hand found Dot's. "Your turn, the hill," she said, nodding at the hat.

"The hill," Dot echoed. "Before the sit-ins, before the practice, there was the letter. *Come if you can.* Signed in a hand I could recognize across a sanctuary. There was also the talk with my parents, Daddy rubbing a thumbprint into the kitchen table and saying, *Hard now for easier later was the bargain. This is one way you pay it.*"

She touched the safety pin. "The first training wasn't dramatic. Two rows of chairs. Ladies who could make you sit up straighter just by breathing. *Write your reason,* the woman said. *When the noise rises, touch the paper. It'll outshout fear.*"

Evie leaned in. "And the hat."

"Packed the night before. Brim for a long day. The way a brim can turn a face into shade and a woman into someone who lasts. We practiced leaving and entering, how to keep the door from telling you who you are. That's where my part starts."

Kris reappeared with the afternoon mail. "A postcard for the Victory Club," she announced, delighted with the address Maggie had wrangled from the front desk. She slid a dog-eared card onto the table: the Lincoln Memorial in forgiving summer light.

"From Cindy," Maggie said, recognizing her daughter's tidy slant. *Mom, I found this in a secondhand bin and thought of Evie's hat. Proud of you. Love, C.* Maggie handed the card to Evie. She ran her thumb along the edge, as if smoothing a wrinkle that wasn't there, a hint of a smile finding her before she could stop it.

"We'll put it in the pocket," Maggie said, meaning the scrapbook sleeve labeled *The 1960s — Artifacts.* She slid the card under clear plastic beside a clipped headline, a church program, and a square of gingham with a bobby pin through it because Evie swore every good story had at least one bobby pin.

"Remind me of our rules," Evie said, more to herself than to them.

Maggie read from page one, where she'd written them in ink and underlined twice:

1. Tell it in order unless the heart needs a detour.
2. Name the small things; people trust you when you remember their elbows.
3. Don't gild; don't flatten.
4. Don't skip the parts that cost.
5. When memory fogs, let the others lend you theirs.

Dot tapped number five. "We made that one for days when the nouns wander," she said, kind and practical at once.

"They wander less when you two are here," Evie said. She fitted the brim over her hair for a second, then set it back where it wouldn't crease. Kris, pretending not to watch, clapped once, quietly.

Mr. Alvarez from the next table leaned over. "You three building a rocket ship?"

"Time machine," Evie said. "Launch in five."

"Bring back oranges," he replied, and returned to his crossword.

The volunteer with grape earrings popped her head in. "Ten minutes to film time. The good seats don't fight for themselves."

"We'll take the middle row," Maggie said. "So we can see and make our notes without being bossy about it."

Dot tucked the pin into the tissue. "We'll leave the Park for next time," she told Evie, not as an order, as a promise—the kind friends keep on your behalf until you're ready.

"Next time," Evie echoed. "Bus, map, strap. I'll tell you the sound the bus made."

Maggie closed the spiral with the satisfaction of a teacher ending a clean lesson. "Summary," she read:

Birmingham — Evie: the call, the bus, the tools; the hinge before the door.

Suburbia — Maggie: lists and casseroles; verbs chosen at a kitchen wall phone.

Atlanta — Dot: the letter, the hill, the reason folded where a hand can find it.

We learned courage in groups. Don't skip the parts that cost.

They rose in small choreography, Maggie collecting cups, Dot settling the hat, Evie smoothing the front of her blouse as if steadying herself. The TV screen in the lounge held still on a crowd and a podium waiting. Dot tipped her hatless head. Maggie squeezed their hands, classroom-style.

"Next time," Evie said to the brim. "Bus, map, strap. Then the morning we walked into Kelly Ingram Park."

The film began to roll.

The chapter they'd promised next opened its palm and waited.

8

THE REPORTER IN THE SOUTH

1963 • EVIE

Bus, map, strap.

Map folded in her pocket. Camera strap biting the back of her neck. Breath tight but legs moving because the day wouldn't wait. The bus had carried her to Kelly Ingram Park.

The park breathed like a held lung, hot, bright, already trembling at the edge of breaking.

Evie paid the cab, shouldered her camera, and stepped into air that tasted faintly of iron. Church bells somewhere. A hymn threading through chants. Chalk on the sidewalk: *FREEDOM*, half-smudged by a hundred brave soles.

She wrote three plain lines. *Tuesday, first week of May. Children marching for days. Hoses expected. Hymns already.* Ink small. Day enormous. She could feel the gap between what fit on paper and what lived in the air.

A girl, maybe eight, knelt to tie her brother's shoe beneath a spindly tree. His sign read *Let us be free*, wrinkled in his fist. The ordinary tenderness of it knocked the wind from Evie. She lifted her camera, Nikon F, Tri-X loaded.

Click.

The shutter sounded indecently clean.

Maggie teaching a toddler to knot laces at a church picnic flickered up, her laugh steady as summer. Then Dot's voice the first time they'd marched for anything at all, sure, level, unafraid. Memory didn't distract; it steadied. The past put a hand on Evie's shoulder and stood with her.

The first hose struck.

Water hit the line of children with a force that made the air grunt. A girl in a yellow dress held one impossible second, then flew backward, dress flaring like a flag before she fell.

Evie ducked behind a light pole, camera to her eye.

Click. A boy's arms over his head.

Click. A policeman's jaw locked like a door.

Click. Yellow mid-fall, water exploding like glass.

A cop turned. "You don't belong here."

She showed her press pass. He slapped it away.

"I do now," she said, voice steadier than she felt, and kept shooting. Not for a byline. Because truth had chosen her.

Miss Clarice, organizer, folder full of names, spine like rebar, tipped her toward a safer door—the back of Leon Wylie's barbershop.

Leon's nephew, fingers nicked from Saturday fades, knew his way around trays and tongs. Developer in a chipped pitcher. Clothespins for clips. Faces rose through chemicals, water ghosts turning back to children.

"Good," the nephew said softly, which meant *true.*

By dusk she'd claimed a corner of the Sixteenth Street Baptist basement—coffee, leaflets, the stubborn patience of people who'd waited their whole lives to be heard. She rolled a sheet into her battered Royal and bled the day onto the page. No euphemisms. No softening. Children knocked down by city water. Mothers shielding sons. Names, not numbers.

The wire tech fed her photo into the transmitter. The machine sang its metallic hymn as the image crawled north line by line, toward living rooms that would swear they hadn't known.

At the pay phone she braced the receiver, a dime and a spare warming her palm.

"City desk."

"It's Evie. Put me through to Max."

"You okay?" her editor rasped.

"I've got copy and the lead shot. Hoses on kids, ten, twelve years old. You'll know the photo."

"We're walking a tightrope. Keep the language—"

"It's careful," she said. "It's true."

A beat. "Don't get yourself killed."

"I'll call tomorrow. If I can."

Backlash came fast—envelopes that stank of rage, words like brands.

"I stood by it," Max said, smoking to the filter. "Don't get used to it. One more step and they'll chain you to wedding copy."

They tried to tame her with tulle.

She argued clean and hard. *The Times* is there. *The Post* is there. History will be, too. Fear of being small beat fear of being hurt. He said yes.

She listened more than she spoke. She learned how news actually moved where power didn't want it to: Miss Clarice, Isaiah keeping kids two by two, Mrs. Dawes singing when voices went thin, Reverend Cole calling the police "our impatient adversaries" with a wryness that kept the room from breaking.

She was a vessel, not the story.

She wrote about the boy who handed his backpack to his sister like a crown. The girl who asked a deacon to hold her shoes and he said, *Ruin them with history, baby.* Mothers everywhere, hands on shoulders, mouths at ears, braiding courage through hair parted straight for school.

Nights taught new reflexes: siren, hymn, the ice machine coughing to life. Shoes you could run in. Two dimes in the pocket. The motel mirror that made her smaller than she was, and the refusal to accept its scale.

In a Montgomery church hall that smelled of paper fans and fried chicken, Dr. King's voice came steady, more weary than thunder.

"We saw our children face the hoses. Now our organizing must be worthy of their courage."

He asked what she'd seen and listened like it mattered.

"We're building a movement, not a moment. The march will be a step. We'll need all the steps."

"Will it change things?"

"It must."

A man with an enamel mug edged close. "You wrote about my daughter."

"The girl in the yellow dress?"

He nodded. "She didn't cry till after. I did, once she slept."

She took his hand, the human seam that keeps a world from splitting.

Back in Birmingham, kitchen tables did the work microphones wouldn't. Sweet tea like sacrament, notes on her thigh when hands needed holding. Mrs. Dawes kept a second ledger in the family Bible—arrests, dates, names in teacher's hand. "Later, we'll ink it."

Mrs. Hill slid over an Easter photo. "This is the face they hosed. I want them to see both pictures when they sleep."

Permission asked plainly, with room for no.

"Use his name," Mrs. Hill said. "Or just my son. Don't let them make him a lesson without a life."

Mothers at the Line ran metro, then page A-1 when letters poured in from women who recognized themselves. Max didn't say she was right. He bought lunch and didn't lift his cigarette.

"You're making me brave."

"I'm just writing down what women already are."

On the National Mall in August, the crowd made its own weather. From the press stand she saw faces knit into one hope, the Lincoln Memorial holding the sky while a dream rose and landed.

Her notebook slid to her feet. Some moments you don't scribble; you keep. Later at the desk:

I saw the dream rise like smoke and settle like ash on the nation's conscience.

May we be worthy of the weight.

Max read it twice, voice cracked. "You sure you're not a poet?"

"No. Just telling the truth. Some days truth sounds like poetry."

TIME ran the yellow-dress photo. It felt less like triumph than being scraped clean and sent back to the line. Hate mail thickened. So did other envelopes—teachers in Ohio, a waitress in Idaho tucking cash for bail, a mother in Boston: *My son is eight. Thank you for making me see.*

The bile went to the trash, the thanks to a shoebox.

Late one night the telephone rang with a sound that knew its own importance.

"Carter," Dot said. "I saw the photo. You did good."

"That means more than Max's yes."

"I saw it in her eyes, the part that wouldn't break. Your picture caught that. They trying to bury you under recipes and hat reviews?"

"Threatening to. I won't let them."

"Don't you dare. Not after this."

Evie stood in her kitchen after, quiet holding her up. She thought what Maggie would've seen first—the mothers. She taped the yellow-dress print to her refrigerator. Not a trophy. A reason.

She wrote two lines for morning: *Mothers at the Line—more interviews. Call Maggie.*

By year's end, she'd learned to park nose-out and choose motels that would swap rooms without fuss. The desk job came with a raise and a threat.

"I want the assignments where the nouns are alive," she told Max. "If I'm wrong, chain me to Style and I'll review hats for a month."

"You'll hate hats."

"I already do."

December snow in Richmond, thin flakes making the streetlights look like patient saints.

"Still good?" Dot asked from a pay phone's other end.

"Still good."

"Light is a practice."

"So is stubborn."

"Come up when you can," Dot said. "Window table. Peppermint tea."

That night, the wire machine in Birmingham sang again, the image crawling north line by line, toward a counter TV in Pennsylvania where a woman rinsing dishes would stop and learn new verbs.

9

SUBURBIA & SILENCE

1963 • MAGGIE

The dishwater was hot enough to pink her forearms. Walter Cronkite's voice carried from the counter set, comforting until it wasn't.

"...children in Birmingham were met with fire hoses and police dogs..."

Her hand stilled. On the snowy screen, a girl in a soaked cotton dress lifted her arms, surrender and defiance at once, before the water flung her backward. Hair stuck to her cheeks in dark lines. Water shouldn't be a weapon, Maggie thought, and something cinched under her ribs.

In the living room, the laugh track warmed up for a world where problems fit between commercials. She dried her hands, but the cotton refused to do the job.

From the easy chair, Charles didn't look up. "Turn that garbage off. We've got enough going on."

Normal life held. Tommy's blanket fort advanced on the armchair. Cindy and Wendy colored, humming *Puff, the Magic Dragon*. Ozzie and Harriet waited in the wings. Meatloaf. Carpet cleaner. Maggie couldn't move.

She used to have a vow, back when she was Maggie Thompson and not Mrs. Miller with a coupon caddy and a dentist-appointment calendar. She and Evie and Dot had written it in Evie's notebook: girls of consequence. The Victory Club. A promise made on a splintered bench.

The tap sputtered. The sink refilled. Water wasn't meant to wound. It shouldn't have to be survived.

The *Manchester Gazette* lay folded by the percolator the next morning. She shook it open and saw the photograph before the headline, a small Black girl mid-step, a white arc driving her sideways. The caption named the place, Kelly Ingram Park. Below it, neat italics read, *Photo by Evelyn Gross*.

Evie.

Brand-new and exactly right. Evie had always walked toward the noise, Maggie thought, and felt the old bench under her knees for one bright second.

All day the beige rotary on the kitchen wall tugged at her. What would I say? *I'm proud of you. I'm sorry I disappeared. I've done nothing.*

By evening, she slid the paper under *Better Homes & Gardens* as if tucking away a relic. Evie's name still glowed through the newsprint.

Routine reasserted itself, lunches, lists, laundry, the six-fifteen slam of the back door. "Those people," Charles said over the editorial page. "Ought to learn to wait their turn." The phrase landed like grit in her shoe.

At the pediatrician she reached for *TIME*. The yellow-dress photo hit her again, Evelyn Gross small but unmistakable. *That girl is somebody's Cindy. Somebody's Wendy.* The recognition came like a clean break—painful and clarifying at once.

She turned into the library without deciding to. Lemon oil, dust motes like small planets. *Stride Toward Freedom*, a pamphlet tucked between thicker books, *Letter from Birmingham Jail. Injustice anywhere is a threat to justice everywhere. Shallow understanding from people of good will... the appalling silence of the good people.* Heat she couldn't blame on July.

"You can take three, dear," Mrs. Ort said. Maggie checked out four and slid the pamphlet inside the King book like a secret. After bedtime, she read until the clock forgot it was late. Silence no longer felt neutral; it felt like choosing not to see.

The scrap-fabric shoebox became clippings. Each morning, she fed it. While shopping in the city, she bought *The Nation* and hid it under the mattress, heart too loud walking back to the car.

September 15. Static, and then four names: Addie Mae Collins, Denise McNair, Carole Robertson, Cynthia Wesley. Her throat went dry. The spoon she was holding hit the counter and rolled. She said their names in the empty kitchen so they wouldn't remain a number.

Still, at church, when the pastor preached law and order and called marches disruptive, her mouth stayed closed. At coffee, Barb said, "If they were grateful, none of this would be necessary." Maggie stirred cream into someone else's cup. "Grateful to whom for what?" she asked, and the spoon stopped clinking. Five beats of quiet. Then a subject change. She told herself she lacked the words. She suspected she lacked practice. She was beginning to understand the difference.

Cherries came in glossy and red. Juice found every cut. "Who's that?" she asked as Cindy drew, tongue hooked in concentration. "Rosa," Cindy said. "We both like purple." A small door swung, not wide, but wider.

A week later, sorting bills, Maggie glanced at the evening news and saw Dot, so fast it could be argued she imagined it, hauled toward a police car, chin up, eyes fierce. The weather returned. Maggie didn't.

When had they stopped telling the truth to each other? When had she stopped telling the truth to herself?

A notice in the *Gazette* tucked itself between washing-machine ads and winter coats: Friends Meetinghouse, gathering for those concerned about the direction of our country. She cut it out before Charles could toss the paper.

She sat in the back on a hard chair, palms damp. Lemon oil, old paper, the quiet settling thick as a blanket, kind as a hand. A young Black woman spoke, calm, specific, about voter suppression and red lines curving around real neighborhoods. "We need allies who are steady," she said. "Not loud for a week. Steady."

Maggie's throat closed around every sentence she didn't ask. She listened like it counted. When the clipboard came, she hovered, then printed her name beside *bake cookies*. A beginning. Not a banner, but a beginning.

At home, Charles spotted the flyer. "What's this?"

"A community thing."

"Don't get caught up in protest nonsense. Not our business."

"It's somebody's business," she said, plain. He looked a moment longer than usual, then nodded once. Conversation postponed, not erased.

Thursday, the kitchen smelled like vanilla. By the next meeting, she was collating a registration-drive newsletter, stapler awkward and then less so. "Steady counts, honey," said the woman beside her, sliding over paperclips like a sacrament. Something in her silence began to unstick.

Changes started in the house, too. "Sometimes I think they forget how good they have it," Barb said. "Good by whose measure?" Maggie asked. When Tommy wondered why people marched, she said, "Because they aren't treated the same, and they should be." "That's dumb," Tommy said, and she let it stand as a lesson.

She mailed small checks in plain envelopes. Invited Rosa after school; when Rosa's mother hesitated at pickup, Maggie met her at the curb. "Please come in. We have too many cherries." A blind across the street twitched. Maggie kept her smile easy and her voice everyday, as if cherries were all that was at stake.

On a Wednesday when Charles worked late, she pulled out pale-blue stationery.

Dear Evie,

I saw your photograph. I see you. I'm learning to look straight on. Thank you for pointing your camera when the world told you not to. I'm late, but I'm here.

Dear Dot,

I've been quiet when I owed you my voice. I'm listening now, really, and trying to become the kind of friend who stands beside you in rooms that once scared me. If you'll bear my late arrival, may I begin again?

She slid a snapshot into Dot's envelope: Cindy and Wendy barefoot in the yard, arms slung around Rosa in a violet dress. Three heads tipped together the way children invent peace.

At the curbside mailbox, the lid clanked and the letters slid out of sight. Her chest felt loose and sore, like a muscle waking.

Baltimore, Three Days Later. Dot read the letter twice, the photograph warm in her palm. "I see you too, Magpie," she said to the quiet, and reached for her own stationery.

Come when you can. Window table. Peppermint tea. Bring the photo so I can put names to laughter.

Washington, D.C., That Evening. Evie nearly missed the mail slot. *Maggie* in a hand she knew before she could admit it. She didn't write back yet. In her cedar-smelling journal she wrote, *October 4, 1963. Maggie wrote to me. Maybe consequence can be quiet and steady and late and still real.* She smoothed the letter so its edges wouldn't curl and looked from it to the yellow-dress photo on the icebox.

"Onward," she said, Dot's word, and meant it.

10

CHAINS & CHANGE

1964 • DOT

Spring 1964. Atlanta on the ticket. The hat came first. Straw brim, narrow ribbon. Shade is a strategy. She lifted Maggie's letter from the mantel, slid the photo of three girls, two familiar and one new in violet, beneath the hat's lining, and set both in the box.

On the bus idling outside Shiloh Baptist, she kept the hat on her lap while the aisle filled with thermoses, paper fans, and last-minute instructions. She'd first worn it the previous August, standing shoulder to shoulder with strangers who became something larger than a crowd by day's end. That was where she met Clara—waiting for water, trading names, discovering they taught the same age and worried about the same quiet things.

When the sun rose over Washington that morning, the hat had done its job. So had she. Ushers in white shirts guided them street by street. Paper cups found their way down long lines. A voice at the Lincoln Memorial reached into their ribs and steadied them still.

She'd learned something there that never left. They weren't brave alone. You learned courage in formation.

Clara's letter had come on a Tuesday, its loops familiar. *Come if you can. Sit-ins at McClellan's. Training in Ebenezer's basement. We need teachers who can keep children steady. Onward.*

Dot taught all day, vowel charts and Baldwin, and graded after dinner. Then she folded her Sunday dress into the suitcase along with the hat and a tin of bobby pins. Station. Ticket. Late train south. Two volunteers slept in their coats and woke to Georgia light.

The Basement

Ebenezer smelled like hymnals and floor wax. Folding chairs scraped. Someone tapped time with a pencil. A coalition trainer, calm as a nurse and with a voice that could quiet a gym, set the rhythm.

"Eyes forward. Hands where they can be seen. If someone pours coffee on you, you don't move. When fear climbs, don't grip the counter. Hands open. If you need to breathe, link with the person beside you and take it together."

They practiced. Sit. Uncross your legs. Fold your hands. Don't let the door tell you who you are.

A girl in a borrowed dress shook so hard the safety pin at her collar worried the fabric. Dot knelt until their eyes were level. "Look at me. You aren't what they say you are. You're strong. You're brave. You aren't alone." The girl nodded. Dot tucked the pin through a second layer and smoothed it flat. Teacher hands, different classroom.

Clara slipped in late with a stack of flyers, blue headband bright as a banner. "Miss Baltimore," she said, grin quick. Dot's mouth answered before she could think. Her laugh arrived before judgment did.

"Remember your reasons," the trainer said. "Write one. Fold it. Then pocket it."

Dot wrote, *My students deserve to sit where they please*, folded the slip, slid it into her dress, and tapped it once like a promise.

They left Ebenezer two by two, collars straight, reasons folded. Heat met them at the door and walked beside them to Auburn Avenue.

McClellan's

The diner hunched under an awning that had seen too many summers. Black-and-white tile cracked at the seams. Red vinyl stools. A jukebox turned down to a private murmur. Grease ticking. A plate-warmer buzzing like a wasp. *You've Really Got a Hold on Me* whispered the root into tension.

They went in pairs, then fours. Dot and Clara took two stools near the middle, hands quiet.

"I'd like a cup of coffee, please," Dot said, a dollar on the counter. Eyes forward.

The busboy froze. The older waitress polished an already clean circle. A man in a straw hat rustled his paper like thunder. The cook reddened as if the heat lived inside him.

"Get out," he said, voice close to shaking. "All of you."

Training is a kind of prayer. Dot didn't move. Clara's knee brushed hers and stayed.

Water hit first, cold, a full pitcher slamming into Dot's lap and sheeting off to the tile. Another splash caught the back of her neck. Mustard followed, sharp where it found a scrape she hadn't known was there.

The girl from the basement two stools down made a sound between a gasp and a sob. Without looking, Dot found her fingers and held on. Breathe in. Breathe out. *Together.*

Chairs scraped. A man spit near Clara's shoe. A glass shattered in back. Then officers burst in, fast and loud, handcuffs clattering on their belts, hands on Dot's shoulders, dragging. Knees to linoleum, a spark up her spine. Metal in her mouth. Fear. Resolve.

"Stand up," someone barked.

She did. Wrist bones learned the neat bites of the cuffs. Her heart pounded toward her throat and then returned to its post.

Clara's fingers found hers for one beat before they were separated. "Onward," Clara said. Dot filed the word where she kept the important ones.

The Cell

Air with weight. Wet cotton, old concrete, breath. Women sat shoulder to shoulder, skirts stuck to their knees, stockings ruined, faces streaked with water, coffee, patience. A hymn under one breath; another voice picked up the second line and let it climb.

Dot took roll the way she did in homeroom, counting without calling attention. Ella with chipped pink polish. Ruthie with cornbread in a handkerchief. The girl with the safety pin, now bent at a brave angle.

Across from her, Clara's headband tilted. "You held," Clara said.

"So did you," Dot answered, voice steadier than she felt.

"Hayes got picked up at the next block," someone murmured. "A pastor went with him."

"We're in good company," Dot said, and meant it.

Silence, not unkind.

"I don't like when people call us brave," Clara said, almost conversational. "Like it's a prize. I don't want to be brave. I want to be free."

"Me too," Dot said, the words catching and holding.

Keys. A door. Noon like a cymbal. By nightfall, a northbound train. Hat on her knees. Wrists sore and hopeful.

Baltimore

Her parents were waiting at her apartment door. Her father clocked the bruise blossoming under her eye. "Another arrest?" he asked finally, anger he was calling fear. He set his hat brim up—his tell.

"I'm trying to teach," she said. "In every room I can find."

"Teach here. Write letters. March on North Avenue. Don't keep going where men with batons are practicing your name."

She thought of the girl with the safety pin and the slip of paper in her pocket. "Some of my students will go south for Christmas and be told where they can eat," she said, gentle and clear. "I don't want to teach courage with a map."

"Promise me you'll come back next time."

She couldn't. "I'll try," she said, because he was her father.

Her mother cupped her cheek at the edge of the bruise. "I'm proud of you," she said, voice steadying. "And I'm afraid. Both are true."

"I know." Dot pressed her hand over hers. "Both are true for me too."

Home and Away.

The work didn't end with the cell door. On Monday, she wore a

scarf over the yellow bloom and wrote *Langston Hughes: Freedom's Plow*
on the board. She underlined *row* and *together* and sent two boys to the
library for extra copies because the class was larger than the room
expected.

Night buses when she could. Weekends when she had them. Atlanta
again. Albany. A teachers' march in Baltimore where the microphones
died and they shouted anyway.

In Washington, when Clara could pry an hour from meetings, they
chose a café between a laundromat and a used bookstore. Ceiling fans
turned lazy circles. Two glasses of sweet tea sweated on Formica. Clara
sat with her back to the wall, door in sight.

"You write with teeth," Clara said, tapping Dot's editorial in the
Baltimore Afro-American. "Ever think about doing more of it?"

"I teach," Dot said, truest sentence she knew.

"So teach and write," Clara said. "Both hands."

With men, Dot had shrunk or shifted, agreeable by reflex. With
Clara, she didn't adjust. She exhaled. She could simply be.

"You don't have to hide with me," Clara said once, palm warm at
Dot's jaw. A door long painted shut moved on its hinges.

The world kept moving. Mississippi called Clara that summer, then
Atlantic City. Fights over who was allowed in the room, arguments held
low over a hotel lamp, names like Fannie Lou Hamer spoken with reverence and urgency. Letters came, ink smudged by heat and the life of the
work. Calls landed at odd hours—static, Clara's laugh, a child singing
while his grandmother cried.

Then calls thinned. Letters took longer. Absence didn't announce
itself; it accumulated. The work has a way of being the loudest voice in
the room.

Dot made herself a rule: no bitterness. She kept teaching. She graded
until the corners of the stack went soft. She taped Zora, Baldwin, Hans-
berry, and Hughes to the wall, eyes steady above chalk dust. She folded
the hat back into its box, slid the bus stub beside it, and tucked the bent
safety pin into a corner like a relic. Beneath the lining were Maggie's
letter and the violet-dress photo, a tether to the girls they'd been and the
women they still were.

On a night when quiet weighed more than usual, she poured one drink she should've skipped, opened her desk drawer, and wrote:

Clara,

I taught Fannie Lou Hamer today. I told them a voice can be a key and a hammer both. I'm still here, teaching, marching when I can. I miss you. I hope you're safe. I hope you eat. I hope you sleep. Onward, always.

Dot

She folded the letter, left the address blank, and slid it into the drawer with the others.

Practice

Years later, a public-television documentary. Grainy streets she'd walked. A voice she knew by shape if not by microphone. No one said her name. That was never the point. She returned the shoebox to its shelf and set her alarm.

Monday, she wrote on the board, block letters:

FREEDOM IS A PRACTICE.

"This week," she said, "write about a moment that changed you. Name it plain. Tell me what it cost and what it gave back."

A boy in row two raised his hand. "What changed you, Miss Carter?"

Dot thought of August sun on a brim, a safety pin worrying cotton, a blue headband, a cold pitcher that didn't move her off her stool.

"A girl in a blue headband," she said, "and a diner that didn't want us."

Paper slid across desks. Pencils began. And Dot felt, just as she had on the Mall and at the counter and in a basement with folding chairs, that something important was being built a small, steady line at a time.

We weren't brave alone, she thought.

Then she began again, because practice is how courage stays, how truth becomes habit, how ordinary becomes holy work.

11

ONWARD

PRESENT • MANCHESTER MEADOWS • EVIE

The common room rested in its afternoon hush. Clouded light slipped through the blinds, laying pale stripes across the carpet and the window table where they always met. The radiator gave a polite throat-clear now and then, as if to remind the room it still had opinions.

Peppermint first, then paper. That was today's arrangement. Maggie set three cups in a small triangle and opened the album. Dot arrived with the shoebox tucked under her arm, the lid penciled 1963–64. Evie came last, cardigan askew, shawl sliding from her shoulder as if she'd outrun a thought.

"Window table," Evie said, small and pleased.

"As promised," Maggie answered. She turned a page, and something thinned and fluttered to her lap. An envelope, yellowed at the edges. *Evelyn Gross*, written in a hand all three of them would've known in the dark.

Evie stilled. "Dot?"

Dot's mouth pressed into its old line. "I sent a lot of those."

Evie lifted the flap with careful fingers. The letter smelled faintly of time and pencil shavings. A few lines in and her breath snagged—news from Atlanta, Clara's laugh written in present tense, how fear and purpose braid if you let other hands hold the rope.

"I didn't know I had this," she said, voice rough. "I didn't read them."

Dot looked out the window long enough to find her balance. "I kept writing anyway."

"I should've answered." Evie slid the paper back into its skin. "I should've come home."

Maggie set a palm over the album, steadying it and the day. "Say it plain," she murmured.

Dot did. "You left, and I was still in the work. I wanted my friend."

Evie met her eyes. "You had Clara. I just didn't know how to be two people at once."

Silence held, not empty but listening. The hall clock hustled the minute hand along, three minutes fast as always.

Maggie nudged the teacups closer. "Then let's try again. Beginning counts."

Dot's shoulders eased a fraction. "Beginning counts."

They drank. The peppermint was sharp and kind.

Maggie turned another page. Three girls beamed under a crooked banner that read *Victory at Last!* The street behind them was quilted with bunting. Evie's arm hooked Dot's shoulders. Maggie's pigtails listed cheerfully off course.

"We were something else," Dot said.

"We still are," Maggie answered, and she made it true with the steadiness in her voice.

Evie's fingers rested on the photo a beat longer, then she looked up. "If I tell you the missing years," she said, "will you keep me honest?"

Dot nodded. "Name streets. Don't skip the parts that cost."

Maggie closed the album, gentle. "Start where it broke and how you kept going."

Evie drew the shawl higher, as if to gather herself. "Paris," she said. "A room that smelled like coffee and rain. And a phone I couldn't bring myself to pick up."

Dot's hand moved, almost without permission, to lay the old bent safety pin on the table. Small. Bright. Stubborn. "Go on," she said.

Mr. Alvarez from the card table lifted his head. "Plotting again?"

"Only in the wholesome sense," Evie said. "Chronology may suffer."

"Bring back lower prices," he replied solemnly, and bent to his cross-word again.

Across the hall, a volunteer rearranged chairs for bingo with the same reverence other people give to altar candles. The television in the corner droned a weather report no one believed.

"The rules," Maggie said, tapping the margin of the album where she'd written them in a teacher's hand. "One: tell it in order unless the heart needs a detour. Two: name the small things. People trust you when you remember their elbows. Three: don't gild, don't flatten. Four: don't skip the parts that cost. And five," she said, softer, "when memory fogs, let the others lend you theirs."

Evie smiled. "That one's saving me lately."

"Us," Dot said. "Plural on purpose."

They were quiet the way old friends can be, no need to entertain the silence. Outside, a sparrow hopped along the window ledge, scolding something only birds understand. Inside, the peppermint cooled, and Evie felt the steadying weight of the safety pin near her wrist, exactly where Dot had set it.

The nurse leaned in with a clipboard. "Bingo in ten."

"No thanks," Dot said without looking up.

Evie groaned. "It's always bingo or chair yoga. I want a whiskey and a typewriter."

"I'll see what I can do," the nurse laughed and moved on, leaving them to their own small climate.

"What I miss," Maggie said into the quiet, "is the sound of high heels on pavement. Us running down Main Street after curfew."

"I always got caught," Dot said.

"Only because you laughed too loud," Evie told her.

"And because Maggie wore perfume like a rose bush in heat," Dot added.

"That perfume was *Evening in Paris*, thank you," Maggie said, and the laughter that bloomed between them felt like a crack in a wall letting light in.

"Some mornings I forget what year it is," Evie admitted. "Sometimes I wake up thinking I'm back in my dorm room at Barnard."

"We'll remember for you," Maggie said.

"Yeah," Dot added. "We've got you."

Evie exhaled. "All right. Paris later. For now—" She tapped the envelope. "Let's take this one apart."

They read Dot's letter aloud in pieces, the way you eat cake slowly to make it last. Every few lines Maggie paused to gloss the names—Clara, Miss Estelle from the dining hall, the girl with the safety pin—anchoring Evie's memory to Dot's ink. Evie heard her own younger self inside the spaces: the way she kept receipts in her wallet in case fear needed itemizing; the habit of parking nose-out; how she bought two pairs of the same plain shoes so her feet never had to learn new blisters on assignment.

"I'm sorry," she said again, quieter. "I thought if I looked back, I'd fall back."

Dot's answer was easy and exact. "Looking isn't falling."

"Besides," Maggie added, "if you'd fallen, we'd have hauled you up by the belt like always."

Evie huffed a laugh that surprised her with its warmth. "True."

They let the album rest and picked up the shoebox. Inside were the kept things: a church program soft as cloth; the diner check Dot paid and kept; a barrette of Maggie's from 1950-something that had migrated into the Civil Rights box as if history needed a hairpin; a postcard of the Lincoln Memorial with a sun-bleached edge. Objects, Evie thought, meant to keep a life from slipping.

"Do you remember the day we made our rules?" Maggie asked. "At the bench behind the library? You two made me swear not to apologize before opinions."

"And we made Evie promise to eat before interviews," Dot said. "She's mean when she's hungry."

Evie lifted her chin. "Accurate."

"And we made you," Maggie told Dot, "promise to let someone else carry the heavy box once in a while."

Dot made a face. "Working on it."

"Still," Maggie said, "we kept most of them. That counts."

From the hallway, the bingo caller's voice sailed in. "B12 like the vitamin!"

"Bless them," Dot said. "May they all win lamps."

"Or those terrifying glass roosters," Maggie sighed. "I had one for years. It watched me make soup."

Evie traced the postcard's edge until the paper warmed under her finger. "There's another rule I need." She looked from one to the other. "When I start the Paris story, if I try to make myself prettier than I was, stop me."

Dot's eyebrows tipped. "We won't have to."

Maggie patted Evie's wrist. "We'll ask for the unflattering parts, too."

They drifted for a while, stories looping and crossing. Dot's first classroom with desks two inches too small. Maggie smuggling novels into the church kitchen to read between casseroles. Evie confessing she still sometimes dreamed in headline fonts. Mr. Alvarez wandered past and donated three butterscotch candies to the cause. "Fuel," he said, and kept going.

Dot vanished with a conspiratorial, "Back in a tick," her slippers whispering down the hall.

Later, the door swung open with a theatrical squeak and Dot reappeared in a towel turban, oversized pink robe, and lime-green fuzzy slippers, balancing three mugs on a floral tray.

"Evening delivery," she announced. "In-flight meal includes lukewarm cocoa and a garnish of unidentifiable cookie crumbs. Buckle up."

"You look like Lucille Ball after a tumble through the laundry," Evie said.

"Fashion is pain," Dot replied serenely. "I've evolved beyond your understanding."

Maggie peered at the tray. "Is that my World's Okayest Mom mug?"

"I liberated it from Mr. Giambalvo," she said. "He's confiscated half the residents' mugs—keeps them hidden in his room. I bartered with tapioca and charm."

They sipped. The cocoa was warm, sweet, and suspicious.

Maggie coughed. "Dot, what's in this?"

"Spicy chocolate. Cayenne, pinch of nutmeg. Sophisticated."

"It's illegal in at least twelve retirement homes," Evie rasped, eyes watering.

"You're welcome," Dot said. "Keeps the blood moving."

They raised their mugs. The clink rang gently, like old glasses in a dance hall, like soda bottles on a summer porch.

"To weird cocoa and stubborn friends," Maggie said.

"And to never letting Dot near the spice rack again," Evie added.

"To the wars we fought, the ones we still fight, and the ones we somehow survived," Dot finished.

Steam curled between them. For a moment, the years fell away, and they were just three girls again—messy, loyal, stitched together by laughter and loss.

The nurse rolled by with a cart of nail polish—Coral Sunset, Cherry Jubilee, Electric Plum—and paused. "Ladies' night?" she asked.

"Board meeting," Dot said.

"Serious business," Maggie added, and accepted Cherry Jubilee like a vote.

The nurse moved on. Evie watched the bottle catch the light and thought of all the rooms where color had been the point—banners, quilts, a hat's narrow ribbon—and all the rooms where color had been the pretext for harm. She set the thought down gently, the way you set down a hot pan, and looked at her friends.

Some mornings, she'd told them, she woke certain she was still twenty. Other mornings, she felt the weight of every year stacked carefully behind her like books. Today, the years made a bridge.

Evie set her mug down, palms flat on the table as if bracing for a takeoff she finally meant to make.

"All right," she said. "Paris."

Maggie reached into the album pocket and slid the small index rule card to the middle of the table. Dot added the bent safety pin on top, anchoring it there.

"Go on," Dot said—not a command, a hand at her back.

Evie took in the room the way she used to frame a shot. The thin afternoon light. Three cups with lipstick crescents. Maggie's tidy handwriting in the margins. Dot's ridiculous green slippers pointing forward. The envelope, already opened, already counted.

"Paris," Evie began, quieter. "A borrowed room on Rue des Écoles. Coffee I pretended to like. Rain that made me think of home. I kept a coin in my pocket for the phone. I didn't use it."

"Name the street," Dot murmured.

Evie did.

"Name the hours," Maggie said.

Evie said them in order, like prayers. She didn't skip the parts that cost.

Outside, the sparrow gave up scolding and flew. Inside, the safety pin caught the light and held it, the way small, stubborn things sometimes do.

12

PROOF OF LIFE

LATE 1970S • EVIE

The attic window stuck in damp weather, and the rooftops looked like folded letters waiting to be opened. Morning smelled of coffee grounds, cold metal, and yesterday's Gauloises. The typewriter, a Smith-Corona that rattled like a valise, sat crooked on a wobbling table. Evie sat on the floor with her knees up, the machine pulled close like a confidante.

She wrote until the keys chattered herself warm, heat ticking through her fingertips. Then she'd stop, crack the window, and let Paris breathe on her—market stalls unfurling, the aproned baker dusting sugar from his sleeves, a schoolchild thumping up the stairs with a baguette like a baton. Rain found the guttering and made it sing. Pigeons bickered along the eaves.

It was finally quiet enough to hear what she'd been dodging.

Not because she didn't love home.

Because loving it had begun to hurt.

At night, the building's metal gate clanged shut and the hallway smelled of onions and wool. The concierge clucked at the draft and at Evie's shoes, sliding mail through her slot with the gravitas of a judge. Sometimes there were clippings from Max, sometimes a thin blue aerogram from a name she didn't expect, sometimes nothing at all. She learned how absence sounds when it lands on the floor.

She learned to cook eggs in a dented pan, to make one good coat pass for three, to ask the grocer for oranges with her hands when her mouth lost French.

What Sent Her: The Long 1960s

Birmingham put a hinge in her life and swung it open. The yellow dress, midair, water like shattering glass, ran in *TIME* with a line beneath: *Photo by Evelyn Gross.* Strangers sent thank-yous. Others sent threats. Editors called it "too raw," which was code for "too true."

Then the cascade: Dallas, an afternoon that changed the country's face. Memphis, balcony silence louder than any speech. A long, hushed nation along Bobby Kennedy's funeral train. In Chicago, tear gas curled into lenses and words. In New York, colleagues talked real estate while she kept tasting a smoke that wasn't there.

She ate from paper cartons beside hospital cots in Da Nang, learned the weight of a nineteen-year-old's name, learned to write with flies on her hands and still spell a mother's address right. One editor killed a piece about a boy who died holding his sister's photograph. "Too much," he said. Evie mailed it anyway to the boy's mother with a note: *He mattered.*

Somewhere along the road, her body adopted new reflexes. Sit with your back to the wall. Scan exits. Park nose-out. Keep two dimes in the small pocket and a third with the bobby pins. When the noise outside finally matched the noise inside, she bought a one-way ticket.

Paris was far enough to hear herself think.

The Work There: Late 1970s

She freelanced from a table that trembled if you breathed too hard. She learned the rhythm of filing from cafés where the coffee went cold and ashtrays filled with other people's stories. A wire editor on the boulevard took her copy if she came with facts, clean verbs, and exact streets. The telex chattered like a flock; she timed her sentences to its breath.

Beirut arrived by telegram and late phone calls—a mother keening through a bad line, the sound a city makes when it braces. Belfast came in rain and hard boots on pavement. Rome arrived in sirens that could, for a certain second, be mistaken for church bells.

She borrowed a darkroom from a friend of a friend on the quai. D-76 in a chipped beaker, clothespins for clips, hands remembering the old motions as if they were prayer. Faces surfaced in trays—grainy, stubborn, undeniable. Paper was dear; she printed the number she needed and no more.

At first, she phoned Dot and Maggie in her mind every night. *Tomorrow* became habit. Guilt, like dust, settled until it felt like part of the furniture. When her mother's birthday came and she only managed a telegram that missed the day by two, she folded the receipt into her wallet as punishment and proof.

A man named Jacques made duck on Sundays and played records with scratches she could map with her eyes closed. He kept bread in a checked cloth, matches in a jam jar, and pain from '68 under brave jokes. He asked for a future. She said no. "You belong to the ghosts," he told her gently, closing the jam jar.

He wasn't wrong.

The Two Notebooks

Evie kept two notebooks. One for facts—names spelled right, streets and dates, the weather's precise mischief, what color a man's tie was when the world changed. The other for what wouldn't sit still: a father's coat absorbing a child's sob, a medic folding a letter and asking her to mail it home if, the angle a widow held her jaw to keep from coming apart.

On some rooftops she tried to write about joy—Bastille Day sparks stuttering into the sky, strangers singing with their whole throats. The words wouldn't land. Joy felt like a language she could still understand but no longer spoke. She practiced anyway. *Practice makes truth a habit,* she wrote, and left it at that.

She didn't schedule tears; they never kept office hours. But there were mornings she woke with salt at the corners of her mouth—

evidence of a body that remembered what the mind refused to calendar.

On Tuesdays, the bookshop on the quai let you drink weak tea if you read in the corner and didn't drip on the pages. She read Baldwin again, slower. She copied one sentence into the back of the facts notebook: *Love does not begin and end the way we seem to think it does.* She let it sit and do its work.

Paris, Lived Small

A neighbor played the same Edith Piaf record every Sunday at 3. The woman upstairs clacked her heels in a steady cadence, and then, after Christmas, stopped; a baby arrived, and the building learned a new tempo. In winter, the stairwell smelled of damp wool and mended gloves; in spring it smelled of oranges and new soap and the wet iron tang of the Métro.

Evie bought bread from a baker who called everyone *ma fille* and oranges from a stall where the vendor weighed honesty with fruit. When she paid in coins, she thought about pay phones—how a single call could reorder a life—and still didn't make one.

On good afternoons, she walked up the hill to the cemetery to read names and let other people's dates argue with her own. On bad afternoons, she made pasta and called it dinner and didn't pretend.

The Call: Bastille Day, 1979

Fireworks stitched the dark. In the street below, someone drummed on a trash can with purposeful joy. The phone rang. Evie let it go six times. On the seventh, she picked up.

"Evie?" Maggie's voice—careful and warm, like a hand at her back.

A thousand apologies crowded the line. None would fit through.

"How did you find me?" Evie asked, sitting hard on the sill.

"Your byline gave you away." Maggie's smile lived in the words. "I miss you. Dot does, too."

Evie gripped the cord. "I don't know what to say."

"You don't have to," Maggie said. "Just listen."

They talked small things—what Paris rain sounds like on zinc, whether spider plants can go dormant and still be trusted with hope. Maggie described a child's solemn fascination with clothespins. Evie described a dog who patrolled the roofline like a mayor. They didn't say *forgive me,* or *why didn't you,* or *I was so lonely I made lists to hear your names.*

When the line went quiet, Evie stayed by the window until the street stopped singing. Then she took the smaller notebook and wrote: *Window table. Begin here.*

Her voice felt safe again.

The Ledger of Coming Back: 1979–1980

The next months were a practice. She mailed a clipping to Dot with a note no longer than a breath: *Still here. Still naming things plain.* She sent Maggie a postcard of a market stall blazing with oranges. On the back: *Save me a cup. I take my tea like confession.*

She began saying their names out loud when she walked—the way a person rehearses for a hard call. Dot. Maggie. Manchester. The words steadied her hands. She practiced answers no one had asked yet. *Where did you go?* To hear myself. *Why didn't you call?* I didn't trust my voice not to break. *Are you coming back?* Yes.

Work still called—Beirut, Rome, Belfast—and she still went. She flew with a coat that could be formal or not, a dress that looked like Sunday, two pairs of the same plain shoes, and the Victory Club photo in her wallet like credit. She carried a safety pin in the little pocket as if it could hold a day together by itself. In hotel mirrors she practiced telling the truth without softening. In airport bathrooms she practiced breathing the way Dot had taught girls in a church basement: together, steady, open hands.

Jacques offered to drive her to Orly once and tried, kindly, one more proposal. "Stay," he said in the car park fog. "We'll buy rugs and fight about nothing. I'll learn to like your bad coffee."

Evie kissed his cheek and answered in the only sentence that didn't lie. "You deserve someone who isn't listening for distant sirens."

He grinned with half his mouth. "You'll come home when the ghosts let you," he said, not unkind, and waved with the jam-jar hand.

On a cold morning when the window stuck and the kettle screamed, she slid open the drawer where she kept the Victory Club photo—three girls under an oak, faces pitched toward a future they couldn't see. She traced their shoulders as if teaching her hand the shape of loyalty.

She put the picture in her wallet instead of back in the drawer.

Proof of Life

There was a day in January when Evie walked down Rue des Martyrs and realized she'd stopped counting exits. The air smelled like butter and wet wool and something green. A woman shoved a pram in one practiced move while lighting a cigarette with the other; the baby laughed like a bell. An accordion player missed a note and grinned at his own fingers. The world went on without her and also, impossibly, with her.

Back upstairs, she made a list with Maggie's tidy numbering:

1. Call on a weekday.
2. Tell Dot the truth in the short version. Save the long one for the window table.
3. Ask Maggie for recipes again. (The good ones.)
4. Pack the notebooks last.
5. Apologize once and mean it. Then tell the story.

She practiced the call by dialing without coins. She practiced putting the receiver down calmly. She practiced not hanging up on her own name.

That afternoon, she climbed the six flights with bread and a ridiculous hope. In the stairwell she met the new father from two floors down, the one who'd once stomped like a military parade at dawn. He held the baby on his shoulder and patted its back like a soft drum. "Bonjour, Madame Journaliste," he said.

Evie felt the word land and not knock anything over. "Bonjour," she said back, and it felt like greeting the world instead of bracing against it.

Packing

Paris didn't argue. It rained lightly, the kind of rain that makes a city look freshly written. She wrapped the Smith-Corona in an old sweater. She tucked the two notebooks into the suitcase and then, heart jumping like a novice, took them out again to copy one sentence onto an index card for her wallet: *We learned courage in groups.*

Into the side pocket she slid a postcard of the Lincoln Memorial, a Métro ticket with no rides left, and a coin for a pay phone in a country that didn't use coins the same way. Let it be a charm. Let it be a promise.

On the table she left a note for Jacques in her neatest hand: *Merci pour le canard. Pour les disques. Pour m'avoir laissée partir.* Thank you for letting me go.

She stood at the window and watched a woman below shake a mop like a banner at a puddle. She watched the puddle lose its argument with the drain. She counted chimneys. She let herself say the sentence out loud to the room.

"I'm coming home."

The room didn't clap. It didn't need to. It held steady, the way rooms do when they've learned your steps.

She packed the notebooks last.

On top of them she placed a folded scrap that had lived, unread, at the bottom of one envelope for years. *Onward,* it said in Dot's hand.

Evie slipped the scrap into her wallet beside the Victory Club photo and the copied line. She whispered the words as if testing them for the first time.

"Onward. Proof of life, " she said, and the words didn't tremble.

13

TWO LOVES
1970S • MAGGIE

The sky outside was the color of old cotton, dull and stretched thin, pressing down on the neighborhood with the weight of waiting. A postcard from Paris—a market stall blazing with oranges—was pinned to the fridge with a magnet. On the back, Evie's handwriting read: *Save me a cup. I take my tea like confession.*

Maggie stood at the counter with a pink floral mug warming her palms. The noon news burred from the little set beside the flour canister. She turned it up the way a person braces for a needle.

"This year's highest lottery number called is ninety-five."

Her lungs forgot their job.

Ninety-five.

Not Tommy—he was too young, born in '55—but the boy next door, Jimmy Acker, had drawn seventy-two. Jimmy, who'd grown up in their backyard: baseball cards traded with Tommy, secret forts in the lilac bushes, two boys who'd shared more summers than socks. His mother would be hearing this same newscast. Maybe holding her breath the same way Maggie was now.

She pressed her fingertips to the soft place above her heart and shut her eyes. Relief hit in a hard wave, salt and lightheaded, the kind that could make a person sit down if she wasn't already seated. She set the mug carefully on the table as if the day might shatter.

Tommy was safe—for now. But the fear wasn't gone. It only stepped back a pace.

In three years, the lottery would reach his birth cohort. And until then, every headline, every rumor, every mother's phone call tightened something low and constant in her chest.

For months, fear had lived in the house like a second shadow—at church beneath the alto line, at the sink with the evening dishes, in the way she woke when the furnace knocked. Even though his turn hadn't come yet, the possibility hovered: draft notices arriving without warning, boys disappearing into uniforms before dinner. Fear took a chair at their table and didn't excuse itself.

She reached for the laundry basket, meaning only to fold a towel or two. But her hands moved differently—tighter, sharper, smoothing every edge with a care that bordered on prayer. A T-shirt, a pair of jeans, one of Tommy's flannel shirts she hadn't yet convinced herself to retire. Folding anchored her, kept her upright inside the news.

A floorboard creaked.

She froze mid-fold, the shirt still warm from the dryer and gripped too hard in her hands.

Tommy padded in barefoot, hair sleep-mussed, pajama pants low on his hips—boy and man braided into one body.

"What was that?" he asked, voice hoarse from sleep. "I heard the TV."

Maggie swallowed. "The draft numbers."

He stilled. "Today's?"

She nodded, or tried to, because her throat had gone hot and thick. "They... they stopped at ninety-five."

He stood very still, reading the rest in her face. "So Jimmy?"

She set the folded shirt on the counter, palms lingering on the cotton as if the fabric could steady her.

"He'll go if they call his number," she whispered. "Seventy-two is... it's close."

Tommy rubbed the back of his neck, the way he had since childhood when fear or guilt or empathy tangled inside him. "His mom's probably losing her mind."

"So is every mother today." Maggie tried to breathe around the truth of it. "But you're safe, sweetheart. For now."

A flicker of relief crossed his face—swift, guilty, human. Then he stepped closer and wrapped his arms around her.

She folded him in.

He didn't pull away.

If anything, he leaned—chin on her shoulder, the way he had at six when thunderstorms found the windows.

For three breaths, he was only her boy.

She didn't pray out loud—not since the year prayers felt like coins tossed into a well. But she sent one up anyway: gratitude, and a plea for the mothers whose numbers landed on the wrong side of mercy.

When Tommy stepped back, he wiped his eyes quickly, pretending he hadn't.

"I'll check on Jimmy later," he said. "Maybe shoot hoops. Something normal."

"Normal's good," Maggie murmured. Her hands ached from how tightly she'd folded the laundry. She eased them open.

"Come on," she said, smoothing the hair off his forehead with the old gesture that never stopped being true. "Let's make breakfast."

Outside, the snow decided and fell.

Inside, the kitchen warmed to eggs and butter and a relief that tasted almost like hunger.

After • 1968–1972

That night, after Tommy slept easy—safe for now, at least—Maggie sat with the absence that safety couldn't touch. The house carried its winter song—furnace sigh, branch tap at the glass, pipes clicking awake and asleep.

She sat at her vanity with the brush stalled halfway through a stroke, the lamplight catching the silver in her hair. She wasn't crying; she'd learned to hold a storm without letting it spill. But her chest felt worked, like a muscle after a long climb.

Charles had been gone four years. A heart that one moment kept time with *Bonanza* reruns and the next didn't. No warning, no last remark to carry like a stone in the pocket. Just an empty cushion and a quiet that didn't know how to behave.

He'd been a faithful man, a list maker and oil changer, careful with towels and paychecks and bedtime kisses. Not grand; steady. Their love had been made of grocery lists and Saturday errands, the kind of safety you don't see until it's gone.

But 1968 carved at him. She could still see him at the kitchen table, coffee going cold, eyes fixed on Walter Cronkite as if the right kind of attention could hold a country together. Body counts delivered like weather. Memphis. Los Angeles. Chicago. "It's coming apart at the seams," he'd say, and his hands would tighten around the mug until his knuckles went chalk white.

Sometimes, she woke in those years to find him in Tommy's doorway, robe pockets heavy with hands, the small curve of his shoulders saying what his mouth wouldn't: *I'm afraid for our boy.*

Maggie set the brush down and picked up the photo on the nightstand—Charles behind Tommy, both of them laughing into the white of a snow day. She touched their faces with her index finger.

"I hope you see him," she said to the quiet. "I hope you know."

She turned the lamp off and lay under the quilt. The wind pressed its soft palm against the window as if to say, *I'm here. Keep breathing.*

Dream • The Doorway

She dreamed she was back in the living room on High Street. Everything was itself and not—sofa a shade truer, wallpaper lit like it remembered summer, snow outside falling in slow, forgiving spirals. She wasn't cold. She wasn't anything but present.

Charles stood in the kitchen doorway. Younger in the face, eyes resting easy on her like the first ten years of their marriage. "Maggie," he said, warm, as if he'd just come in from shoveling.

Her throat wouldn't start. She lifted a hand.

He crossed without sound and cupped her cheek with the palm she knew—callused at the base of the fingers, warm from life. For a second, time behaved.

"It's okay now," he told her. "You can go."

Tears started without instruction. "Go where?"

Behind him, the kitchen filled with a soft radiance that didn't come from any lamp, a rectangle of light like a door standing open.

"You'll know him when you see him," Charles said.

Maggie turned toward the light.

She woke at first color. Snow tapped the glass like polite company. Her heart wasn't racing. It was awake.

Late 1970s • Downtown York

Years moved the way grief does—slow at first, then suddenly gone.

They met at Creatives on King, paper cups of wine and someone's cousin playing tasteful guitar. Maggie had come to the art gallery because the house felt too quiet. She drifted past landscapes and ceramic bowls, letting her breath fall into the slower rhythm of a room full of looking.

Then the painting stopped her. Crimson and storm, a weather system caught mid-turn. It felt like the moment before a confession.

"Looks like somebody's emotions got into a bar fight," she said, not meaning to say it out loud.

A voice at her shoulder chuckled. "That was, more or less, the intention."

She turned. Jeans, paint-freckled shirt, dark curls pulled back, hands that knew how to make, eyes that knew how to see. The gallery softened at the edges. Her body did that small, private thing it does when truth taps on the door.

She didn't believe in fate. But she did believe in the body's quiet yes.

From the first second it wasn't infatuation. It was recognition.

Eli was younger by nearly ten years and careless about it. He'd never married. "I haven't met anyone I wanted to share silence with," he said, and Maggie hadn't realized silence could be an invitation until that moment. She laughed and then cried and then let herself do both at once.

They unfolded gently: used bookstores, late walks that gave them back their knees, the tenderness of washing someone else's coffee cup and putting it back where they like it. When she told her children, the house tilted again.

Tommy went still. "He's too young, Mom. What's he want with a widow and—" He stopped himself. "—with all of us."

"My children aren't baggage," she said, hearing the steel in her voice.

Cindy, cautious by habit, asked over tea, "Is it real? Are you sure?"

"I'm alive again," Maggie said. "That I'm sure of."

Wendy, who always saw the heart of a thing, loved him immediately. "He's like the character who shows up halfway through and makes the story honest," she said, squeezing her mother's hand.

Holidays were awkward, then less so. Eli never reached for ground that wasn't his. He brought flowers and washed dishes and learned that Tommy hated mushrooms, that Cindy needed a phone call before a surprise, and that Wendy double-salted popcorn. He stood beside what came before and honored it.

Tommy cracked eventually—first over jazz, then over a fence they fixed together. On a chilly Saturday, Maggie watched from the porch as they lined the posts.

"You set or guessing?" Tommy asked.

"Listening," Eli said. "Wood tells you when it's true."

Tommy shifted the level, not quite hiding his smile. "All right, Picasso."

Later he told Maggie, "He's all right." Then, after a beat, "Still hate the ponytail." Eli laughed when she relayed it and brought Tommy a hat —an olive branch, disguised as a joke.

Illness • The Studio Fall, The Diagnosis

Then the body betrayed him. Fatigue that didn't make sense. A cough that wouldn't leave. A slip from the studio step he'd taken a thousand times without thinking.

In the exam room, the fluorescent light hummed like a bad thought. The doctor's pen hovered, touched down, hovered again. "We're looking at lymphoma," he said, voice lowered as if the word might startle.

Eli's hand found hers and squeezed once, steady. "Okay," he said, as if agreeing to weather.

"Stage four," the doctor added, careful. The second hand on the wall clock ticked far too loud. Maggie noticed everything—the scuff on the linoleum, the way Eli's thumb traced a crescent into her palm, the folder sticker that read INTAKE when nothing about any of this felt like a beginning.

They made a fortress together. Maggie became advocate and nurse and harbor. Her children pivoted in: Cindy arrived with a color-coded calendar and pill organizers snapped into neat weeks; Wendy brought records and played the Ella he loved until the apartment softened; Tommy came by after work, sat quiet with a hand on Eli's shoulder, and one night said, "Thank you for loving my mother."

Near the end, when breath came in careful portions, Eli took her hand. "I would've married you," he whispered.

"I would've said yes," she said, and meant the whole word.

His last breath was a release, not a fight. Afterward, she closed her eyes and saw the lit doorway again. *You'll know him when you see him,* Charles had promised.

She had.

Afterward • The Studio

The studio behind the house waited in a hush, the kind that settles after a life leaves. Maggie pushed the door and went in alone. The air carried the ghost of linseed oil and coffee and the small, familiar whisper of the radio that had once lived on the windowsill.

She trailed a finger along the backs of canvases, the nicked edge of an easel, a jar of brushes gone to splay. In the corner, behind a leaning stack of gessoed boards, was the painting from the night they met. Crimson, shadow, weather about to turn.

It startled her how it still moved her—breath catching, eyes prickling—as if Eli had stepped back to say one more true thing.

"I would've said yes," she told the room.

Something in the air settled, and for a second she felt him beside her—the way you feel a person before you see them. A rectangle of afternoon lay across the floor like a door standing open, a light that didn't come from any lamp.

Now • Manchester Meadows (Present Day)

A soft squeak and the steady thock-thock of rubber tips on linoleum broke the quiet. Maggie sat tucked into her recliner beneath the lavender throw, Eli's painting hanging across from her bed where the light could find it.

Evie negotiated the doorway with her walker, muttering about knees and barometric betrayals. Dot followed with a crinkly plastic bag of contraband: salted cashews, chocolate-covered raisins, and the particular glee of rule-breaking.

"This weather makes my joints feel like they're on backward," Evie said, lowering herself into the chair by the window.

From the hall, the intercom pinged and a nurse's voice floated by: "Medication rounds at two, folks," cheerful as a train schedule. A cart rattled, then the corridor settled again.

Dot set the bag down and studied Maggie's face. "You okay, Magpie? You look like your soul watched a sad movie without snacks."

"It's his birthday," Maggie said. "He'd have been seventy-eight."

Evie's gaze slid to the painting and softened. "Those dates keep their hooks."

"They do." She let the quiet hold a minute, then added, "I didn't believe in second chances. Not really. Then Eli walked in and turned on every light."

Dot reached over and squeezed her hand. "You fell in love with a painter who made you feel like a sunrise. We approved."

"Did your kids ever make peace with the ponytail?" Evie asked.

"Eventually," Maggie said, laughter moving under her voice. "They fixed a fence, and each other."

Dot produced three plastic cups of vanilla pudding like an altar and three plastic spoons like sacrament. "Art and poetry are swell," she declared, "but nothing honors a man like pudding and gossip."

They ate pudding as if it were rare and precious. They traded small stories—the kind that look like nothing and turn out to be the spine—Tommy's first paycheck, Cindy's careful lists, Wendy's insistence on extra butter, Charles's neat towels, Eli's way of standing quietly beside a person until they believed in themselves.

When the cups were empty and the light outside had softened into a patient gray, Maggie looked at the painting again. The storm within it seemed suspended, as if waiting for the next brushstroke.

"I had two loves," she said, not to brag, but to mark. "Charles gave me a life. Eli gave me myself. Both cost. Both count."

"Greedy," Evie said, but her eyes were wet.

"Blessed," Dot corrected, tucking a raisin into Maggie's palm like a charm. "Also greedy."

Maggie smiled. "With Tommy drawing one-six-zero in the draft and only the first ninety-five called, you'd think we wouldn't have been so lucky." She glanced at the spiral on her bedside tray and then back to the canvas that had started it all. "But we were. Luck turned out to be us."

Outside, the rain thinned to a silver mist. Inside, the room held a small, steady glow, the kind that lingers where women tell the truth and find it enough.

14

CRACKS IN THE MIRROR

1970S • DOT

The mirror on the windowsill was cracked into a spider of light that caught the afternoon and turned it into rivers, bright where memory ran fast, gray where it pooled. Dot studied the woman who looked back. Once her hair had been a tight, no-nonsense Afro that matched the edge in her voice. Now, it fell in silver-threaded curls that brushed her shoulders, still natural, softened by seasons. The flame in her eyes hadn't dimmed; it had learned where to live—warmer now, steady, the kind that heats a room instead of burning it down.

Honesty first, she told herself. She owed herself at least that.

Baltimore pressed in outside: the long wail of a siren, the ordinary rattle of a bus, then the pause that was sometimes worse than noise. The walls around her carried a paper chorus: clippings from *The Sun,* her name in stubborn serif, a photo of her elbow linked with Angela Davis's at a D.C. rally, a pamphlet from the first National Black Feminist Organization conference framed in black. A life you could point to. Proof she hadn't just watched history; she'd handed out pencils and courage while it was being written.

Some nights, those proofs sang. Tonight, they felt like guests who didn't know when to go home.

The 70s had asked for everything, and she'd answered with callused hands. School board nights pushing for Black Studies and a library that didn't hide Black authors on a shelf nobody visited. Saturdays canvassing for Shirley Chisholm until her arches whined. Weekday mornings riding the integration bus with children whose courage hadn't been asked for and was asked for anyway. She kept extra hair ribbons in her bag and learned which boys threw up when the route took too long.

"Ms. D" taught history as a live wire. She taught like tomorrow would take attendance.

Progress came in inches, and some days even those slid backward. Men with spectacles gripped procedure like a life raft and pretended not to hear her. Funding vanished inside drawers. Paper victories curled at the edges. Dot kept showing up with chalk on her sleeve and a safety pin in her pocket, small things that held more than they looked like.

The movement wanted everything. She'd given it. Time. Peace. Love.

Clara.

Dot braced a palm on the painted sill and let the name rise without flinching. She'd always told herself she understood; the work had a mouth and a hunger. Tonight, in the cracked glass, she admitted the other piece: she hadn't just lost Clara to the cause—she'd been left. She didn't know whether it was for the cause or in spite of it.

She touched the cleanest shard and met her own gaze head-on. "Truth," she whispered. "No trimming."

Night Work: Shards

When sleep stayed standoffish, she graded essays at the kitchen table and let the city's after-hours begin. A cop car idled two blocks over. Somewhere a radio insisted on Al Green. She kept a notebook open beside the stack and let memories land the way they wanted to—out of order, like rain.

August 1963: paper fans and paper cups, working the March, hat brim tilting against the sun while a voice at the Lincoln Memorial reached into the ribs of a crowd and kept time.

Spring 1964: Atlanta, basement of Ebenezer, singing while they practiced keeping their voices calm; McClellan's Diner where the coffee was cheap and the sheriff's eyes cheaper; Clara's hand squeezing hers under the table when someone hissed.

1973: a hotel ballroom where the NBFO conference wrote a future with ballpoint pens and borrowed typewriters.

Oakland: a winter she never finished telling, even to herself. A raid at dawn. Stairs. Boots. Clara's voice, steady until it wasn't. After that, blanks.

Sometimes you couldn't fix the chronology. You didn't force it neat; you lived around the jagged parts.

The Call

The phone rang. Once. Again. A third time that sounded like a dare.

"Hello?"

A breath, familiar as a song she hadn't heard since summer. "Dot?"

Her knees softened. "Clara?"

A small laugh, worn at the edges. "Still know my voice."

"Where have you been?"

"Everywhere and nowhere," Clara said. "Panthers for a time. Oakland. Now clinics in Atlanta. I'm tired." A pause that carried years. "But I'm here."

"I tried to reach you," Dot said. It came out smaller than she meant.

"I know." Quieter. "After the raid that winter, I only knew how to run. I didn't know how to come back, not after leaving."

Dot let the quiet show its use. "I needed you," she said at last, finding the center of the sentence and staying there. "Not the movement. You."

"I'm sorry."

Silence opened between them, not empty, but useful.

Then Clara: "There's still time, Dot. Not everything has to be behind us."

Dot looked at the mirror again. Lines, yes. Also something bright under the surface, like a coin at the bottom of a clear river.

"You still listen to Coltrane?" she asked.

"Every night," Clara said. "And I think of you."

"Okay," Dot answered. The word didn't tremble. "Let's talk."

They stayed on the line until the radiator clicked itself to sleep. After they hung up, the house felt an inch taller. The cracks in the glass were still there, but now they carried light.

Choosing a Dress: After the Call

She pulled three hangers from the closet and laid them on the bed like test answers. Navy shirtwaist, her default; a burnt-orange sweater dress that made strangers grin; the black skirt that had argued with many a school board. She touched the orange and felt brave. Then she added a scarf Clara had once bought from a sidewalk market and left on Dot's chair "by accident." She had kept it like a contraband heartbeat.

Before sleep, she dialed another number.

"Mags," she said when Maggie's voice came through the static. "Do I look foolish in orange?"

"You look like sunrise in orange," Maggie said without missing a beat. Dot could hear the smile. "Are we celebrating?"

"Reconsidering," Dot said. "I'll tell you soon."

"You will," Maggie said. "And you'll be gentle with yourself in the telling."

Union Station: One Month Later

Union Station held the city's pulse the way only old buildings can, marble catching shoe-slap, announcements stitching strangers into a temporary choir. The air smelled like coffee and stone and travel. Dot stood just beyond the arrivals and held her purse strap the way you hold a railing on a moving bus. Ridiculous to be nervous, she told herself. They had faced horses and hard hands together. But facing someone in ordinary light, with nothing between you but the past, some bridges require a breath before you step.

And then Clara was simply there.

Hair cropped close into a neat natural with a thread of silver. The bright headband, always a flag, still making its small declaration. A denim coat. A rust scarf. A new limp, slight and honest about miles and years. The stride was slower. The gaze was the same: searching and direct. So was the smile that found Dot like it had been trained to find her across a crowd.

They moved toward one another and stopped at the same time, close enough to feel heat, far enough to look, two women taking inventory: laugh lines they'd earned, tired they hadn't, the steadiness they still recognized. Then Dot exhaled and reached, and they stood in a quiet that forgave.

Lavender and paper, that was the smell of Clara's hair. Dot memorized it again.

"You're here," Dot said.

"I'm here," Clara answered, not letting go.

"Hungry?"

"Always."

H Street Diner: That Afternoon

They found a narrow diner, the kind with scuffed linoleum and a waitress who called everyone *hon* and meant it. Burnt coffee in the air, the clock above the pie case five minutes off. They slid into a booth and let the silence fill, soft but certain, like breath remembered. Dot's knee bounced; Clara steadied it with a palm against her shin and left it there, a small brave thing.

"I thought you'd be different," Clara said, stirring cream into her cup.

"I am," Dot said. "And I'm not."

"Still good at riddles."

"Still good at leaving," Dot returned. Not cruel, just accurate. It made Clara flinch, then square her shoulders.

"I deserved that. After Oakland, I didn't know how to stay when the fight kept calling." She looked up. "I never stopped loving you, Dot. I just didn't know how to love you and the world at the same time. I thought I had to choose."

"And now?"

"Now, I run clinics for reproductive justice. Less shouting, more building." She hesitated, brave in a new way. "I'd like to build with you, if it's not too late."

Dot studied the face she'd carried like a folded letter. Clara had stared down sheriffs, smuggled bandages into basements, written Dot's name in every margin. Here she was with her hands open.

"I don't know what it looks like," Dot said, sliding her palm across the table until their hands fit the way old truths do. "But I'll find out."

"Me too."

The waitress arrived with grilled cheese and tomato soup, steam making halos. "Anything else for you two?"

"Time," Clara said softly.

"If I could ring that up, I would," the woman said, grinning.

District Walk: Evening Coming On

They walked the city as if reading old notes in the margins. Steps outside the Capitol that remembered their voices. The Adams Morgan mural they'd helped fund, still bright. Paper cones of roasted peanuts. Laughter at nothing in particular. On a park bench, a young couple dozed with a baby asleep across both laps, a small domestic miracle that Dot felt in her throat.

"Sometimes I think about the life we didn't make," she said.

"I think about it, too," Clara answered.

"Would we have been out?" Dot asked, testing the word. "Or tucked behind a door only we knew how to find?"

"Both," Clara said. "Whatever kept us safe and honest."

They stood at the edge of the Mall where the grass gives way to gravel and watched a boy practice skateboard turns until he stuck the landing and whooped. The sun dropped into a copper bowl; the city exhaled.

"I'm tired of choosing between the world and the person I go home to," Clara said quietly. "I want both."

Dot didn't kiss her. Not yet. When the light leaned toward blue, Clara pressed her forehead to Dot's and whispered, "Come next weekend. I'll cook. *Coltrane* on vinyl."

"Only if you make cornbread," Dot said, smiling with her whole face.

"With your secret recipe," Clara promised.

Baltimore: Between Weekends

Back home, ordinary life kept up its end of the bargain. The radiator clanked; the mail brought flyers and the thin blue of an overdue notice; Miss Loretta downstairs burned something sweet and apologized through the vent. Dot ironed a blouse for Monday's class and sharpened pencils until the shavings made a small mountain.

In third period, Jamal raised his hand and asked, "Why do they keep calling it progress if it keeps getting taken back?" The room went quiet the way it does when someone finds a door nobody noticed.

Dot drew a line on the board: forward, backward, forward. "Because the world has a short memory," she said. "Our job is to remember on purpose. And to keep the receipts."

At lunch, she wrote Clara a postcard she'd hand-deliver: *Baltimore is gray today. I'm wearing orange under a sensible coat. Send Coltrane, hush, and your laugh.*

That night, she stood at the mirror again and decided not to replace it. She cleaned the glass with vinegar until every vein shone. When the cracks caught the lamplight, they looked almost like a map.

Weekends: A Small Pattern

Three weekends made a pattern. Morning coffee that went lukewarm because talking went warm. Walks that memorized new routes through old neighborhoods. *Coltrane* as background, the way love is when it settles into the furniture without disappearing.

Dot peeled carrots at Clara's kitchen table while Clara flipped through a binder of clinic notes. Sun slid across the stove and found the nick in the enamel Clara never bothered to fix. The room smelled like onions and possibility.

"You ever think about moving here?" Clara asked without looking up, casual the way a brave thing sometimes pretends to be.

"I've got my life in Baltimore," Dot said, naming the loyalties, students who counted on her steadiness, neighbors who knocked when the porch light stayed off too long, the church ladies who pretended not to know and loved her anyway.

"It doesn't have to be everything or nothing," Clara said. "Just... think."

Later, they sat on the front steps, knees almost touching, city hum braiding with a child's thump-thump-thump of a ball against a stoop. The sky turned that deep blue that makes streetlights look courteous.

"I don't know what we're building," Dot said.

"Something worth the time," Clara answered.

Dot reached. Fingers, then palms, then the quiet agreement of two women who had learned that practice makes a life.

"Then let's take the time," she said.

One Hard Weekend: The Meeting

Not every weekend was cinematic. One Saturday, Clara dragged Dot to a coalition meeting in a church basement, clinic workers and neighborhood organizers trying to stitch a safety net from thin yarn. Folding chairs. A coffee urn that tasted like tin. A man in a corduroy jacket who spoke like a pamphlet and looked past both of them when he said "ladies."

Dot raised her hand and kept it there until the chair noticed a whole person attached to it. "Why does the budget list security after signage and refreshments?" she asked.

Corduroy blinked. "We're trying to build community."

"So am I," Dot replied. "I'd like the nurses to get to their cars."

Afterward, Clara hugged her in the hallway that smelled like lemon oil and hymnals. "I forget how good you are at buildings," she whispered.

"Buildings?"

"Taking a ramshackle thing and giving it a frame," Clara said. "I've been so long in the street I needed a reminder."

They argued late that night anyway, about where each of them stood when danger visited, about the old fear that one would choose the road over the room. It ended with Clara's back to the sink, eyes wet and stubborn, and Dot saying, "I'm not asking you to shout quieter. I'm asking you to come home whole."

"I'm learning," Clara said, raw. "I'm still learning to stay."

"Me too," Dot admitted, and they let the truth be the apology.

A Call to Maggie

At the train station the next morning, Dot dropped a dime into a pay phone and dialed. "I nearly told a man his pie chart needed a conscience," she said when Maggie answered.

"And did it?" Maggie asked.

"It did."

"How are you?"

"Terrified and lit up," Dot said.

"Then you're on the right street," Maggie replied. "Choose the life that keeps you whole, not just useful."

Dot closed her eyes. "You always did prefer the exact word."

"It's cheaper than therapy," Maggie said, and they both smiled.

Threshold: Keys and Calendars

A month later, Clara pressed a brass key into Dot's hand. "Spare," she said, and looked scared about it.

"I can't promise more than weekends and the occasional rogue Wednesday," Dot said. "My kids need me."

"I know." Clara tucked a curl behind Dot's ear. "I want what you can give with both feet under you."

They hung a small calendar on the fridge and put saints' days no church had canonized: Report cards. Clinic audit. Dot's Wednesday. Coltrane fix needle. They wrote in pencil so the future, not because they doubted—because they'd earned the right to edit their future without apology.

On a hot Sunday, they bought a plant together, stubborn, green, all elbows, and set it on the sill.

"We'll find out if we're responsible people," Clara said.

"We've been responsible for entire movements," Dot replied. "Surely we can keep a fern alive."

"That's not what the fern heard," Clara murmured, and they laughed until it became a rule: laugh before the problem gets a name.

Steps at Dusk

Back in Baltimore after one of those rogue Wednesdays, Dot climbed the stairs and paused at the mirror. The cracks were still there. So were the rivers of light.

She didn't replace the glass. She learned where to stand so the fractures made a crown across her reflection, learned how the window's evening sun found each vein and set it to shimmering. On the sill she placed a small jar of safety pins, a leftover protest button, and the spare key on a strip of red ribbon.

From the street, somebody's radio sent *Coltrane* floating up like proof. Dot smiled, picked up her school bag, and set tomorrow's coffee. The day's work hadn't made her smaller. It had made her roomier.

Some fractures don't end a thing. They just show you how the light gets through.

She pressed her fingers to the glass, then to the steady, ordinary pulse at her collarbone, and whispered the true inventory: "Work. Love. Time." Then she added a fourth word she hadn't dared in years.

"Home."

15

RADIUS

PRESENT • MANCHESTER MEADOWS

L ate-autumn light slicked the garden gold. The common room carried its usual murmur: rubber soles on linoleum, a TV whispering weather, a cart's loose wheel rattling. Dot let the sounds drift past. She sat by the window, palm on the cool glass, letting her breath learn steadiness against it.

Two days after hearing it in the hallway, she still tested the words for edges.

Gracie was gone.

The nurse had used the practiced voice people kept for endings— peaceful, in her sleep— and Dot had nodded, two feelings tugging the same rib: gratitude and fury sharing a chair.

Gracie had been the first person to pull Dot into the rhythm of Manchester Meadows, a wiry woman with a laugh that snapped like a match and eyes that kept their own light. When Gracie told a story— Selma, D.C., Baltimore—her hands sketched the air until the march came back alive. Dot had loved her for that, loved the way she saved the soft chair for anyone new.

Gracie kept bringing memories of Clara back.

The thought rose like music from another room, soft at first, then everywhere. Clara's kitchen arrived: skillet cornbread hissing in oil, cayenne waking the greens, *Coltrane* leaning through a doorway. There had been a small limp by then, and there had been the same unspent grace. Dot remembered the phone call that had stitched decades into a single thread. She remembered Union Station, how the crowd had parted and there Clara had been, older and exactly the same, blue head-band bright as a flag. They had walked the city, paused at the mural they had raised money for, the bench where they had once planned the world. The next weekend they had cooked. They had danced on tile. They had relearned each other gently, one smile, one silence, one song at a time.

I want to build with you, Clara had said, fingers trembling against Dot's cheek.

Then we begin, Dot had answered, taking that hand like a vow.

They had begun: Sunday dinners, clinic flyers, a couch that felt like a harbor. Dot had let herself imagine a future measured in ordinary things, peppermints tucked in a pocket, kettle whistles, the late-after-noon light settling on Clara's shoulder.

A crash took it in a sentence. Years ago, and still near.

Dot had stood graveside, rain slipping under her collar, umbrella handle wet in her fist. The family's grief had risen loud and righteous; the obituary had edited the life into something polite. No one had said Dot's name. There had been no slot for her in the neat rows of chairs. She had swallowed her sorrow because there had been nowhere to set it down.

Only Dot remembered Clara humming while she cooked. Only she had later found a peppermint in her pocket, small, round, a planet she could hold.

Now, the garden moved in a hush of wind. For a second, she thought she saw a figure at the hedge, blue headband, the beginning of a smile. She blinked. Only wind, only the hour.

"I missed you," she whispered.

Her thumb found the nick on her old blue pen. The ridge steadied her.

The Memorial: The Next Afternoon

The memorial for Gracie the next afternoon was simple: a border of gold marigolds in a galvanized tub by the window, a photo of her mid-laugh, eyes catching light, residents drifting in with cardigan sleeves to their wrists.

Someone had set out paper cups of fruit punch and a tray of lemon cookies that tasted like school fundraisers. Maggie stood on Dot's left, steady as a tree; Evie on her right, gaze far and kind. The big TV had been switched off, even the loose-wheeled cart had kept its distance, as if it understood ceremony.

Nurse Jen spoke first, practical and gentle in the same breath. "Gracie taught us to put the microphone closer," she said, adjusting it as if in tribute. "She wanted people to hear."

Mr. Alvarez, who wore ties as if every day requested respect, told a story about Gracie relabeling the bird feeders after the grounds crew mixed seed types. "She said, 'Even sparrows deserve clarity,'" he managed, then dabbed at his eyes with a folded napkin.

The room learned a new draft: grief passing through.

"Gracie would've liked this," Maggie said quietly. "Especially the flowers."

"She would've asked who watered them, then bossed them about drainage," Dot answered, and the smile they shared didn't fix anything but let the ache breathe. "Remember when she smuggled in that foil pan of seedlings last spring? 'Contraband hope,' she called it."

Evie cleared her throat. "She saved the best chair for new people," she said to the room, voice thin and true. "That's a kind of marching."

A nurse's aide rang a small handbell at the end, one bright note that lifted and hung, then left them to the ordinary air.

Room 1C: Turnover

On her way back to the nook, Dot paused at the open door of 1C. Gracie's room stood bright and bare, the way rooms looked when memory had been shaken out of them. The bed had been stripped to its undecided mattress; a faint half-moon marked the wall where a picture had hung for years.

Jen appeared with painter's tape and a fat black marker.

"We're turning it over," Jen said, not unkindly. "Families don't like to wait. Would you like a minute?"

Dot stepped inside. The window still wore a thumb-smudge where Gracie always rested her hand. On the sill sat a mug with a yellow rim, a jar of buttons, a cardboard box labeled PHOTOS—MARCHES in Gracie's big, uncompromising hand. The lid sat crooked.

She lifted it and her breath caught. Gracie in a wool coat, arm looped with another woman's, eyes laughing. A line of them shoulder to shoulder, signs gone soft with rain. In the corner of one frame, almost out of sight, was Dot herself, jaw set, hat low, a peppermint wrapper flashing silver. She hadn't known anyone had caught that.

"Keep what you need," Jen said softly.

Dot took only one: Gracie mid-chant, mouth open, light making a small crown in her hair. She slipped the photo into her cardigan pocket and covered it with her had, where Clara's peppermint had once rested.

Footsteps sounded in the hall, careful lipstick, grief tucked into posture. A woman peered in, then straightened.

"My mother's moving in," she said. "She liked the bed by the window."

"Good light there," Dot said. "Tell her the gold border gets bossy about four o'clock."

The woman blinked, then smiled. "I'm Lani."

"Dot," Dot said. "We kept an eye on Gracie. We'll keep an eye on your mother. It's what we do here."

Lani's voice shook, then she nodded. "Thank you."

Dot watched as Jen positioned blue tape on drawers and wrote in bold marker: MORA, E. — 1C. The letters looked too new, like a bandage too white. But there was mercy in order. Someone would sleep under that window tonight. Someone would learn the timing of the dining room and the trick to the TV remote. The world, stubbornly, would keep going.

The Window Nook: Precision

Later the three of them claimed their window nook, their chairs everyone avoided out of respect or fear of Dot's stare. Conversation came in small waves: one memory, one joke, the quiet settling again.

"I didn't know how much longer I could do this," Dot said at last, soft as confession. "And then today stretched the feeling."

"Do what, baby?" Maggie asked, thumb circling Dot's knuckle in a way that felt like an old lullaby.

"Pretend," Dot said, keeping her voice even. "Pretend I was fine. Pretend it was enough to sit and knit and wait for the mail. I fought my whole life, and then I was tired. And also, God help me, restless."

"Both were true," Evie said.

"The world didn't even look like the one I marched for," Dot added.

"It didn't," Evie agreed. "But it was still yours to touch."

Maggie threaded her fingers through Dot's. "We could make our radius smaller," she said. "Closer in. That wasn't surrender. That was precision."

Dot held on. Outside, the first garden lamp clicked on; inside, her pulse steadied against two warm palms.

"Precision," she repeated. "I could work with that."

They put their heads together like girls at a lunch table. What could a small radius hold? Phone calls to the city about the crosswalk paint the bus drivers kept missing. A letter to the library asking for a quiet hour for the hearing-aid crowd. A sign-up for a Tuesday story circle so the new ones didn't think they had to audition for belonging. Maggie insisted they add potluck pudding to the agenda, which made Evie snort and then dab her eyes.

"Precision," Maggie said again, sounding pleased. "Like embroidery. Tight stitches keep a quilt together."

"Like editing," Evie said. "Give me the long mess; I'll find the line that carries."

"Like a map," Dot said, touching the blue pen. "We could draw one small block and still get someone home."

They wrote the list on a napkin with the dining room's stubby pencil. Dot tucked it into her pocket beside Gracie's photograph and felt the weight of both, the gone and the going-on.

Evening: A Room Like a Mirror

That evening in her room, the garden a dark mirror beyond the glass, Dot smoothed a sheet of paper and uncapped the blue pen with the nick by the clip. She had turned the chair so the lamp fell across her good hand. Down the hall, left on by someone who liked company, the radio murmured a station ID and then a saxophone line that curled like steam.

Clara, she wrote.

Gracie is gone. You would love her trouble. Today, they emptied her room. I took one photograph. It's in my pocket, like a small heart.

She paused and watched the garden lamps blink in sequence, one, two, three, as if the night knew how to keep time.

I'm still angry sometimes that the world makes no space for how I loved you. Then I catch myself showing a new daughter where to sit, like it's church, or coaching staff on where to place a microphone, and the anger loosens. I'm still building. Different lumber. Same hands.

She stopped for the sound of the medication cart rolling past, its drawers rattling, the tidy tap of little plastic pill cups set one after another. Someone laughed in the hall; someone else answered with, "Hush, you'll wake the babies," meaning the men who napped after dinner.

Dot smiled and wrote again.

We were going to meet in the flowers at 4, remember? Today, the wind pushed the gold heads all to the same side, like women leaning into a photograph. If there's a place you can hear me, come stand there tomorrow. I'll look for your blue headband and call it the breeze.

Either way, I keep going. The work is the size of my hands and the length of my breath. Friends bring pudding like sacrament. Women tell me the world still asks for me. I carry a photograph in my pocket and a memory of a peppermint memory. I'm not done.

She signed, folded, and tucked the letter inside her old CD wallet for company, zipper frayed, edges softened by thumb. She pressed play. The small player warmed and clicked, and the room filled with a tone that found the corners and cleared them. It wasn't loud. It didn't need to be. She let it run while she washed her face and lined three safety pins along the dresser edge the way she had in every apartment since 1964. The pins glinted like three thin spines.

When she turned back toward the window, movement pricked her eye, the blooms shifting, late wind riding low. For a heartbeat, the hedge looked like a blue ribbon. It wasn't. It was only evening rearranging itself. Still, Dot lifted her fingers and touched the glass.

"Tomorrow at 4," she said to the garden, and to the woman she'd loved, and to the world that had never known what to do with that love. "We had a list. We chose what we could reach."

Radius.

The Next Morning: Radius

Morning came thin and exact. Dot put on the cardigan with the firm elbows and felt for Gracie's photo inside the pocket. In the dining room she laid out three sign-up sheets on a table—Story Circle, Library Letter, Crosswalk Calls—and borrowed a pen from the activities cart.

By 9, Mr. Alvarez had added his name, neat cursive, Alejandro underlined twice. At 10:30, Lani wheeled her mother out of 1C and into the common room, then waved shyly from the door way; Dot waved back and pointed to the good chair. At 11, Maggie convinced the kitchen to part with an extra box of vanilla pudding "for community purposes," and Evie wrote a single line at the top of Story Circle sign-up sheet:

Don't skip the parts that cost.

Before lunch, a new scrawl appeared beneath the Story Circle list, careful letters printed with effort: *Elena Mora (1C)*. Lani's steady hand, Dot thought, making space on purpose.

Dot stood back and looked. It was nothing, and it was something. It was a map of one small block.

At 3:38, she took her place by the window. The flower bed leaned as if listening. Four o'clock came honest and on time. A breeze tipped the petals and ran on. Dot watched until the minute moved and then longer. The ache in her chest behaved itself.

When she finally turned away, she felt taller by a half inch, the way she always had after a march, not because the world had changed, but because she'd remembered how to stand inside it without shrinking.

She took the napkin list from her pocket and carried it back to the table, adding a fourth sheet: *Pudding & Gossip, Thursdays, 2 p.m.* She laughed, hearing Maggie's voice in the back of her mind. *Precision, baby.*

Dot smoothed the page flat and then returned to her chair by the window. The fractures of her life didn't blur. They caught the light— and gave it back.

16

THE REVOLT OF THE RECLINERS
PRESENT • MANCHESTER MEADOWS

It started with Jell-O. Lime. Electric. Missing.

Maggie reached the dessert station and stared at the empty Jell-O tray as if it had broken a promise. "They ran out again," she said. Her fork hovered, tines up, like a tiny white flag.

"Room 207 has been taking four," Evie murmured. "He bragged at bridge."

Dot stopped her fork midair. "Four? He building a bunker?"

"With load-bearing gelatin," Evie said.

"We're not going down without dessert," Dot decided, feeling the old flint strike and welcoming the spark. Ten minutes later, they moved like a slow, stylish heist crew. Maggie stationed herself at the water fountain, the gentlest lookout alive. Evie drifted to the nurses' station and unfurled a bright, slightly inaccurate story about the March on Washington, dates approximate, spirit correct. Dot slipped through the swinging kitchen door, cardigan flaring like a cape.

She reemerged with one wobbling relic of lime perfection, rescued from the back of a stainless-steel pan. Back in Maggie's room they shared it with plastic spoons and the giggles of teenagers who should've known better and didn't care.

"To crime," Evie toasted, the green square trembling like a compass.

When nursing aide Bonnie found the empty cup, Dot only said, "Scientific experiment. Results inconclusive."

It might've ended there, a sugar-high memory filed under Mischief. Instead, the meatloaf arrived. Three days running. Lukewarm, grayish, a brown gravy that refused to identify itself.

"This isn't dinner," Dot said, her fork refusing to puncture. "This is a human-rights violation."

"I'd rather eat my shoe," Maggie said.

"I'd like to eat it near a working radiator," Evie added, rubbing her hands together.

"They cut the heat at night," Dot said quietly. She'd heard the aides whisper it. Two weeks before, Gracie had stood at the edge of bingo with fingers wrapped around a flimsy cup of cocoa, blowing on her hands between numbers, just to keep the sting off, she'd said. Dot had laughed with her then. Now, the chair that had been Gracie's held the absence without apology.

"She froze," Dot said. "And we were polite."

"We played by their rules," Maggie said, flint under calm. "But we can make noise."

"Then we make noise," Dot said, and felt the decision settle into her bones like heat.

The Petition

That night, beneath the jitter of fluorescent lights, Dot laid a borrowed clipboard on the activity-room table and uncapped her blue fountain pen. Her hand remembered how to move. The ridge by the clip steadied her grip.

The petition read like a backbone:

We, the residents of Manchester Meadows, deserve basic human dignity. We are old, not voiceless. We demand functioning heat in every room, meals prepared with care, and a formal Resident Council empowered to speak and act on behalf of the people who live here.

She added one line of evidence, neat and precise:

Night checks recorded temperatures below sixty-eight degrees in rooms 112 through 120 after 11 p.m.

She signed: *Dorothy Louise Carter.*

Maggie printed Margaret Ann Thompson in tidy letters that looked ironed. Evie added Evelyn Ruth Gross, pressing hard enough to emboss the paper.

By breakfast, there were twenty signatures. By lunch, thirty-five. Crossword Curmudgeon in 3B signed after Dot accused him of "hiding behind thirteen-down." (Clue: abdicate. Answer: relinquish. He scowled and relinquished.)

At 1B, Mr. Hoover frowned at the paper. "In my shop," he said, voice thin but sure, "customers complain, I listen. I lose face otherwise." He signed with practiced strokes. "Make them listen."

At 2D, a nurse's aide named Marisol hesitated. "We're not supposed to sign."

"Then don't," Dot said gently. "But tell me which nights the heat drops worst."

Marisol exhaled. "Tuesdays and Thursdays. After ten."

"Thank you," Evie said, writing it down carefully. "That matters."

They gathered testimonies the way women gathered recipes—careful, specific, full of substitutions that still fed people. Mr. Alvarez checked the draft by his blinds with the little thermometer he'd gotten at his church picnic and announced the reading with the satisfied pride of an engineer. Mrs. Kapur described how her arthritis flared when the temperature fell below "sweater plus shawl." Lani signed for her mother, Elena Mora in 1C, and tucked a note under the signature: *Window seam leaks. Sounds like a whistle after midnight.*

Room 207 opened as they rounded the end of the hall. The Jell-O baron peeked out, hair like dandelion fluff. "You're back," he said, narrowing his eyes at the clipboard.

"We're here about heat," Maggie said.

"And desserts," Dot added, because accuracy mattered.

"Diabetic," he announced.

Evie lifted a brow. "And still an engineer. You, of all people, know about fair distribution."

A beat stretched, then—grudging, almost pleased—he plucked the pen from Dot's fingers and signed in block capitals. "I'll bring chess on Wednesday," he muttered. "If you don't gloat."

"We'll absolutely gloat," Dot said, already moving.

Due Diligence

The kitchen door swung. Inside, steam fogged the high windows; a woman in a hairnet stirred a vat that smelled like onions and apology.

"You the ones with the petition?" she asked without looking up.

"We are," Dot said.

"Name's Patrice." She tapped a paper tacked to the wall: *BUDGET HOLD – VENDOR SUBSTITUTIONS* printed in a font that apologized for nothing. "They cut our supplier. We do what we can with what we get."

"We're not here to blame you," Evie said. "We're here to give you cover."

Patrice's mouth softened. "Then ask for a produce line. Doesn't need to be fancy. Just real. And a second steam-table pan so we can keep the late trays warm."

Maggie nodded. "We'll make those asks clear."

Dot copied the bullets under the petition, letters straight as fence posts. She added another line: *Replace 'meatloaf entrée' with rotating protein—chicken, beans, fish cakes. Residents request fruit with every meal; sugar-free gelatin acceptable as alternate.* She underlined *alternate* twice.

That evening, they cross-checked. Mr. Alvarez produced the same flimsy little thermometer he'd gotten at his church picnic and showed Dot how to tape it near a vent without skewing the reading. Evie called Annie, a friend from her reporting days who knew a reporter at the *Chronicle*—not for a story, for advice—and hung up with a list of words administrators respected: *audit trail, compliance, variance, posted metrics.*

Maggie worked the phones with the patient ferocity of a woman who'd wrangled toddlers and politicians: adult children of residents, church friends, anyone who'd ever organized a bake sale. By 10 p.m., fourteen family members had emailed the front desk requesting that heating logs be posted publicly.

When Dot finally slept, she dreamt of Gracie in a knit hat, palms held out to a bonfire of marigolds, the petals lit like embers caught midair.

The Meeting

Monday brought the chalk-scratch of cold on the windows. The administrator shuffled papers as if noise could make time. His tie listed. His smile tried policy before sincerity.

"We appreciate your passion," he said. "We'll need time."

"You've had time," Dot said. "Now you need dates."

He brightened as if offered a raft. "Let's form a task force to explore—"

"We formed one," Dot said, nodding toward the hallway. "It's standing in your office."

She tipped the clipboard toward the door, where Maggie, Evie, Mr. Han, Mr. Alvarez, Lani, and two church ladies from down the hall arranged themselves with the soft, immovable politeness of grandmothers at a bake sale table. Behind them, Marisol pretended to wipe the counter while absolutely not leaving.

The administrator tried again, stalling with procedure. "Any changes must go through a policy cycle and legal review."

Dot twirled the blue pen like a baton. "Great. Put the dates for that on the wall. Along with nightly temperatures, posted by the mailboxes." She let the word *posted* land.

A facilities manager with rolled sleeves finally spoke, looking at Dot instead of the administrator. "We can log night temps this week," he said. "Start with the East Wing."

"Good," Evie said. "Post them nightly. Transparency warms a building."

The administrator hesitated, counting invisible hurdles. Then he sighed. "My father's in a place like this two towns over," he said, voice briefly unguarded. "I know heat shouldn't be a negotiation."

"Then let's stop negotiating," Dot said.

They set dates. Heating audit: begin Tuesday night; first results posted Thursday morning. Kitchen changes: pilot produce line by Friday; revise the vendor order the following cycle. Resident Council:

first meeting Wednesday at 2 p.m. in the activity room, microphones provided. Maggie requested a podium less than four feet high. "For visibility," she said, and no one argued.

Patrice slipped in late, hairnet in hand, and added a practical grace note. "We can do oatmeal with toppings at breakfast if I get an extra serving scoop," she said. "Cinnamon, nuts, raisins. Folks can build it how they like."

"Agency," Dot said, underlining *build it how they like* in the notes. The administrator looked at the pen as if it were a power tool.

He tried one more hedge. "We'll try."

"We'll calendar it for you," Dot said, smiling.

The Week Work Began

Within a week, maintenance checked every heater and logged temperatures after lights-out, tacking the chart to the cork board by the mailboxes. The first night, the log didn't appear ("IT issue," the administrator claimed), and by noon, half the building stood by the cork board with coats on. Patrice marched out with a clipboard copy and thumbtacks; the online log appeared the next morning and never missed again.

Extra blankets arrived, stacked like clouds and smelling faintly of industrial sunshine. Evie offered a tutorial in the lost art of the hospital corner; half the East Wing gathered to watch her tuck and flip and pat the edge. Mr. Alvarez clapped.

A Resident Council took shape: agenda, minutes, microphones, a laminated suggestion sheet with a line that read *Don't skip the parts that cost.* Maggie chaired the first meeting with a wooden spoon she carried in for moral support. The spoon looked like a gavel that had learned kindness.

Meatloaf retired without ceremony. Fish cakes introduced themselves and stayed. Rotating proteins became a thing. Sliced oranges brightened plates like small suns.

A local news crew came after someone's niece sent a tip. The headline along the bottom of the screen read: *THE REVOLT OF THE RECLINERS.* Dot pretended to scowl and secretly loved it. The reporter asked what they wanted most. Dot said, "Respect you can feel without reading a sign." Evie added, "And Jell-O with integrity." Maggie smiled at the camera the way a good mother smiled at a company she intended to outlast.

That evening, they tucked fleece across their laps in the common room. The sky rinsed lavender beyond the windows and the outside lamps clicked on in sequence like beads on a string. The air held a bite that felt honest instead of dangerous.

"Gracie would've eaten this up," Maggie said.

"She's why we did it," Dot answered. She touched the photo she kept in her cardigan pocket—Gracie mid-chant, light making a small crown in her hair—and felt steadier.

Evie lifted her mug. "To Gracie," she said. "And to Dorothy Louise Carter—precision and volume."

Dot laughed, surprised by the warmth rising through her. This wasn't surrender. This was focus.

Aftershocks

The changes didn't fix everything. Tuesday nights still dipped, but now there was a clipboard and a number and a man with a wrench who knew why he was there.

Patrice's produce line wobbled (bananas played favorites, spinach sulked) and then found a rhythm with apples, carrots, and the occasional pear so fragrant it slowed the lunch line.

The Resident Council met again the following week. Mr. Han proposed an "accountability hour," which sounded like detention and turned out to be a cheerful posting of progress notes beside the thermostat log. Mrs. Kapur requested "quiet time in the afternoon for those of us whose hearing aids make the TV sound like a swarm." The administrator said, "We'll try," and Dot said, "We'll calendar." A printed sheet appeared the next day: *Quiet Hour, 2–3 p.m., Common Room.* It felt like a small country changing its flag.

Lani brought Elena to the window nook one morning and settled her by the good light. "She says the whistle stopped," Lani reported, eyes bright. Elena nodded, then fell asleep with her hand fanned on the armrest like a pale leaf. Dot tucked a blanket over her knees and felt the relief like a hand on the back.

Room 207 arrived for chess with a notebook labeled *Resource Allocation*. He set the board with grudging grace and offered Dot the white pieces. "To offset Jell-O inequities," he said. She took his bishop in nine moves and thanked him for his service.

At night, Dot wrote to Clara again.

We asked for dates. We got them. The line for fruit made me cry for reasons I refused to explain to the evening news. You would've said, "Of course it was the food," and then told me to wear thicker socks. I'm wearing thicker socks. I'm also considering a pudding caucus.

She slipped the letter into the sleeve of the Coltrane CD, the zipper frayed where her thumb liked to find it, and let the saxophone clear the corners.

The Vote

When the council voted on a set of standing priorities—Heat, Food, Quiet Hour, Mobility (Evie: "Stop blocking the door with the linen cart, for the love of dignity"), and New Resident Welcome ("Best chair first," in Gracie's honor)—Dot looked at the paper and saw a map of one small block. It was exactly her size.

After the vote, the administrator lingered near the doorway as if waiting to be released by a bell. "Thank you for your input," he said.

"You're welcome for our leadership," Dot replied, and smiled because she didn't need him to approve the word. She noticed, though, that he'd already posted next week's dates before she could ask.

On her way back to her room, she paused at 1C. Elena dozed, mouth soft, the late sun catching the blue tape on the drawer that read *MORA, E. – 1C.* Lani looked up from her knitting.

"How's the heat?" Dot asked.

"Better," Lani said. "She didn't wake shivering last night." Her knitting needles clicked. "I keep thinking how quickly everything can change, and then I think how slowly it does. Both are true, I guess."

"They are," Dot said. "But we can make one faster."

Lani smiled. "Thank you for the list."

"It's what we do," Dot said, and touched the tape—new, too white, but getting friendlier by the day.

Coda with Lime

Two Fridays after the revolt, the dessert tray arrived like a joke with timing. Lime squares trembled in perfect rows. Orange shimmered behind them, a sunset insurance policy. Sugar-free wore a small sticker like a Scout badge.

Bonnie lifted the lid with a flourish. "Equal-opportunity gelatin," she said. "Two per person, no exceptions, and may God have mercy on our souls."

Room 207 tried to hover. Maggie cleared her throat. Dot raised an eyebrow that had survived the Johnson administration. He took two and saluted with his spoon.

They ate under the soft whirr of a fan that had finally stopped pretending to be a heater. The common room was warmer. The gravy was better. The boxwood along the garden border leaned in a small wind and looked, for one long blink, like a crowd in bright hats.

Dot set her palm flat against the cool glass and watched her reflection share space with the outside world. The fractures didn't blur. They caught the light and gave it back.

"To precision," Evie said.

"And volume," Maggie added.

"Both," Dot said. "Always both."

She lifted her spoon. The square quivered, faithful as a marching line. And when she tasted it—lime, electric, present—she felt, for the first time in a long time, that the place she lived could hear her when she spoke.

17

THE OPEN WINDOW

PRESENT • MANCHESTER MEADOWS

Night settled in layers: the elevator's sigh, carts parked, a hallway as quiet as a library after hours. The building exhaled its long day. Evie sat by the window with peppermint steam rising from her mug and knew what the room needed—a sentence that opened space, not a fist that broke it.

"I'm going to do something," she said.

Dot peered over *Les Misérables*, finger holding her place at a barricade. "No petitions tonight. My pen needs a nap."

"No petitions." Evie smiled. "A letter."

Maggie looked up from a magazine full of porches that promised breezes and a view. "To who?"

"To everyone." Evie slid the tray table closer. The act steadied her—margin, breath, the pen tip's first soft touch. She wrote:

To the residents of Manchester Meadows:

We're still here. We sit in armchairs and wheelchairs and by windows with good light. We play bingo and lose at cards and some days nap through movies, but we're still here. We've been teachers and welders and parents and cousins and quiet friends who brought a casserole. We've voted and marched and baked and grieved. We've held hands in hospital rooms and at bus stops.

This place is ours. It isn't perfect—no place with people in it is—but for now it's home. Home should warm you, feed you, see you.

Let's ask for what we need. Let's notice what's good. Let's help each other speak. We've earned our say.

With respect,

Evie Gross, Resident

She set the pen down. Her hand trembled the way it used to when she sent a piece to print—ink fixed, no more edits, a moment perched before response.

Dot nodded once, slow. "Balanced. Strong."

"At the meeting?" Maggie asked.

"At the meeting," Evie said, and felt something align, like a frame finally straight.

Wednesday at 2, the activity room filled: folding chairs, a sign-in sheet, the administrator with his careful tie and careful smile. The new Resident Council agenda sat in neat stacks. Someone had set a pitcher of water beside paper cups that collapsed if you squeezed too hard. Maggie tapped the wooden spoon once, called the meeting to order, and nodded to Evie.

After quick updates—heat checks posted by the mailboxes, kitchen menus revising with a pilot produce line, Council elections on Friday— Evie stood. Her hands didn't shake. The years had burned the tremor out of her in stranger rooms than this.

"I wrote something," she said, and the microphones caught only enough of the wobble to make everyone lean closer. She read. Her own voice sounded older than the one that used to boss around newsrooms and police spokesmen, and kinder too.

The room stayed quiet the way a field stayed quiet before wind moved through it. Then one hand lifted. Then another. A murmur gathered at the edges, then stepped forward.

"Draft under my door when the wind changed," Mr. Alvarez said. "But my granddaughter brought weatherstripping. The maintenance man said he could help install it. I just wanted to say thank you."

"Bonnie puts flowers on the dining tables," Mrs. Kapur added, fingers curved around her walker like parentheses. "They make dinner feel like dinner."

A man in the back—Mr. Rizzo, who'd told Dot more than once that meetings weren't his hobby—cleared his throat. "Not my thing," he said. "But sign me up for Story Hour." He shrugged, surprised at himself, and the room warmed a notch.

"Marisol sang while she changed my mother's linens last night," Lani said from the back. "She didn't know I was there. I want that in the minutes. That kindness."

Aides listened. The facilities man took notes, head down, pen real. Someone laughed at an aside about the chess bully in 207; someone dabbed a cheek when a soft-spoken woman admitted she'd been afraid to ask for an extra blanket. Something in the air shifted—less complaint, more claiming. The administrator cleared his throat less and less.

In the hallway after, Nurse Jen caught Evie's elbow the way you catch a friend crossing ice. "Thank you for how you said it," she murmured. "It helps us, too."

"It's everyone's home," Evie said, a little embarrassed, a little proud.

Maggie touched her arm. "You cracked a window. Fresh air's coming in."

Dot tapped the folded letter with her knuckle. "You brought us back to ourselves."

By Friday, the letter had sprouted company on the bulletin board: a neat half-sheet labeled *Story Hour: Bring One Memory*. Someone had tied a pen on a string through a thumbtack. Names appeared like crocuses. Evie didn't overthink it. She booked the sunniest corner of the lounge for 3 p.m. and wrote it on the calendar with a flourish that made Dot snort.

"Hostess flair," Dot said, fond.

"Practice from church bake sales," Maggie said. "Also from wrangling my fellow Republicans."

Evie laughed. "From newsrooms that thought coffee made meetings shorter."

She arrived early, scouting light the way she used to scout a shot. The corner offered a square of sun that warmed the carpet and made even the plastic fern look briefly credible. She dragged two extra chairs into the circle, just in case, and asked Bonnie for a plate of cookies that tasted like a memory even if you couldn't name whose.

Ten people came—five residents, three staff on break, two daughters visiting. Nurse Jen sat on the arm of a chair, chart tucked away like a secret, hair escaping its clip in a way that made her look almost off-duty. Mr. Han set his thermos beside his ankle and patted it once, as if to reassure the tea they'd get through this together.

Evie opened with something small. Big stories were trick doors; they slammed. Small ones stayed ajar.

"The first pie I ever burned," she said, "taught me patience and the smell of October."

Laughter rippled, not because it was hilarious but because everybody had stood at a stove and wished time backward.

Mr. Han told about the summer he learned English from teenagers who wanted free soda and taught him slang that made him accidentally swear in church.

Marisol shared her grandmother's cough remedy—honey, lime, a song whispered into the tea until the steam lifted the notes.

Patrice from the kitchen sat on the floor, back against the radiator, and talked about her son's first apartment and the miracle of a working stove that didn't trip the breaker.

A new woman, Esther, who wore her wedding ring on a blue ribbon, described the whistle of a train that passed her childhood porch at night and how the sound told her the world was larger than her block.

When it was Dot's turn, she didn't say Clara's name. She talked about a blue headband and the sound of cornbread releasing from a skillet like a sigh. She described the lint-back taste of white bread and the way protest songs found harmony on buses not built for it. She let the room fill with steam and the memory of soap on cotton and the relief of a door unlocking. The circle went quiet in that bright way that meant everyone was remembering something of their own.

Maggie, who claimed she didn't like talking in groups, followed with a story about the day she realized the best seat at any table was the one you pulled out for someone else. She made them laugh with a picture of toddlers and peas and a husband who believed casserole covered a multitude of scheduling sins. She made them hush with a line about how love sometimes sounded like a car turning into the driveway five minutes late and still coming home.

Afterward, a visiting daughter lingered near the cookies. "I didn't know my mom marched," she said, eyes wet with pride and a little grief. "She never told us."

"She told us today," Evie said, pressing the woman's hands between hers. "Sometimes we need an audience to remember we were brave."

On the way back to the nook, Evie found a folded paper taped to the bulletin board. She recognized the careful block print of someone who filled out forms for a living.

Ms. Gross,

Thank you for Story Hour. We're tired sometimes. Your stories make the halls feel like porches.

— Night Shift, East Wing

Evie stood there a moment longer than she meant to, letting the kindness land. The years had taught her how to read a crowd—where a laugh would land, where a headline would turn—but she'd forgotten that hush could be a headline, too. She peeled the tap free, smoothed the fold and carried it with her like a bouquet.

"Frame it," Dot said when Evie set the paper on the table.

"Put it by the thermostat," Maggie added. "Proof that some things change the temperature."

They settled by the window as the late light went the color of tea. The building sounded different to Evie—lighter, as if the walls had shifted to make room. The small flame that took work to keep lit felt steady for once, protected by three pairs of hands.

That weekend, Story Hour became Story Hours without anybody quite deciding it. The bulletin board collected sign-ups and a doodle of a microphone wearing sunglasses. Evie made a rule: no speeches, no apologies, three minutes and pass the plate. She broke it immediately for Mr. Alvarez, who needed five to explain how his father taught him to fold a newspaper to the exact width of a subway pole so he could read and still keep his balance. She broke it again for Lani's mother, who dozed through the beginning and woke at the part about tamales and asked, "Did we use the green sauce?" (They had.) Exceptions, Evie decided, were just another kind of noticing.

The administrator hovered once and then—after Dot nodded in a way that meant *you're allowed if you behave*—pulled up a chair. He listened with the face of a man who'd finally found the instructions folded into the box. Patrice took notes on recipe cards and pinned them on a cork strip in the kitchen: Esther's beans, Mr. Han's tea. Marisol sang more. The facilities man started greeting people by name and stopped calling them "unit numbers" when he thought nobody heard.

In quieter hours, Evie copied her letter in larger print for the big-type binder by the front desk. She added a second page—questions more than statements:

What made you feel seen this week?
Who do you miss that you could call?
Which corner needs a chair?

People began answering in the margins. Bonnie's daisies. My grandson's dumb joke. The bench by the fish tank—put it back, please. Dot underlined that one twice. The bench returned, scooted an inch away from the emergency extinguisher, compromise and oxygen sharing the same square of floor.

On Tuesday evening, Evie walked the long loop of the East Wing, counting quiets. Television hums softened at two; a whistler in 1C stopped; laughter leaked under a door in a good way. In the alcove by the vending machine she paused—half from the ache in her knee, half because the buzzing lights trembled like heat over asphalt, and a summer from fifty years ago rose through the waxed floor. She remembered the first time a picture she took had given strangers the courage to speak. She remembered the phone calls after—thank-yous and threats and the ragged breathing of a country learning its own shape aloud. She'd believed then that the work was to hold the megaphone steady. Maybe now it was to pass it around and hold the cord so nobody tripped.

She didn't say any of that out loud. She only stood in the not-quite-cold and let the building's new rhythm fold around the old one until they kept time together.

By the end of the week, the Resident Council posted its first minutes with a brisk little font and a title that made Evie grin: *Standing Items: Heat, Food, Quiet Hour, Mobility, Welcome.* Someone—Maggie, obviously—had added a line at the bottom in handwriting you could iron a shirt with: *Don't skip the parts that cost.* Evie slipped her letter into the plastic sleeve behind the agenda so newcomers would find a voice waiting for them beside the rules.

Late Sunday, rain stitched the windows. The three of them took their usual chairs by the glass. Dot pretended to read, which meant she turned two pages at a time and watched reflections. Maggie compared two porches and declared both perfect if you added people. Evie tucked the Night Shift note behind the frame of the thermostat after all; it made Maggie happy to be technically correct.

"Reckoning sounds loud," Maggie said, eyes on the rain. "But sometimes it's just a list and a light on."

"Sometimes it's a letter," Dot said.

"Sometimes it's a pie you burned and served anyway," Evie said. "With extra whipped cream."

They laughed. The fan above them hummed like a friendly hive. Somewhere down the hall, a kettle clicked off and a door clicked open. The air felt easy in her lungs. It had taken a lifetime to learn that gentleness could carry as far as fire if enough people leaned into it.

Evie set her palm to the glass. The window gave back a faint cool, not the bite of last month, not the ache of that night with Gracie's knit hat and the too-thin cocoa. The fractures in the pane caught the light and handed it on. The building listened in its way—slow, institutional, stubborn—and still, it listened.

"Same time next week?" Nurse Jen called, passing with a cart that jingled like bracelets.

"Story Hour never sleeps," Dot said.

"Story Hour naps," Maggie corrected.

Evie lifted her mug. "To windows," she said.

"And to doors that open," Maggie added.

"And to a thermostat with taste," Dot said.

They drank their tea. The hallways breathed. The ember stayed.

18

A QUIET STORM

PRESENT • MANCHESTER MEADOWS

Day 1 – The Thread

The cough arrived like a loose thread Maggie kept meaning to snip—soft, persistent, easy to ignore. She blamed the dry heat that hissed from the baseboard, the ficus dust, the way winter air slipped under the east doors even after Maintenance taped the seam. By afternoon, her laugh rode on a rasp. By evening, even her breath was thin.

"You okay?" Dot asked, watching the quilt tucked around Maggie's lap.

"Fine," Maggie said, which had always been code for *please don't fuss*.

Evie poured tea with honey and handed Maggie her favorite World's Okayest Mom mug—the one Dot had rescued from Mr. Giambalvo, the facility's most notorious mug thief.

They watched the hall settle toward Quiet Hour. The television down the corridor murmured at a polite volume. A cart rolled past, its jingling briefly bright, then gone. The thermostat by the mailboxes clicked once—habit or promise, impossible to tell.

At dinner Maggie didn't appear in the dining room. Evie and Dot traded a look, then moved down the hall with that particular speed older women knew—urgent, careful, proud. Maggie's room smelled faintly of eucalyptus and lemon cleaner. She lay tilted against pillows, cheeks too pink, lips too pale.

"Mags," Evie said, cool fingers on a hot forehead. "We're calling Jen."

"I can—" Maggie tried, and coughed instead, a sound that curled in her chest and wouldn't unhook.

Nurse Jen arrived with the calm of someone who'd seen many storms. She brought oxygen tubing, a stethoscope, a pulse oximeter, and a kind voice. "Deep breath for me," she said, and listened long with her eyes focused, her head bent the way people bent when they were deciding between three truths and one necessary action.

"It's pneumonia," she said at last, easing the soft green cannula under Maggie's nose. "Oxygen's at eighty-nine to ninety. Let's bring it up."

A portable chest x-ray confirmed it: a right-lower-lobe pneumonia like a small cloud in a corner of sky. They drew labs, started IV antibiotics, and paged Respiratory. The little screen numbers climbed a notch, then another, as if persuaded by company.

They wheeled Maggie to the medical wing, the corridor unexpectedly long, like a story you thought you knew until you had to walk through every sentence. The monitor kept a small steady chord. Dot held the rail like an anchor; Evie smoothed the blanket, then the hair at Maggie's temple, as if neatness could negotiate with fever.

"I thought it was nothing," Maggie whispered once the plastic taste of oxygen turned ordinary.

"Nothing wasn't allowed," Dot said, fierce to keep from crying.

Evie leaned close. "We overruled you. It took a quorum."

That first night stretched and then folded the way nights did in places where machines counted breath. Patrice sent broth in a paper cup with a lid that refused to stay. It tasted like salt and the memory of chicken and came with two crackers and a note: *Beans behaving tomorrow. Don't tell administration.* Room 207 sent a pawn from his chess set "for luck," then knocked on the frame and pretended he hadn't.

When the sky finally lightened, the world felt as if it had blinked and chosen to keep going.

Day 2 – Learning to Breathe

Morning brought a respiratory therapist named Nate, rolling a cart of tidy instruments and patience. He looked barely old enough to have opinions and sounded like someone who trusted the body's willingness to be coached.

"We're going to help those lungs remember what good work feels like," he said, and set the incentive spirometer in the tray as if it were a bell to be rung.

He taught Maggie to purse her lips on the exhale, to count the seconds out. Dot sat forward, counting along on her fingers. Evie timed rests on the watch she hadn't worn since her daughter moved to the coast, the second hand stroking its circle with unbothered certainty.

"Again," Nate said gently. "In—two—three—four. Out—two—three—four—five—six."

Maggie closed her eyes. She saw a clothesline in a backyard thirty years gone, sheets like sails. She breathed them full; she let them go. The little blue float in the spirometer rose and hovered. The numbers flirted with one another and settled in a better place.

"Better," Nate said. "You're stubborn; I like that."

"So do we," Evie said, and Dot snorted softly as if stubborn were a family heirloom they'd polished together.

When Nate left, Maggie whispered, "I hated needing help."

Dot brushed a thumb across her wrist. "Needing wasn't failing. It was trusting the circle."

Maggie nodded, though her eyes shone. "The circle had a loud opinion."

"Precision," Evie said, "and volume."

That afternoon, Cindy called first, voice brisk with worry that arrived like a to-do list. "Should we come? Is she eating? Did they check for fluid?"

Evie answered steady. "She was eating pudding, dictating demands to the kitchen, and yes, they checked."

Wendy called after dinner, soft with apology and a laugh that tried to be brave. "Mom would say she was fine when she wasn't."

"She already tried," Dot said. "We ignored her."

Wendy laughed for real then. "Thank you for that."

"Bring the quilt she likes," Evie added. "When she's back in her room, she'll want something familiar."

When the calls ended, Maggie looked at them with that familiar mix —gratitude, embarrassment, love. "I didn't want to scare them."

"You wanted to carry what wasn't meant for one set of shoulders," Dot said. "Even your fine ones."

Evie tucked the sheet a little tighter, the way she'd taught the East Wing to do last week. "We'll share the weight," she said. "That's the whole point of growing old with people."

Residents passed quiet messages through the staff the way neighbors passed casseroles across back fences. From the kitchen, Patrice sent a sliced pear that smelled like a whole orchard. From Housekeeping, Alma tucked a lavender sachet into the drawer because sometimes rooms forgot how to be rooms. From Mr. Han came a folded paper crane made of last Sunday's circular—ink smudged, wings clean. On the back he'd written, *Balance.*

Evie taped a note on the bulletin board in her square, practical hand: *No Story Hour today—send one sentence of home to Room 112.* By dusk ten slips sat beneath the tape.

The oranges at lunch looked like suns.

I fed the goldfish; he acted like I owed him rent.

Patrice says the beans behaved today.

Heat held all night. Posted.

Evie read them aloud. Maggie listened with her eyes closed and held the words the way you hold a warm stone in your pocket—weight and comfort at once.

Day 3 – Turning the Corner

On the third morning, Nurse Jen checked the numbers and smiled for real. "Turning the corner," she said. "Ninety-four and climbing."

Nate returned with his spirometer and his patience. "Let's make that float jealous of the ceiling." Maggie inhaled as if she'd been saving that breath for a good day. The blue piece rose and hung there like a hat on a peg. The blood-pressure cuff sighed and loosened. The antibiotic pump clicked done with an almost comic sense of accomplishment.

They let *Casablanca* play low on a tablet propped against a water carafe. At the airport goodbye, Maggie stirred.

"Not yet," she murmured, not opening her eyes. "We weren't saying goodbye to anything."

"No, ma'am," Evie said. "We're just practicing the lines."

Dot scrubbed the clip back twenty seconds with a little flick that felt like a magic trick. Outside, the wind worried the hedges. Inside, the scene played again and again, and each time Ilsa stepped toward the plane, Maggie breathed out a little easier—as if even old stories could work the lungs.

By late afternoon, the room felt less like a ward and more like a living room—blanket, low light, a promise made. Patrice smuggled in a contraband wedge of lime Jell-O. "Integrity assured," she said, and winked like a conspirator. Room 207 arrived with a notebook labeled *Contingencies* and tried not to cry when Maggie called him a fusspot.

Day 4 – Thresholds

The next day was for thresholds. Jen turned the oxygen down a notch and watched the numbers behave. Nate signed off on fewer hourly checks. The fever, having made its point, packed up like weather and moved on.

"Here's what we'll do when we take you back to your room," Dot said, listing like the chair of a sensible committee. "A chair by the window and the humidifier running. The thermostat at a number that won't make me call Facilities in the dead of night. A glass of water with a straw you tolerate. *Casablanca* cued to the airport scene because you insist. And a sign on the door that says Knock Softly and Bring News."

"You forgot the quilt," Evie said.

"I wouldn't forget the quilt," Dot said, injured. "The quilt is the point."

Maggie smiled without opening her eyes. "You're both ridiculous."

"And effective," Evie said.

In quiet stretches Maggie drifted. When she slept, she swam

through rooms from other years—the parlor where her mother kept the good doilies, the little room behind the sanctuary where Dot had fastened a row of satin buttons up her spine on a June morning that smelled like soap and peonies, the night she sat at her own kitchen table and wrote a letter to Dot she never mailed, the words too tender and too true for the life she was living then. In every room someone opened a window. In every room the air moved.

When she woke, Dot sat with a legal pad and made a list titled *After-care*. It included "extra pillow," "pursed-lip breathing reminders," and "evict dust from ficus." Evie added "letters home—to families," wanting to keep people steady the way the notes on the bulletin board had steadied Maggie. Then she drew a lemon with a ridiculous smile, because the cleaner's lemon scent still lingered—and for once, even the trace of it felt friendly.

Day 5 – Home

By the time the sun slid low on the fifth day, the medical wing had started to release its hold. On team rounds, Jen, Nate, and the PA agreed Maggie could transfer with oxygen off and the spirometer at the ready.

"You'll ring if breath feels short," Jen said, signing the transfer with the daisy pen. "No being brave in private." She said it to Maggie but looked at Dot and Evie, earnest as a promise.

They wheeled Maggie back down the long sentence of corridor to her room. It had been aired, dusted, and rearranged by friends who knew the choreography of return. The quilt waited—blue, of course—folded like a welcome. The chair stood in the good light. The thermostat, recently persuaded, held steady at a number that made Dot nod.

Evie set the tablet on the sill and opened the film to the airport scene. The three of them waited through the first line as if it were a grace.

"When I'm back in my bed," Maggie said, eyes closing, "we'll start with *Casablanca*. The airport."

"The airport," Dot echoed, and reached for the remote the way she'd reached for bullhorns once, for clipboards last week—for whatever worked.

The building moved around them—carts and sneakers and the careful laughter of night shift swapping stories at the desk. In the garden, the evergreens held their dark shine against the early evening. Inside, steam curled from a fresh mug. Patrice's beans arrived behaving. Someone—probably Bonnie—had tucked a daisy into the plastic cup where the straws lived, because dignity sometimes looked like a flower drinking from the wrong vase and making it work.

Life was fragile, yes. But it was also this: a peppermint in a pocket, a hand that knows where to find yours in the dark, a thermostat with decent taste, a list on a legal pad with boxes that can be checked. It was staff who learned your name and residents who learned your tells. There was the daughter who pulled the quilt high, Dot who wouldn't let silence win, and Evie who set the small things right without being asked.

Ilsa took a step toward the plane. Maggie breathed out and let the air replace itself, faithful as tide. The blue quilt warmed her legs. Evie's fingers tapped the arm of the chair in time with the softened room sounds. Dot sat very straight, the way she'd always sat when she was keeping watch and pretending she wasn't.

"Tomorrow," Maggie said, eyes still closed, "we'll plan the menu. No meatloaf. Fruit with every meal."

"Agency," Dot said.

"With integrity," Evie added.

They smiled. Somewhere down the hall a kettle clicked off and a door clicked open. The pilot light kept burning.

19

A VOICE OF HER OWN

PRESENT • MANCHESTER MEADOWS

The library cart squeaked as if it knew secrets. It rounded the corner with a wobble and a sigh, a little parade of paperbacks stacked like row houses—sun-faded spines, curling covers, that faint perfume of basements and winter coats that belonged to every book that had waited patiently for years. Marisol steered with her hip and grinned at the three women gathered near the window.

"Treasure delivery," she announced. "And look what hid in the back."

A navy-blue hardcover rode on top, its cloth rubbed thin at the corners. Evie recognized the weight before she saw the title. Some books were heavy because of their paper; others because of what they'd held for you. Marisol turned it so the silver letters flashed: *A Voice in the Wind: The Anne Harbison Story.*

"Your name's inside," Marisol said, delighted. "Was it really you?"

Evie laughed, the kind of laugh that steals a bit of breath from memory. "It was," she said. "It is."

They claimed the sunny corner by unspoken agreement. The afternoon did that golden thing the building was so good at—light pooling in squares on the carpet, lavender from the courtyard leaking through the cracked window. Somewhere down the hall a kettle clicked off; farther still, a television whispered game shows to an audience of dozing men. Someone had propped open the lounge door with a stack of old *National Geographics* so the good air could wander.

Evie opened the cover. The inscription gleamed dull with time:

Evie—thank you for seeing me, even when I didn't want to be seen. For giving voice to the truths I wasn't always brave enough to say aloud. — A.H., October 1992.

Dot and Maggie arrived with their usual rustle of cardigans and the soft whisper of slippered feet. Dot's hair had gone the color of salt; Maggie's wool throw—spring blue—waited folded over her arm like good manners. Maggie was still building herself back after the pneumonia week; her cheeks held color without fever, her breath measured itself carefully, learning steadiness again.

"Was that the senator?" Dot asked, already leaning in. Her curiosity was a hand on Evie's back.

"It found me," Evie said, and the words felt like a small mercy.

Maggie settled, the throw across her knees, careful as always with her hips. "I remember when you came back from D.C. talking about rooms with flags and men who called you dear," she said. "You said the truth mattered even when the microphones were tired."

"That sounded like me," Evie said, smiling.

Dot tapped the page with one capable finger. "And did it?" she asked. "Matter?"

"Some of it," Evie answered. "Not all. Enough." The old tug arrived —admiration braided with argument, the ache of what she couldn't put on the page because someone had to keep living with it.

Outside, a bare branch tapped the glass, patient and insistent. The building breathed. In the hallway a call bell chimed, a laugh rang, two nurses compared dinner recipes in quick Spanish. Patrice passed the door carrying a crate of oranges that brightened the corridor like small lanterns and called, "Fish cakes stayed on the menu. Cumin ratio improved."

Evie turned the book so Maggie could see a photograph: Anne Harbison in a soft suit, hand lifted mid-sentence, the camera catching the exact moment conviction found its light. The caption credited Evie

—Photo by E.R. Gross—and the name pulled at her the way a thread did when you feared what might unravel and yet kept tugging.

"There's still a story in me," Evie said, more to the room than to either of them. "Not someone else's. Mine."

Maggie's smile turned warm and bossy. "Then you should start. Before we begin filling in the ending for you."

Dot nodded. "We'd proofread and heckle in equal measure."

Evie ran her palm over the navy cloth—an old habit, as if she could iron the years smooth—then closed the book. Not like closing a door; more like saving a place. In her hands she felt the keys again: the Royal that had demanded muscle, the Smith-Corona that purred like a promise. She smelled the lavender and leather of Anne's office, heard the antique clock that never quite kept time, saw the pink Post-it flagging the chapter everyone had wanted to demote to a footnote.

"Go," Dot said softly, as if Evie were poised at a starting line only she could see. "We'll keep your seat."

Evie stood, the book tucked under her arm, a little buoyant, a little afraid. The hallway waited—bright as a fresh page. She carried the inscription like a note folded once and kept close.

Time tilted.

She was back in the office with the honeyed lamp, the folder labeled *1979—Defense Vote,* the version of herself who still believed a sentence could change the temperature of a room. She had put her fingers on the keys.

Mr. Han paused at the lounge doorway on his way to chess and raised two fingers in a small salute. "Good words today?" he asked.

"Work in progress," Evie said.

"A good store always kept a sign like that," he replied, and moved on, his thermos thumping lightly against his ankle.

They watched her go. Dot lifted the blue throw up around Maggie's shoulders and wagged the senator's book once in mock threat. "We'll test you later," she called after Evie. "On chapter headings."

Evie waved without turning. Quiet Hour signs rustled on their plastic tacks, the building's promise that afternoons could still be gentle.

Later, after supper trays and bingo numbers and the soft click of evening meds, Evie's room held its own kind of dusk—amber from the vintage lamp she insisted on keeping within reach. The ceramic base had crazed with hairline cracks; the shade frayed at the seam. It had lit smoke-thick motel rooms and press tents near runways, borrowed desks in borrowed cities. It had watched her draft obituaries and speeches and half a dozen first paragraphs that had pretended to be hers before one finally was.

The Royal was gone—misplaced in a move she hadn't supervised—but her hands remembered it, the way truth used to require muscle. The Smith-Corona, ribbon dry, sat like an altar on the credenza with a polite layer of dust that Dot would scold tomorrow. On the desk, her laptop woke with a groan and a fan that whirred like a small plane taxiing for courage. A piece of clear tape held the corner where life kept catching. The Night Shift note from last week—*Your stories make the halls feel like porches*—was tucked under the lamp's base like a talisman.

She opened a blank document. The cursor blinked, patient as a pulse. Her fingers hovered, then lowered. The ache in her knuckles arrived early and was welcomed.

She typed:

This time, it's mine.

No assignments. No managing a senator's margins. No ghosting someone else's courage. Just memory and truth and whatever remained between them with her name on it.

She backspaced once, twice, and tried again.

I was born loud and handed a pencil. They tried to tame both. I kept scribbling. I kept speaking. Especially when the room turned away.

Her mouth tilted. Warmth lifted behind her ribs—not nostalgia, not yet. Something like arrival. She paused to sip the tea Maggie had left —lukewarm now, still sweet—and set the mug back on a square of paper towel folded into quarters the way Dot insisted civilized people did it.

A soft knock sounded. "News," Marisol whispered through the door, obeying the sign. She slipped in with a small plate: two slices of orange and a sugar cookie the kitchen called house. "Patrice said fuel for chapters."

"You're an angel," Evie said.

"Tell the Council that at the next meeting," Marisol grinned, and vanished.

Evie ate the orange and kept going. She wrote the day she'd smuggled the Royal into the back seat and driven three hours to stand outside a courthouse where a custody case had needed someone who didn't flinch when the lawyer raised his voice. She wrote the night she'd photographed a candlelight vigil and blurred the first dozen frames because her hands had refused to behave around grief. She wrote the morning she'd sat in Anne's office and argued for the paragraph about the funding vote because context, she'd said, was also a kind of truth.

Her battery warning chimed at twenty percent. She plugged in and smiled at herself—prepared, at last. Someone laughed in the hall; a door clicked shut; the building settled into the hour. She felt like a journalist again—curious, awake, accountable to the truth and to herself. She felt like the girl who'd believed stories could change a room's weather. She believed it again.

She sketched the chapter names on a scrap:

- Rooms with Flags
- The Royal and the Road
- What Wouldn't Fit in a Press Release
- Quiet Hours
- The Revolt of the Recliners
- Aftercare

She laughed at herself for titling anything and titled them anyway. She wrote three paragraphs about the first newsroom that had paid her in bylines and bad coffee. She wrote a sentence she loved and immediately distrusted and then let it stand, because perfect, she reminded herself, wasn't an item on the Resident Council agenda.

Dot appeared in the doorway with her book and her eyebrow. "Status report?"

"Two pages," Evie said. "A structure that might not embarrass the ancestors. A cookie."

Dot smiled and touched her shoulder, firm as punctuation. "Be fair to yourself, too," she said, and went to fetch warm water for the humidifier because she couldn't leave without fixing a small thing.

Maggie arrived with careful steps, set a fresh tea bag beside the laptop, and tapped the desk. "Five minutes," she said.

"Four paragraphs," Evie bargained.

"Four," Maggie agreed, and left, because kindness didn't require hovering.

Evie wrote five.

Her document ticked past a page count she hadn't seen in years. She saved in three places—habit, superstition, survival—and touched the senator's book on the bedside table, the inscription cool under her finger.

She titled the document *Rooms with Flags* and began.

20

GHOSTWRITING THE REVOLUTION

1983 • EVIE

When her fingers met the keys, the room remembered 1983. The office was small and stubborn with its own weather: lamplight honeying the corners, paper stacked in small cities, a window cracked to the restless chorus of horns and a far-off dog. Evie sat at the secondhand desk she refused to replace. Her Smith-Corona rattled softly like a patient animal. Beside it, Anne Harbison's archive bloomed in tidy folders: clippings, speeches, calendars with careful stars, the onionskin copies that always felt like they might float away.

She ran a thumb over the keyboard as if greeting an old friend and still thought of the Royal she had muscled through war zones and motel rooms. That machine had wanted proof. Each letter demanded the weight of a wrist, the truth struck into the page with a clack you felt in your bones. The Smith-Corona was smoother. Sometimes, the ease unnerved her. Sometimes, she missed the resistance.

City noise threaded through the open inch of window. In her thirties, that sound had read as possibility; in her fifties, it sometimes read as a dare. Solitude used to be chosen: airports and deadlines, nights in borrowed rooms, months holding a story like a lantern through dark places. Lately, solitude felt like a curtain. She wasn't ready for the lowering, not yet.

She was ghostwriting a legacy. Senator Anne Harbison of Maine: quick mind, quicker smile, one of the first to kick at the marble ceiling while men in committee rooms called women dear and patted their hands as if testing for fever. Decades later, illness whispered around Anne's edges. The book was meant to fix what time smudged: a life, preserved.

Evie admired Anne. She could say that without flinching. But timelines told their own truths if you let them, and the gaps were loud. Missing months. Positions that pivoted without leaving footprints. It was as if Anne had lived two lives, one broadcast, one seamed tight.

Evie sorted through notes and stopped at a pink Post-it she refused to label footnote: *1979—The Defense Vote.* Turning point. Fallout. The year the phone rang in the middle of the night and the caller forgot she had a child sleeping down the hall. If Evie was going to write this story, it had to breathe.

She typed a paragraph that admitted cost. Then she sat inside the quiet that followed a sentence she knew would be argued with. Down the hall, a copier warmed up and a dot-matrix printer chattered to itself; on a staffer's terminal, green text blinked in slow command prompts.

Evie knew it was only a matter of time before she traded ribbons for screens—before the room learned a new kind of keystroke. But for now she kept to her Smith-Corona, its hum and heft still truer to the way she thought. She promised the younger version, dust on her shoes, press pass more stubborn than polite, that she wouldn't disappear inside someone else's version of the world.

The Meeting

Anne's office on the Hill was all polish: mahogany and orchids, floor-to-ceiling windows courting the Capitol's clean angles. Lavender and leather rode the conditioned air. Evie kept a hand on the worn briefcase she'd carried since Saigon, the one with a rip in the lining where she used to hide notes when hotel safes felt like suggestions.

"Evie," Anne said, smiling the way people did when rooms were used to tilting toward them. "You're early."

"More to cover than an hour wanted to hold," Evie answered. She set the draft on the desk, flagged, annotated, loved and challenged in the same ink.

Anne flipped straight to the pink Post-it. "The vote again."

"It wasn't a footnote," Evie said. "You went against your party. Donors turned. Your staff slept on the office floor to answer phones that wouldn't stop. If leadership costs something, this was the receipt."

A shade passed through Anne's gaze. "We'd talked about this."

"And we'll keep talking," Evie said, steady. "Because a legacy without friction reads like myth, and you didn't live a myth. You lived a life that dared people to argue with you."

Anne leaned back. Her fingers tapped the chair—once, twice. "Do you know how long it took to recover? Not the polling. Me. I stopped taking my mother's calls for a month. Strangers sent threats to my sister's house. A veteran spat at me in Bangor." She exhaled, measured. "I nearly lost everything."

"That's why it belongs on the page," Evie said. "Not as spectacle—*as context*. People need to understand that conviction doesn't pay in applause."

Silence threaded the room. The antique clock ticked its soft disapproval. From the street, a protest chant rose and faded like a tide. Anne closed the draft and studied Evie as if weighing two stones in one hand.

"I hired you for your integrity," she said at last. "I also hired you to guard the parts of me I still need to live with. There's a line between honesty and damage. Keep me on it."

Evie didn't look away. "That was the line I intended to write, yours and mine."

Weariness showed then, unguarded and human. "Maybe the truth isn't always the whole story," Anne said quietly. "Maybe it's the part a person can bear."

Evie stood, heart heavy and clear. "You didn't want a fairy tale."

"No," Anne said. "I wanted a version that wouldn't haunt me."

Evie's hand found the doorknob. "Then let's choose the truths that earn your sleep."

Outside, the carpet hushed every step. Vivian, the chief of staff with the marathoner's stride, fell in beside her.

"You push her," Vivian said, not unkindly.

"She hired me to," Evie replied.

Vivian nodded toward the window where the dome interrupted the sky. "Just remember, history gets edited twice. Once by the people who lived it, and again by the ones who read it between errands."

"I was trying to write for both," Evie said.

"Good luck," Vivian said, and somehow it was a blessing.

Fallout

That night, Evie's apartment smelled like onions and the neighbor's television. She dropped the briefcase by the door, set her day-planner by the phone with its long coiled cord, and called home.

"Mom?"

"I'm here," she said, and closed her eyes at the relief tucked inside the word.

Later, she sat at the kitchen table with a bowl she wasn't hungry for and spread the transcripts, vote counts, and clipped editorials that used to make her stomach burn. She wrote in the margin: *This hurt. It mattered.*

She called Dot after ten, against the rules of considerate friendship.

"So?" Dot asked, no hello necessary.

"She wanted the truth gentle," Evie said. "Gentler than it was."

"Truth rarely thanks us for telling it," Dot said. "But it does keep us company."

Evie laughed, surprised by the sting in her eyes. "You were getting that embroidered on a pillow."

"I'd put it on a shirt and wear it to church," Dot said. "Now sleep. You can argue with a senator tomorrow."

When the apartment finally quieted, Evie returned to the draft. She didn't sand the edges off the chapter. She did change two verbs that had felt like verdicts. She added one line she knew Anne would hate and another Anne might secretly be grateful for. She removed a sentence that was only there to prove Evie had been brave.

She read the pages aloud. The words felt lived in, not lacquered.

When she turned off the lamp, it left a coin of light on the desk, bright enough to find again.

Aftermath

Two weeks later, Anne signed off on the chapter with a short note in the margin: *All right. Leave it. If the tide rises, we'll mark it together.*

Evie kept the page—not for the archive, but for herself.

On press day, she stood in a hallway outside a greenroom and watched a young staffer rehearse talking points. The girl, twenty-something and hopeful, caught Evie's eye and blurted, "Do you think it matters? Books like this?"

Evie thought of the veteran in Bangor, of phones that wouldn't stop, of girls who would stand where Anne stood and need to know they weren't the first to shake.

"Sometimes," she said. "Sometimes it tells someone they aren't crazy for caring."

The staffer nodded, blinking quick. "That's enough," she said.

"It is," Evie agreed.

Back at her office, she packed the folders carefully, leaving the pink Post-it for last. She smoothed it flat and filed it under *Kept Promises.*

On her way home, she bought peonies from the woman on the corner who never had change but always remembered faces. She set them in a jar on the windowsill and opened a new document. A line that had waited for years finally let her type it.

This time, it's mine.

And when the cursor blinked, steady as breathing, she kept going.

Now • Manchester Meadows

Late light softened the common room. Evie traced the edge of a photocopy in her lap, Anne's margin note creased from years of keeping. Vivian's line threaded through her mind: history gets edited twice. Evie smiled at the third edit, the one you made in the quiet with the life you actually lived, and closed her eyes for a minute, grateful the truth still kept her company. Then she opened them, steadied her hands, and kept typing.

21

THE DETAILS THAT REMEMBERED US

MANCHESTER, PENNSYLVANIA
• SPRING 1984 • MAGGIE

T he house wore its holiday best.

Honey-glazed ham warmed the air, scalloped potatoes breathed butter, and rolls cooled on the rack like little pillows. Maggie moved through her kitchen in the tulip-embroidered apron Cindy had made in high school, conducting timers and serving spoons with a maestro's certainty. Flour dusted her cheek; she didn't notice. A green-lidded Tupperware deviled-egg tray waited like a promise. The good silver, polished on Thursday because Friday was for errands, glinted from a tea towel as if it knew its cue.

She'd been up since five. Holidays always woke her early—excitement dressed as purpose. The vintage ivory damask cloth lay smooth across the dining table. Water goblets stood like little bells. Cloth napkins, folded into rabbits, waited beside pastel chocolates. Place cards in tidy script sat on the plates, even though everyone knew where they belonged. In Maggie's house, love spoke in details.

Outside, the backyard held its secrets: plastic eggs tucked into flowerpots and the low limbs of the dogwood, quarters and jellybeans rattling softly inside. Yesterday's rake marks still lined the grass. The tulips she'd planted in October stood at attention, pink and yellow, as if hoping to please. She'd swept the back step twice and left the broom leaning like a chaperone.

At 11:03, right on time, the front door sighed open.

"Happy Easter, Mom!"

Cindy, twenty-nine, breezed in with daffodils and a bottle of Riesling, day planner under one arm, beeper clipped to her belt. It chirped once; she tapped it mute and set it face down like an apology. Maggie kissed her temple, pointed to the green vase by the sink, and circled her wrist once with a smile that said: one hour off the clock, please. Cindy mouthed sorry and actually meant it.

Tommy followed, baby carrier in one hand and a grin in the other. Nathan slept hard, cheeks the color of new apples. Rachel trailed with a diaper bag and a carrot cake, anxiety bright in her eyes. "He napped early in the car. Did I ruin the schedule?"

"We'll let him write the schedule," Maggie said, taking the cake and the worry both. "You're here. That's what matters."

Wendy arrived last, sunglasses pushed up like a movie star, scarf red as a robin's breast, a crescent of cobalt paint drying on her cuff. She produced a small watercolor of a nest. "For the breakfast nook."

"It's beautiful," Maggie said, feeling her heart do that quiet squeeze. "I'll hang it where the morning can brag on it."

Grace came with the clink of forks settling and everyone remembering how to be in a room together. They bowed their heads without discussion.

"For food and hands that made it, for the people who sit here and the ones far away," Maggie said, thinking of Evie in D.C., who would call after supper, the long-distance hush now part of their holidays. "Amen."

Lunch was a symphony—chatter, clinks, stories that started over each other and made room anyway. Maggie sent bowls around, green beans almandine and deviled eggs dusted with paprika, and let herself watch more than speak: Tommy's steadiness, the way Rachel kept checking Nathan and then letting herself laugh, Cindy's quick hands already planning dessert, Wendy pausing mid-sentence to listen to some thought only she could hear. A cassette of '70s Road Mix clicked to side

B in the living room. Sun warmed the edge of the tablecloth; shadow inched across the sugar bowl as the hour turned.

"Remember when Dad hid the giant egg in the mailbox?" Cindy said, already smiling toward the punch line.

"And the mailman ate the jellybeans," Tommy added.

"He apologized," Maggie said, "and then asked for the recipe—as if jellybeans were an art."

"They were," Wendy said gravely. "Placement mattered."

When the plates were cleared and the dishwasher sighed to life, they wandered to the backyard.

Rachel stayed on the porch, Nathan warm against her shoulder, bottle tipped just so. "I'll watch," she said. "Someone should keep score."

Maggie met her eyes and nodded—agreement, not exemption. Then she clapped her hands on the back step.

"All right, egg hunters. This isn't any old hunt. It's the Egg-Cellent Scavenger Hunt." She held up three cards. "Each clue leads to your next clue and eventually to your basket. Find your basket and win bragging rights till next year. Tommy, blue. Cindy, yellow. Wendy, pink. Here's your first clue."

They were grown, but their smiles made them briefly twelve.

They scattered across the lawn, reading as they went. Cindy darted toward the azaleas, her Swatch glinting in the sun. Wendy trailed a fingertip along the dogwood as if greeting it. Tommy pretended not to race and absolutely did.

Cindy reached the azaleas first and crouched, reading aloud as she searched.

"*Where coffee began before you knew better—check the tin with the dent,*" she read.

She straightened, already turning toward the potting bench by the shed. Maggie used to set the coffee there in the mornings, mug balanced on soil bags while she worked.

The dented tin sat on the lower shelf, exactly where it always had. Cindy lifted the lid and found the folded yellow card inside.

"Second clue!"

Wendy's pink card sent her drifting toward the side yard. "*Where* summers cooled—*check the hose that kinks when it's stubborn.*" She followed the green coil to its inevitable bend, lifted it gently, and found her next clue tucked beneath. She paused, as if composing the moment, then smiled and moved on.

Tommy's blue clue led him straight to the tool bench. "*Where things were fixed instead of thrown away—look where your father kept the square.*

He checked the pegboard, smiled, and crouched. Taped beneath the bench, out of sight, he found the next card and held it up like evidence.

"I overthought it," he said, laughing.

A small snag, on purpose. The second clue for yellow sent Cindy to the gate that stuck. She wrestled it, laughed, and called out, "Mother!" Maggie hid her grin and passed her the oil can. "You always were my fix-it girl," she said. Cindy freed the latch with a triumphant *hah* and, for a heartbeat, looked exactly like the kid who'd taken apart the toaster to understand heat.

The final clues converged at the swing set. One by one, they reached beneath their swings and came up grinning, baskets in hand.

They lifted their prizes like trophies.

Tommy's held a bar of dark chocolate, a tiny tool-set keychain, and a folded coupon good for "one Saturday of Dad-level help from Mom." Cindy's had a bag of good coffee and a paperback she'd been meaning to read, plus three quarters taped together with a note: *for laundry when the world forgets you're important.* Wendy's offered new sketching pencils and a *Road Trip '79* mixtape Maggie had found at the back of a drawer, labeled in blue Bic: *Open Windows.*

Rachel's welcome basket—lemon cookies and soft spa socks with a note in Maggie's neat script—waited by the picnic table: *For feet that carry more than they admit.* Nathan's basket was a flannel blanket square with a ribbon corner—chewable, washable, celebratory.

They drifted inside reluctantly, the way people did when weather begged to be a room. Coffee steamed. The carrot cake surrendered its first neat slice and then chaos. The beeper dared to chirp—one look from Maggie and the thing thought better of it. Track three on the mixtape, "Brandy," made Tommy sing harmony badly on purpose until Rachel snorted tea.

"Next year," Cindy said, "I'll beat both of you."

"Bragging rights noted," Maggie said, and wrote *CINDY, 1985* on the back of a grocery list because records mattered even when they didn't.

After they left and the house exhaled, Maggie set the dishwasher for the good cycle and sat on the porch step. The afternoon slid toward gold-gray; the neighbor's wind chimes practiced one note until they found three. Her hands and feet ached; she couldn't remember sitting during the meal. She noticed a napkin she'd folded crooked, reached to fix it, then let it be. Imperfect could still mean beloved.

"This," she whispered into the new-cool air, "this was what I was meant for."

She went back inside, wrapped two rolls in foil for the freezer that fed everyone sooner or later, and wrote the scavenger clues into the cookbook margin, because future Maggie liked instructions from past Maggie.

She tucked Wendy's nest watercolor into the nook frame and angled the lamp so morning would catch it. She laid the baskets by the door to put away for another year—evidence that a day had been well and truly lived.

Now • Manchester Meadows

The common room rustled with soft conversations and the quiet shuffle of footsteps. A silk tulip in the windowsill leaned slightly askew; Maggie left it that way. The wall clock ticked toward late morning, and when the hands met at 11:03, memory arrived warm as ham and bright as the dogwood.

So much had changed since that bright day. Tommy, steady and kind, had been taken by a widow maker in his late sixties. One minute coffee, the next a silence that rearranged the world. At the funeral she had stood straight for Rachel and Nathan, then sat down in the quiet days after and learned where grief kept its weight, on stairwells, in grocery aisles, beside the hose that still kinked for old time's sake.

Cindy's life had turned sleek and sure—suits, flights, a phone that bossed everyone. The month before, she'd led a campaign that made the business pages; yesterday, she'd sent a bar of Swiss chocolate from an airport shop with a scribbled heart on the wrapper. *Wish you were here,* her note said. *Or that I were there.* Maggie had laughed and tucked the napkin from the package away like legal tender.

Wendy had stayed Wendy, moon pulled, earnest, two states away. A padded envelope had arrived that week with a new sketch of a robin mid flight and a note: *For spring.* The bird looked like it knew where it was going without needing to explain.

Nathan, no longer the baby in the carrier, was a kind, tired ER doctor with a spouse and two Pomeranians who wore bandanas. When shifts allowed, he visited and asked for stories about his dad he hadn't heard yet. Maggie told him about the mailbox egg and the day Tommy brought home a stray turtle because "it followed me," even though it very much hadn't.

Outside, April leaned green. Inside, the season had shifted for Maggie too. The days were gentler and quieter. She understood now that she had chased perfect out of love, not fear. Still, some nights she wondered what she had hurried past, the mess that made its own kind of memory.

She folded her hands, pressed her palms together, and let the question rise like prayer. *I did the best I could, didn't I?* The old tears came without heat. She patted them dry and answered herself aloud, smiling. "I did the best I could."

Bonnie had rolled by with a tray and paused. "Need anything, honey?"

"Only more stories," Maggie had said.

"That we have," Bonnie had promised, and jingled on, a one woman parade with better shoes.

Later • Manchester Meadows

That evening, Maggie, Dot, and Evie sat at a round table near the window, the Manchester Meadows version of a feast: sliced ham, sweet potatoes in their own little crocks, green beans set like fences. Cups lifted. Plates nudged. They ate slowly, in no hurry to let the hour end.

"Remember the year we actually made it to your house?" Evie asked, eyes bright. "1962. The one time."

"The only Easter we ever caught," Dot said. "You kept that door open every spring; life kept closing it."

Maggie laughed. "The backyard looked like it had secrets back then, too."

"It did," Evie said. "And we all pretended not to stare at the coconut cake with jelly beans."

"I was policing the deviled eggs," Dot announced. "People cheated with deviled eggs."

"You patrolled the table like a union rep," Evie said. "Fair allocation."

Maggie's laugh made her feel young. "Tommy tried to snake the giant egg before Cindy even knew there was one under the peonies. And Wendy sang to a ladybug and forgot she was hunting."

"Balance," Evie said fondly. "Steady, spark, and song."

Dot set down her fork. "We arrived on the bus," she remembered. "Two transfers and one driver who thought our tickets were optional."

"And you still brought carnations," Maggie said. "Pink. You claimed they were on sale and lied to my face."

"Strategic truth," Dot said. "The part a person could bear."

They let the memory open like a window. Outside in 1962, the dogwood was younger, the neighbor's radio carried a ballgame, and Maggie's mother tried to press five dollars into Dot's palm for the bus, which Dot refused twice and accepted once because pride could be stubborn and friendship smarter. The cake leaned. The eggs were dyed in coffee cups and stained everyone's fingertips. It was perfect, which was to say, not.

Dot reached across and squeezed Maggie's hand. "You gave them good days, Mags. That's a kind of wealth."

For a few breaths, the room seemed to hold more sound, quick feet in grass, the rustle of bushes, the joyful chaos of a yard full of small victories. Then it settled again, gentle as a hymn.

Evie lifted her tea. "To open doors, even if we only walked through one."

Dot tipped her cup. "To showing up."

Maggie touched hers to theirs. "And to the details that remembered us."

They finished the meal in companionable quiet, then and now stitched together by memory, another egg tucked safely into the basket of a life well loved. Perfection could visit; belonging stayed. And the door, as always, stood open.

22

THE WEIGHT OF LOVE

1986–1993 (AND AFTER) • DOT

Dot had always been the one who held.

In school, she steadied their trio when tempers flared. As a teacher, she held classrooms full of kids who needed lunch and a fair shot. In the streets, she held the line, voice even. For Dot, strength was never loud—it was reliable.

Which was why the letter on her kitchen table made her hands shake.

I messed up. I'm trying. Call me?

—June

Cousin by blood, sister by everything that mattered when they were girls. Bare feet on their grandparents' farm. Secrets whispered under quilts. Constellations learned by heart. Then life forked. Dot chose lesson plans and organizing meetings and a future she could name. June chose fast love and faster jobs, hope stitched to late notices.

Before Dot could dial, the phone rang.

"Dot... it's me," June said, pride swallowed down to a pebble.

"It's been a long time," Dot answered—careful, not cold.

"I wouldn't be calling if—" The words broke loose. "The company downsized. I thought I could land on my feet. I didn't. And the drinking..." A torn breath. "I slipped."

Dot closed her eyes.

"They took James," June said, the sentence breaking in the middle. "He's in foster care. They say it's a good family. He's scared. He asked why I wasn't coming to get him." Another breath, shredded. "I'm getting help. Meetings. A counselor. But I can't get him back until I'm steady. He's ten, Dot. He needs someone solid."

Silence pressed warm to Dot's ear. She could hear June breathing, thin as thread.

"You should've called sooner," Dot said.

"I know." A whisper falling. "But I'm calling now."

Dot had planned many things: syllabi, budget meetings, a life with space if she and Clara ever got their timing right. She hadn't planned on a boy with a backpack and a history, needing a door that stayed open.

After they hung up, Dot sat very still. Daisy, the calico, blinked from the windowsill. The radiator ticked. On the table, her students' essays waited in a neat stack—*Persuasive Argument, Draft Two.* She thought of James as a toddler at a reunion, sticky hands, cake on his cheek, and of the way June's voice had cracked around his name.

A room could be made. Groceries could be bought. Schedules could bend.

Dot stood and pulled spare linens from the closet, the motion a way to breathe. Then she called social services.

"I'm Dorothy, June's cousin," she said when the line picked up. "I can take him."

By afternoon, a social worker had arranged an emergency kinship placement—temporary, pending the home study, interstate paperwork to follow. Paper first, then James.

Dawn rinsed Baltimore in pink. At 7, Dot slid the essays aside, left coffee cooling in the sink, and headed north on I-83. Rowhouses gave way to hills holding the last of the night. An hour to think—maybe too much. She told herself she was capable of hard things. She told herself again.

York was a map her feet remembered: Central Market, Penn Park, the Queen Street exit. She turned left on Pennsylvania Avenue and found the red-brick duplex near the end of the block. The sidewalk was cracked; a tricycle leaned on its side. From inside came the soft murmur of a daytime talk show—Phil Donahue mid-sympathy—and the lemon bite of pine cleaner, home by effort rather than ease.

A woman opened the door before Dot finished knocking. "Ms. Dorothy? They said you'd come."

"Yes," Dot said, smoothing her palms on her skirt.

"He's ready. Quiet kid. Likes to read." She stepped aside. "James?"

He came down the dim hall, cautious and taller than memory—faded navy hoodie, sleeves over his hands, eyes older than ten. A wall clock ticked too loudly.

"Hi, James," Dot said, keeping her voice low and ordinary. "I'm Dot. Your mom's cousin."

He studied her, wary but not shut. "You sent me the space book."

"I did." She smiled, surprised at what had stuck. "Still like that stuff?"

He lifted one shoulder. "It's cool."

"Well, I've got more books. And a room. And hot chocolate I make too sweet."

A beat. Then a nod. He didn't look back as they stepped into the light.

The drive south was mostly quiet. Dot pointed out a hawk riding a current, the sign for the science center, the corner store where she bought cocoa. James watched the window as if it might hand him a map.

"Let's go home," she said when the city gathered around them.

She gave him the spare room and let him choose a poster—planets, of course. She stocked peanut butter and jelly; he declared Frosted Flakes the only cereal worth buying, as if this were a settled fact of the universe. Those first weeks were a classroom with no lesson plan. He picked at food. Avoided her eyes. Pretended not to hear boys shouting in the courtyard. At night, he curled small under the covers and didn't cry where anyone could hear.

Dot practiced a new kind of patience. She left notes in his lunch box: *You've got this. Your brain's a good place to be.* She sat beside him through math that snarled. She set a schedule and let him knock it crooked with his life. After dinner, they walked to the park. On the third night, he said, "I like basketball," as if confessing. On the fourth, he asked if she could play. She lost spectacularly and pretended not to gasp; he laughed out loud—the first time.

A week later came their first supervised visit with June—fluorescent lights, a mural of a rainbow done by many small hands, vending-machine coffee that tasted like it held a grudge. June's hair was pulled back too tight; her hands shook when she smoothed James's sleeve. She had a new coin chip from a meeting and the fragile brightness of starting over.

"Hey, baby," she said, voice snagging.

James nodded, gaze fixed at her shoulder. They played Connect Four at a table with a nicked edge. June asked about school. Dot watched the board fill—red, black, red—praying for a path that would hold. Afterward, in the parking lot, June leaned against the car and pressed her palms to her eyes.

"I'm going to keep going," she said. "I am."

"I hope so," Dot answered, and meant it.

Visits went from supervised, to short and supervised, to short and unsupervised, to delayed—each change a tiny weather report. Through it all, James tested and tried and grew.

He began to speak. Small details at first—teachers' names, a joke from homeroom, how the bus smelled of vinyl and morning breath. He asked for seconds. Carried his plate to the sink like someone who belonged in the room. One evening, after a day of nothing in particular, he sat beside her on the couch and set his head on her shoulder like it had always belonged there.

"I'm glad you're here," she said into his hair. "We're gonna make it."

He tilted his face up. "Do you think my mom will get better?"

Dot's heart thudded once, then steadied. She wouldn't lie. "I hope so," she said. "And no matter what, you're safe here. I'll make sure."

Love, she learned, was less a feeling than a practice: a pot of chili on the stove, a ride to a meeting, a quiet chair outside a counselor's office, a calendar with the important dates circled twice. Strength, she realized, could look like staying.

Years rose and fell. Middle school loved him back a little: a teacher who noticed his quick wit, a stage where he became a comedic pirate with a yardstick sword. Dot clapped until her hands stung, louder than anyone.

Then the shadows lengthened.

It started small. Missed curfews. A dullness moving across his eyes like cloud. Calls from school: tardies, bathroom doors that stayed closed too long. Dot asked, then insisted, then pleaded. *I'm tired. I'm stressed. I'm fine.*

Until he wasn't.

She found the pills by accident—an old sock in the back of a drawer, label torn. The floor tilted under the life she'd built. "James?" she said, not trusting her voice. "What's this?"

He sat on his bed, hands locked between his knees. "I just wanted to feel... something else."

Dot did what she could. She learned. Rehab, counselors, group rooms with bad coffee. Acronyms that tasted like chalk—IOP, NA— lodged in her mouth. Family Night meant folding chairs and hard stories, a basket of stale cookies, the reminder that love wasn't the same as cure. She locked the medicine cabinet. Searched his room with shaking hands and hated herself and did it again.

He did better. Then worse. Then better. He worked at the grocery store, stocked shelves, charmed old ladies in Produce. Went to meetings and laughed at jokes Dot wasn't supposed to understand. Moved into a small apartment close enough to walk to. Picked curtains with ridiculous blue stripes and sent Dot a photo. A VCR on his dresser blinked *12:00* like a tiny lighthouse. She let herself breathe.

A quiet Tuesday in November, the phone call didn't make sense. She drove without remembering the trip. His apartment smelled clean —citrus and something like laundry. His face was too still. The blue around his lips was the wrong color for the living. The sound she made didn't belong to language.

The funeral was small and honest. Co-workers who knew his kindness. People from meetings who knew his fight. In the front pew, Dot held a photo: James gap-toothed, clutching a basketball bigger than his head.

"I tried," she told the boy in the picture. "I really tried."

That night, the answering machine blinked. June's voice arrived in pieces.

"I heard. I was in a place without phones. I'm... I'm sorry, Dot. I should've been there. I should've been a thousand things. I'm still going to meetings. I've got sixty-two days. I wanted to say his name out loud. James. I wanted to say thank you. And I'm sorry."

Dot sat in the dark and pressed the button again. She didn't need more than once.

Afterward, friends said the right things. *Not your fault. A disease. You gave him years.* Nights were longer. The hall clock insisted on every second. Dot lay awake and asked the questions love asks when it's alone. *What else. What if. Should I have—* No answers. Only memory.

A lopsided birthday cake at twelve, chocolate chips collapsing the middle. They ate it with spoons from the pan, laughing until it hurt.

A photo strip of silly faces from the carnival, both of them cross-eyed in frame two.

A sticky note tucked in her recipe book: *Thanks for not giving up on me.*

The night he tried "Mom" on his tongue like a new word, then shook his head and smiled. "You're Dot. That's better than Mom."

In the living room, a shoebox held these pieces: program from his school play, the photo strip, the note folded safe. She talked to him sometimes on walks, by the high school where she'd taught. "I still see you," she'd say to the air. "You were the best thing I ever did."

For a moment then, she didn't feel like a failure. She felt like a person who'd loved a boy with her whole, breakable heart.

Present • Manchester Meadows

Late afternoon draped the common room like a soft shawl. Two televisions played softly in distant corners. Evie dozed, her breath soft, one hand rising and falling on her chest. Maggie pretended to read hydrangea tips without her glasses, thumbing pages like old habits.

Dot sat by the window, blanket over her knees, not reading, not sleeping. Remembering.

A boy had passed in the hall earlier, a nurse's grandson, lanky, ten or close, hugging a small basketball to his chest. Somewhere, rubber had scuffed tile, and the sound had threaded through Dot like a stitch.

"Thinking about him?" Maggie had asked, eyes still on the magazine.

Dot had nodded. "I can't seem to stop."

"You don't have to," Evie had said without opening her eyes. "That's how we keep them."

Silence settled the way it does with friends who know the whole map of you.

"I had ideas when I took him," Dot said. "If I poured in enough love and structure, it'd fill the cracks. Undo the early hurt."

"You did give him that," Maggie said, setting the magazine aside. "Seventh-grade play. You in the front row with flowers bigger than your purse. He saw you."

"But it didn't save him," Dot whispered.

"No," Evie said, turning her head now, gaze steady. "But you saved him anyway. You gave him years and a home and a person who never hung up. That's a kind of saving."

Dot's eyes warmed; she didn't look away. "He called me Dot till the end. Never 'Mom.'"

Maggie reached for her hand. "He knew. And you knew. That's what mattered."

Dot let the smallest smile come. "Seventeen," she said. "We were fighting. I said, 'You're breaking my heart,' and he said, 'It's already broken, Dot. I'm just living in the pieces.' I didn't know what to do with that truth."

Evie took Dot's other hand. "We've all got broken pieces," she said. "Yours made room for someone else."

The three of them sat like that awhile, hands linked, the old lace of years threaded between them—girls who once chased a white kitten, women who'd paid the price and held the privilege of loving stubbornly.

Down the hallway, a ball bounced once, just once, and quieted. Dot closed her eyes and, for a breath, felt the weight of a boy's head settle against her shoulder. Not heavy. Certain.

Strength, she thought, feeling their fingers laced with hers. *This is what it looks like.*

She closed her eyes, and the sorrow thinned to salt—to music on the car radio, to the first wave that made them shriek and then laugh. Not gone. Just gentled. Held.

23

SALTWATER SUMMER
1950 • REHOBOTH BEACH

They left before the sun had the chance to warm the porch steps. Mrs. Thompson clicked the kitchen light off with battlefield satisfaction: ham and cheese wrapped in wax paper, check; a dozen deviled eggs settled into crushed ice, check; a jar of lemonade whose round slices floated like small suns, double check. She had ironed the cloth napkins, corners crisp enough to salute.

Outside, Mr. Thompson admired the seafoam '49 Ford Custom Tudor the way a man admired a job that had finally gone right. Chrome bright as a whistle. Whitewalls clean enough to see your face. "Everybody in," he said, tapping the steering wheel while the AM crackle hunted for a station. When Nat King Cole's "Mona Lisa" found them, he crooned like a man conducting his own good day.

In the back seat, the girls ricocheted between giddy and unsure. Dot wore a navy one-piece with a white belt and a small bow—her mother's choice, "respectable." She kept a towel around her shoulders like a cape, even in the car.

Evie had borrowed a red halter suit with polka dots from an older cousin; it smelled faintly of *Evening in Paris* and mischief. Maggie's suit was brand-new and sunny yellow, paid for with S&H Green Stamps carefully pasted into booklets that lived in a jar on the kitchen counter.

The straps kept slipping; each time she tugged one up she felt like a movie star caught by a camera flash she hadn't planned for.

Fields flattened and the sky opened, a lid lifting off a pot. Telephone wires stitched past in steady black slashes. Mr. Thompson pointed out a roadside stand that would have peaches in August, the kind that dripped down your wrist, and Mrs. Thompson passed back butter mints as if joy needed just a little more fuel for the last hour.

"It'll smell different," Maggie said, forehead pressed to the window.

"Like a new idea," Evie agreed.

Dot tightened her towel cape, pretending not to smile.

Then the world unstitched at the edge: water, and more water, and a wind that tasted like anything could happen.

The boardwalk boards knocked softly under their sandals. Mr. Thompson rented an umbrella, a folding chair, and a striped windbreak from a man who had opinions about weather. The girls stepped onto the hot white sand, hopping and yelping until the heat gave way to damp. They stopped together where the tide drew its lace and left it at their toes.

"Oh," Dot breathed, towel loosening without her permission.

"It looks like the world is about to begin," Evie whispered.

Maggie squeezed their hands. The wind stole her laugh and tumbled it down the beach like confetti.

"Girls!" Mrs. Thompson called, passing Mr. Thompson the Kodak. "Picture first."

They found their old choreography without thinking—heads together, shoulders bumping, Dot's towel still caped, Evie already wind-blown and daring, Maggie grinning too wide. The shutter clicked. None of them knew it would be the keeper.

Then they ran.

The first wave slapped cold at their shins and made them shriek, which made them laugh harder, which made the next wave take them by surprise. Evie dove and came up crowing, hair like black seaweed. Dot tried to be cautious and failed, its own kind of joy. Maggie learned the ocean's math: hold your breath, trust the lift, find your feet. A life-guard's whistle spiked the air; a gull heckled them like an aunt who'd seen it all. Sun turned their shoulders into warm bread.

They made a small city of their things beneath the umbrella Mr. Thompson staked into the sand. A family on one side glanced over, took them in, and shifted their blanket a few feet without comment. Mr. Thompson pretended not to notice, then set his chair a shade closer— close enough to be there, far enough to let them be. It was 1950. The ocean felt endless; people didn't.

"Only to your chests," he called, shading his eyes with the flat of his hand.

"To our elbows," Mrs. Thompson amended.

"Which is higher?" Evie murmured, and Maggie snorted so loudly the gull judged her.

For a long time, it was only sun and salt and the reliable pulse of the tide. Evie tucked shells into the hem of her towel and declared each one a treasure. Dot peeled off her towel by degrees and, after a double dare, gave up and waded to her waist. Maggie tried floating on her back and memorized the sky, a blue so complete it felt like a secret she'd been allowed to overhear.

They collapsed at last, damp and glittered with sand. Evie stretched like a cat and wiggled her toes.

"Evie," Dot said, squinting. "Your second toe is trying to climb over your big toe."

"It's mutiny," Maggie declared. "Your toes are staging a coup."

"It's a hammer toe," Evie said, flicking a pinch of wet sand with imperious dignity. "Very fashionable."

Dot extended her own foot. "Now these are the gold standard. Each one shorter than the last. Perfect little staircase."

"More like a ski slope," Evie said.

"At least they behave," Dot sniffed, then nodded at Evie's foot. "Unlike Captain Crooked over there."

Maggie lifted her foot for judgment. "Second toe's longer than my big toe. I read that means I'm destined to rule."

"Rule what?" Evie asked. "A kingdom of flip-flops?"

"A dynasty," Maggie said, chin tipped up. "Egyptian queens had this toe."

Dot executed a dignified bow from the towel. "Then, Your Majesty, please lead us to the snack stand when we rise."

"I'll require an escort," Maggie decreed, flinging another pinch of sand that made them squeal and duck.

"The Marvelous Foot Sisters," Evie proclaimed, carnival-barker loud. "Captain Crooked, Princess Long-Toe, and Dot the Dignified."

Two men dragging a beach cart looked over and, despite themselves, smiled. Mrs. Thompson waved her sunhat like a flag.

"Lunch!"

They trooped back to the umbrella, toes tunneling into the soft sand, and ate with the wind tugging at their ironed napkins. Wax paper crackled open to ham-and-cheese sandwiches, the mustard sharp enough to wake the tongue; deviled eggs went fast, dusted with paprika that clung to their fingers. Lemonade cooled their throats.

Mr. Thompson told a story about trying to surf in the Army, which made no sense and delighted everyone. He took another photograph, closer this time: three girls mid-chew and mid-laugh and entirely themselves.

"What do you think we'll be like when we're old?" Evie asked through a bite of sandwich.

"Old how?" Dot asked. "Old like my grandma? Or old like a church lady who tells you to hush?"

"Old old," Evie said. "Counting-clouds-on-a-porch old."

Maggie kept her eyes on the horizon. "I hope we're still... us," she said. "Even if we forget things."

"You don't lose people like us," Dot said simply.

"We'll probably get into trouble," Evie added, satisfied.

"Evie," Dot said dryly, "you already do."

They napped in the net of afternoon, lulled by the steady pull of waves and the soft percussion of the boardwalk behind them. When the sun tilted, Mr. Thompson walked the girls up for soft-serve swirls. The shop door stuck, then gave. Behind the counter, a teenager with a paper hat and a face full of storms asked, "Vanilla or chocolate?" He said "girls" but looked at Dot like the word might not belong to her.

Mr. Thompson placed his palm on the counter—steady, ordinary— and named three cones. The boy's mouth flattened, then he pulled the levers and the ribbons rose, neat and cold. They ate outside, cones dripping onto their knuckles, the small sting of what the world would and wouldn't allow tucked beneath the sweetness.

They tried the arcade because Evie said no good story ever started with prudence. Skee-Ball swallowed their nickels and spit out tickets that smelled faintly of cardboard and miracle. Maggie won a tin whistle that sounded like a seasick sparrow; Dot chose a packet of bobby pins shaped like stars. Evie saved her tickets for a fortune, which the machine dispensed with a cough: *You will travel far on words.* She tucked it into her suit like a pact.

Back at the water, the tide had changed its mind. It came in stronger, the kind of insistence that rearranged sandcastles without apology. Dot waded out only to her knees this time; she'd found the right amount of daring for the day. Evie chased a set of waves farther than was wise, and the lifeguard's whistle peeled the air again. She came back breathless, eyes on fire, and Maggie—half mad, half relieved—grabbed her wrist.

"You're not indestructible," Maggie said. "You're a person I need alive."

"Copy that," Evie said, contrite for exactly four seconds.

A quick summer shower shouldered its way over the horizon, the drops fat and warm. The beach turned into a constellation of umbrellas popping open. Mr. Thompson taught them the trick of sitting behind the windbreak to watch rain hit the ocean, how the water darkened, then brightened, then pretended nothing had happened. When the cloud heaved its last and trudged inland, the sand steamed like a pie just pulled from the oven.

Afternoon shifted to gold. The girls returned to the boardwalk for saltwater taffy that glued their molars together and a minute in the photo booth where the curtain stuck and they howled while the camera snapped anyway.

Evie tried on sunglasses the size of saucers and declared herself profoundly anonymous. Dot found a straw hat identical to the one she'd admired that spring in a magazine and, after counting her coins twice, bought it; dignity, she'd decided, could have a brim. Maggie stood at the railing with a paper sack of still-warm fries and promised the horizon they'd come back.

"What will you remember about today?" Maggie asked, their shoulders pressed together, salt drying on their skin.

"The rain on the water," Dot said. "And the part where I forgot to be embarrassed."

"The whistle," Evie said with a grin. "And the way *Mona Lisa* will sound when we drive home."

"The moment the ocean said hello," Maggie said softly.

Sun slid down in soft bands. The three of them held hands ankle-deep and swore—on shells, on songs, on the smell of vinegar fries—that this wouldn't be the last.

Packing to leave felt like trying to fold a day into a suitcase. Towels held half the beach. The umbrella resisted. Mrs. Thompson shook sand from the napkins and laughed at herself for ironing them. Mr. Thompson returned the rental chair and listened politely to a lecture about wind shifts and undertow he'd never need again.

On the drive home, everything smelled like fried dough and salt and sunshine. Evie spread the photo-booth strip across her knees and titled it in pencil: *The Marvelous Foot Sisters*. Dot fell asleep with her mouth open a little, hat tilted over one eye, towel finally surrendered to the floor. Mr. Thompson took a detour down a road lined with scrub pines to buy some cherries bruised with sweetness. Mrs. Thompson passed back tin cups so the lemonade could be decanted from its sweating jar without catastrophe.

Mona Lisa played again, as if the radio had been waiting for the return trip.

Maggie counted the first stars, stubborn about keeping the day. When the last light of the ocean gave way to dark fields and crickets, she pressed the photo strip into her palm and decided she'd put it on the first page of whatever life came next.

The map had ended in water; the day went on in them.

Now • Manchester Meadows, Present

Late afternoon sifted through the common room blinds, stripes of gold banding the floor. Dot's straw hat, its twin bought somewhere along the way and gentled by years, hung on the back of her chair. Evie dozed, mouth slightly open, one hand rising and falling like a small tide. Maggie paged through the scrapbook, the plastic film lifting with a sound like a wave pulling back.

"There it is," she said, tapping the photo from the Kodak. Three girls at the very edge of a beginning—Dot caped in a towel, Evie untamable, Maggie grinning as if the horizon had told her a secret.

They let silence do the explaining. A boy rolled a mop bucket down the hall; somewhere a cart's loose wheel rattled. The tide, faithful even here, kept time inside their chests.

"Do you think you can carry a day for seventy years?" Maggie asked.

"You can," Dot said. "If you pack it right."

Evie, eyes still closed, smiled—a small, certain crescent. "We packed that one," she murmured. "Tight."

Outside, beyond the manicured hedges and the parking lot patched in tar, the sky darkened toward the same blue they'd once memorized from their backs on a beach. Inside, three old friends sat shoulder to shoulder, and their laughter, when it came, ran, tumbling, farther than the hall.

24

WHEN THE OCEAN COMES TO US

PRESENT • MANCHESTER
MEADOWS • NEXT MORNING

K ris had been carrying their beach all morning with her: the way Dot's straw hat caught the light, the way Evie, without opening her eyes, smiled at the word keeper, the way Maggie traced the photograph's edge and whispered, "I'd give anything to feel sand between my toes." She took that sentence to Mr. Aughenbaugh with a folder and a plan.

She waited outside his door with too much hope and a thin stack of logistics, pressing the damp corners flat. A year at Manchester Meadows had turned hallways into a kind of map: med carts and bingo boards, yes, but also lives still burning bright behind papery skin. She'd fallen hard for Evie, Dot, and Maggie. They weren't merely residents; they were her trio, her found grandmothers, her balcony seat to braver decades.

Again and again the same place rose like tide: the beach. Sand that clung. A sky so big it chose you back. Waves that arrived and left and arrived again, like a heartbeat you could hear with your feet.

She stepped in. Mr. Aughenbaugh looked up over his glasses, kind eyes, careful jaw, a man who counted risks for a living.

"A day trip," she began, laying the folder down. "To the coast. Doctors sign off. Hydration schedule. Wheelchairs with beach tires, I found a rental. Luis will drive. We'll leave after breakfast and be back by supper. They talk about the ocean every week. Let's give them a real day."

He scanned the pages, then closed the folder. "Four hours each way. Liability. Staffing. Heat index." He sighed. "Kris, the answer is no."

The word landed like a closed door. Kris nodded. Closed was still a door you could knock on later.

In the break room, the first tear surprised her; the rest arrived on cue. She blotted with a paper towel and studied her reflection in the vending-machine glass until something reknit. Her grandmother had wanted to see the ocean one last time and never did. Kris wouldn't let that be the whole story this time.

If she couldn't take them to the beach, she'd bring the beach to them.

By midmorning, heartbreak was a list. Determination looked good on her; Dot would've approved.

She raided the storage closet and returned like a party pirate, dusty summer banners over one shoulder, a tangle of plastic seashells looped like leis, a half-deflated beach ball under her arm. She called a landscaping company with an odd request: two bags of clean play sand. Pickup arranged.

Luis, the van driver with a soft spot and a collection of antique radios, leaned in the doorway. "What's the caper, K?"

"Operation Keeper," she said. "I need muscle and discretion."

He grinned. "I've got both on Thursdays."

The kitchen crew was next. "Can we do lemonade with the slices floating?" she asked. "Hot dogs wrapped in foil. Watermelon so cold it aches your teeth. Popsicles if we're feeling dangerous."

"Dangerous is our brand," Patrice said, already hauling out the cooler.

Kris hit the dollar store like it was a mission brief. Neon pails and plastic shovels. Two inflatable palm trees with questionable posture. Strings of faux shells. A Bluetooth speaker shaped like a conch. She added sunscreen because scent is memory's fuse.

Back at Manchester Meadows, she built a coastline.

Beach towels bloomed across the courtyard like parade bunting.

Folding chairs circled a patch of sand she and Luis poured by the bag and smoothed with a cafeteria tray. A kiddie pool sat in the shade; she filled it with hose water and tested it with her wrist. Fans angled to send a steady breeze; she misted the air with sea-salt spray. Old banners hung alongside new, cheerful kitsch and color. Somewhere under the decorations, the courtyard remembered how to be a party.

A palm tree listed; a fan unplugged. She steadied the trunk with twine and clicked the fan back to life. Competence, she thought, was its own kind of grace.

Inside, Patrice set pitchers of lemonade on ice. Someone found a box of pastel paper umbrellas that had been waiting in a drawer for their moment. The smell of grilled hot dogs slipped under the courtyard door like a dare.

By midafternoon, Manchester tilted. The courtyard wasn't a courtyard anymore. It was a small, sincere beach.

Kris wiped sand from her palms, checked her list twice, and headed to the common room.

The trio sat at their corner table, halfheartedly playing cards. Maggie watched a pale square of sun creep across the carpet. Evie tapped a rhythm only she could hear. Dot's eyebrow did the thing it did when the world disappointed her.

"Ladies," Kris said, trying not to vibrate, "field trip. Please bring your curiosity."

Dot squinted. "What's the catch, kid?"

"You'll see."

They set off. Nurses passed with winks and small, conspiratorial thumbs-up. The courtyard doors swung open.

For a breath, no one moved.

Sand glowed under the sun. The conch speaker pulsed with surf and gulls. Palm trees leaned like they had stories. A line of gaudy towels shouted in color. The faintest whiff of Coppertone waltzed with lemon and grill smoke.

Evie lifted her hands to her mouth. "Oh," she said, the same oh from the photograph.

Maggie let out a laugh that cracked in the middle and kept going.

Dot blinked hard, then harder. "Well, I'll be," she muttered. "You did it."

"If I can't get you to the beach," Kris said, shoving her hands into her back pockets so she wouldn't hug them all to the ground, "the beach can come to you."

Evie was first. She toed off her slippers and stepped into the sand. Her feet sank. Her face changed. "It's warm," she said, wonder making her younger. "It's really warm."

Maggie lowered herself to a towel with careful hips, lifted her face to the fan-breeze, and closed her eyes. Dot knelt, scooped sand, and let it sift through her fingers. "It even smells right," she said, gravel in her voice and gratitude behind it.

"Trade secret," Kris said, tapping the sunscreen. "Two spritzes of ocean, one of childhood."

The afternoon opened like a window.

Patrice and Luis paraded out with a tray of wrapped hot dogs, a mountain of sliced watermelon, and a cooler of lemonade. Kris tucked paper umbrellas into their cups because every detail counted. Then, just because she could, she cued Nat King Cole. *Mona Lisa* spilled into the courtyard, and three faces tipped toward the sound as if a door had quietly opened.

They ate popsicles that stained their lips and pretended not to care about the drips. Maggie dropped hers twice and laughed at the pink polka dots forming on her towel. Evie asked Kris to tear the stubborn wrapper, and when the first cold bite shocked her gums she giggled like she wasn't surprised by delight.

Neighbors came, too. Mr. Hargrove rolled up with his crossword and told Dot she owed him a seven-letter word for "briny." Mrs. Alvarez chose the brightest towel and painted everyone's thumbnails coral, a shade named Beach Please that made Evie cackle. A nurse carried out a shy tabby in a harness, the building's unofficial therapy cat, and set him under the shade of a palm. He blinked at the fake gulls like a critic who would allow it on a technicality.

They built a lopsided castle at the edge of their artificial shore. Dot directed with the authority of a woman who had shepherded a hundred classroom projects past the bell. "No, Luis, pack the wall, don't pet it."

He saluted and obeyed, and Dot granted him a rare, satisfied nod. Maggie patted towers that leaned with personality. Evie tucked a plastic shell above the doorway like a blessing.

Between songs, Maggie said, "This reminds me of that day when we were fifteen, comparing our toes."

Evie opened one eye, mischief lighting it. "The Marvelous Foot Sisters."

"Don't encourage her," Dot said, but she was smiling. She arranged her feet just so. "For the record, mine are still museum quality."

Evie lifted her foot, the second toe still ambitious. "Hammer toe, present and accounted for."

Maggie wiggled her longer second toe with pride. "Royalty, as previously noted."

They held their feet up like offerings and dissolved into laughter that startled a sparrow into flight.

Safety threaded through the fun. Kris checked hydration, settled sun hats, and set a timer to prompt position changes. A nurse slipped out with a finger-clip oxygen monitor and pretended she was only there for popsicles. The heat behaved. The breeze held.

When the Beach Boys crooned "Wouldn't It Be Nice," Maggie's voice found the harmony she remembered. It trembled but didn't break. Evie stretched full-length on her towel, eyes closed, a smile like a small sunrise. Dot tipped her head back and let the sound sit inside her, the way a person let a truth be true.

"Kid," Dot said to Kris when the song ended, "you're dangerous in the best way."

"I'll take that," Kris said.

As shadows lengthened and the lemon slices sank to the bottom of the pitcher, they migrated to the kiddie pool one by one. Kris laid a non-slip mat beneath each chair, locked the brakes, and lowered their feet into the water like a small ceremony. She pinched in a little Epsom salt and a drop of sunscreen for scent.

"This might be my favorite part," Maggie said. "No undertow. No lifeguard judgment."

"Just tide enough," Evie murmured.

Dot looked toward the courtyard gate as if, beyond it, the horizon waited. "Once," she said, "I thought grown-up meant staying put. Turned out it meant making a way through anyway."

Kris felt that sentence attach to a rib and live there.

Cleanup proved easy. Joy, it turned out, didn't leave much trash. On her way past the back office, Mr. Aughenbaugh glanced up. Through the window he could see a plastic palm tree and a last scrap of towel flapping on the fence.

He lifted a hand in a small salute. "Nice work, Kris."

"Thank you," she said, surprised by how the praise landed.

"That courtyard," he added, voice kind, "hasn't sounded like that in a while."

"Like what?"

"Alive."

Kris nodded, her throat tight for a different reason. "We'll clean up before supper."

"Leave the sand till tomorrow," he said. "Let people step in it." Then he looked back at his paperwork, pretending he hadn't just said a poetic thing out loud.

Kris returned with warm washcloths and a bowl of water. She wiped their hands, palms first then fingers, like a rite. The three of them leaned back, content and a little sun-stunned.

"Same time next summer?" Evie asked.

"Next good-weather day," Kris said. "And when my sister drives up from Lewes, she'll bring a bucket of the real stuff. We'll top off the shore."

"Perks of knowing the right people," Dot said, which was Dot for thank you.

Maggie reached for the others' hands, habit now, not decision. "It's enough," she said.

For a while, with the ocean moving inside their remembering and the courtyard holding the last of the light, the day held.

25

NOON NEWS

PRESENT • MANCHESTER MEADOWS • EVIE

The dayroom TV was already on Channel 8 when Kris wheeled in a tray with lemonade and a bowl of ice wrapped in a dish towel like a small glacier. The noon block always felt the same: sun bars on the linoleum, the soft clink of pills in plastic cups, a volunteer singing off-key as she folded warm towels.

Dot preferred the local anchors, less fuss, more facts. Maggie liked the weather map because it looked like a quilt. Evie tolerated the whole enterprise for the news crawl at the bottom: names, places, motion.

"Breaking at the top of the hour," the anchor said, smile neat as a straight pin. "A look back at the women who changed state politics, beginning with former Senator Jennifer Ashford."

Evie stilled.

On screen: a campaign office from another century, yard signs propped against a wall, phones with curly cords, a white blazer at a podium. Voiceover: discipline, message control, values that were said to resonate.

Dot lifted a brow. "Values, hmm."

Maggie's hand found the arm of Evie's chair. "You okay?"

Evie couldn't look away. The past arrived the way weather did, first a pressure shift, then wind under the door. Once upon a time, newsrooms had trusted her to name what was happening. Later, campaigns trusted her to name what they wished was happening. The muscle memory confused the heart.

"I wrote that line," she said, surprised to hear it out loud. "The 'values that resonated' one."

Kris eased the tray closer. "You wrote for her?"

"Ghosted," Evie said. "Speeches, mailers, a TV spot I still dream about. It felt like history from the inside." She hesitated. "Sometimes it felt like erasing."

The segment cut to an archival clip: the senator at a church-base- ment breakfast, steam lifting off foil trays. The camera found a hand on a Bible. The mic found the word family and stamped it twice for good measure. Evie flinched.

"I'll turn the sound down," Kris said, remote in hand, gentle.

"No," Evie said. "Leave it. I should hear it to the end."

They kept listening. There was the county-fair shot, babies kissed, a ribbon cut, flour dust in a borrowed apron. There was the kitchen-table ad Evie had written in a blender of exhaustion and pride, promising pragmatism over partisanship while a knife chopped onions on beat. She'd trimmed out two sentences that might've offered a door for people like Dot, and for herself. The ad won awards. The door stayed shut.

She'd told herself it wasn't so different from journalism—just another way of arranging facts, another story under deadline. But jour- nalism had asked her for consequences. This work asked her for loyalty.

The piece wrapped with a glossy photo of Ashford mid-wave. Applause track. Commercial for stairlifts. Life resumed.

Kris set a glass beside Evie's elbow. Condensation made a small comet on the table.

"Write it," she said softly. "Whatever the it is."

"I tried this morning," Evie said. "Hands wouldn't let me." She flexed; ache answered back, a dull throb beneath the thumbs. There had been a time she could draft a front-page lead with coffee gone cold and a city storming outside her window. Words used to show up like colleagues. These days, they arrived like witnesses, and she was never sure which of them would testify.

"Then we'll bribe them," Kris said.

She disappeared and returned with a shallow bowl of warm water and a rolled towel. The steam smelled faintly of eucalyptus. "Ten minutes in heat, then a cool wrap," she said, setting a timer on her watch. "And—" She produced a fountain pen from her pocket like a magician revealing a coin. "Borrowed from Luis. He says it writes like memory."

Evie laughed once, surprised by the lift of it. "He would say that. He names his radios."

"He does," Kris said. "The Philco is Rita. She only gets jazz."

They retreated to Evie's room. The desk was neat, journal centered, a small dish of paper clips, a framed photo of three girls on a beach with their heads tipped together as if listening to a joke only they could hear. On the bookshelf, a shoebox held the life she kept avoiding: clippings rubber-banded into eras, a press badge clouded with scratches, one campaign button with its enamel chipped like a tooth. A manila folder, its tab thick with use, read in block letters: *LATER*.

Evie soaked, then wrapped, then tested. The pen moved smoothly, like breath.

She slid the old *LATER* folder to the back of the desk, close enough to feel, far enough not to lead, and opened the journal to the first page where she'd tucked a typed sheet months ago. She read it again before she began:

This time, it's mine.

No assignments. No interviews. No ghosting someone else's glory.

Just memory, and truth, and whatever's left of me between the two.

She thought of the newsroom buzz she used to live inside—the smell of ink, the click of wire copy, the discipline of telling it straight because somebody's life depended on someone not lying. She missed that steadiness. She missed herself inside it.

She wrote *Later* → *Now* at the top corner, set the sheet aside, touched the pen to paper, and the first sentence came like a tide, hesitant, then sure:

The room was sterile and cold, and the first thing they asked me to ghost was a prayer.

The fluorescent hum returned; the coffee on the hot plate turned bitter in memory. A staffer whispered, "Make it sound like she believes it." Evie could feel the legal pad under her wrist, the moment she crossed out mercy and wrote grace because polling liked it better. Somewhere in the past a woman cleared her throat before speaking grace over scrambled eggs and sausage links, and Evie, twenty-nine, quick as a match, made the cadence sing.

"Start in the room," Kris murmured from the doorway. "Then go wherever you need."

Evie nodded without looking up. Lines gathered. A paragraph unspooled.

We said family and meant a shape some families couldn't hold. We said small business and meant the kind with a ribbon to cut. We said future and meant a face in a mirror with a pearl clip and a practiced smile.

Her hands ached; she breathed through it and kept going. Copier toner and winter wool. She remembered editors who argued with her in good faith, who circled verbs and demanded proof. No one circled verbs here. They circled polling. The office manager who taped a photo of her son inside a drawer so she wouldn't have to explain. The county chairman who winked like complicity. The intern who slipped her a note, *My sister thanks you*, and how Evie wasn't sure either of them was right.

In the hall, Dot and Maggie waited with their lemonade and their patience. Dot jotted a crossword clue on the back of an old grocery list and slid it under the door as if language itself were a vote of confidence: Seven letters, honest. Maggie, believer in the sacrament of snacks, sent two sugar cookies on a napkin with violets around the rim.

"Give her an hour," Kris had said.

"Give her two," Maggie had answered.

Kris hovered without hovering. She refreshed the warm bowl when the water cooled, then switched to the dish-towel glacier and wrapped each hand the way you bandage a sprain or a courage you don't want to lose. She rubbed a drop of lavender into Evie's wrists because scent can be a ladder. The timer chirped and quieted. A sparrow fussed on the courtyard fence. A cart squeaked past with someone's afternoon meds and someone else's crossword dictionary.

Evie turned a page.

The mail piece with the oak tree took six drafts. We kept the roots and cut the branches where the birds lived. The TV spot that won the award cut my favorite line, the one about people who don't show up in photos. I saved it in a folder named "Later."

Ink carried her forward. The letters sat like small decisions she could finally keep. She remembered the night she and the field director ate cold lo mein on the floor and admitted they were tired of winning the way they were winning. The morning the senator hugged her and said, "You make me sound better than myself," and how something inside Evie tilted at the compliment, as if a picture had shifted on its nail.

Kris reappeared with a glass of water and a joke about Luis naming a transistor radio Dolores because she once shocked him. Evie grinned without looking up. "He deserved it."

The clock in the hall chimed the half hour. Her tendons throbbed; she set the pen down, rolled her wrists, and lifted it again.

If this is confession, let it be useful. If it's history, let it be plural. If it's a letter to the girls I used to be, Maggie with the stubborn star-counting, Dot with the hat and the steady spine, and me with ink on my fingers, let it say: we did our best until we knew better. Then we tried again.

Evie kept at it, sentence by sentence, true where she could manage, braver where she must. The ink shone, then dried, blue-black like a bruise loosening.

At last she stopped, flexed her hands, and blew gently across the page. What lay between the margins was a beginning she chose.

In the doorway, Dot's hat appeared first, then Dot. "How'd it go?" she asked, as if the answer might set the room's temperature.

Evie turned the journal so the fresh page faced the light. "True," she said, and let the word stay. "Feels like the first honest byline I've earned in years."

26

POLITICAL GAMES

1994 • HARRISBURG, PENNSYLVANIA • EVIE

T he campaign office looked clean enough to squeak. Carpet that smelled like new glue. Walls the color of copier paper. A ficus by the door, glossy and brave, pretending warmth. Phones with curly cords sat in tidy rows, coiled like waiting snakes. The sound here wasn't a newsroom's living chorus; it was fluorescent lights and a dot-matrix printer grinding out *ASHFORD FOR SENATE* banners in perforated sheets that begged to be torn.

Evie missed mess. She missed desks with coffee rings and the soft, hard music of typewriters—keys snapping like tiny doors, bells chiming at the end of thought. The Royal that raised a ridge on her finger. The Smith-Corona that purred when she landed a cadence. Machines used to feel like partners. This IBM PS/2 felt like a gatekeeper, pages that needed permission to exist.

She woke the blue screen. WordPerfect's cursor waited, polite and relentless.

The race mattered. Jennifer Ashford—camera-ready, disciplined, ambitious—was running to become the first female senator from a state that preferred its history ironed flat. A win would crack something open. Evie believed that. Or wanted to with the kind of wanting that pressed on her ribs. History had weight; you felt it even when the words were wrong.

"Morning, team." Warren Tate, the campaign manager, cruised past with a clipboard and a coffee he'd forget to finish. "Schedule change. Faith-leader breakfast at 9. County picnic at 2. We need a tighter family-values frame. Glenn, pull lines from the op-ed. Evie, new close for the breakfast remarks. We want 'neighbor,' 'faith,' 'tradition,' in that order."

"On it," Evie said, keeping her face easy.

She could braid rooms into paragraphs in her sleep now—image, breath, promise. She wrote:

My father taught me you don't talk about faith to win an argument. You live it, quietly, daily, in the way you carry your neighbor's load. That's the work I'm asking to do for you.

Clean. True enough. A promise you could hold without cutting your hand. She printed, ripped the perforations in one satisfying pull, and slid the page into the black binder that traveled everywhere with the candidate, essential as a wallet.

The binder made its rounds and came back heavier with sticky flags. Glenn set it on her desk, still smiling. "Good bones. Let's add signal—church, tradition—and swap father for grandfather. In our breakdown tables, 'father' counts as an urban voter."

Evie stared at the note. How strange to turn kinship into a dog whistle. "Her grandfather died when she was six," she said.

"Then he taught her something by dying. Work with me."

The sentence bruised as it landed. She felt the ache bloom in the old writer's bump on her finger. Facts first, the newsroom self insisted. But this was television with chairs. She rewrote. She hated it. She delivered it anyway.

A staff memo slid across her keyboard while the printer chattered: *Scrub "domestic-partnership" from the Q&A. Substitute "support for all families."* The asterisks looked like flinches.

Five minutes before the breakfast, Warren stuck his head into her cubicle. "One more thing. Pastor Hollis is hosting. He'd love a closing prayer—ten seconds, tops. Can you give her the words?"

Evie's fingers hovered over the keys. "We can honor faith without borrowing God's voice," she said. "I'll craft a close that nods without trespassing."

Warren squinted, already halfway down the hall. "Make it land."

In the copy room, Carmen was feeding paper into a jam-prone machine. "Tell me you're not writing a prayer," she said.

"I'm not," Evie answered. "I'm writing mercy."

Together they scraped adjectives, trimmed anything that sounded like a pulpit, and built a line that breathed without kneeling:

I was raised to leave the porch light on, because faith isn't a speech, it's the mercy we practice when no one's looking.

"Better," Carmen said, handing over the page like a secret.

The church-basement breakfast smelled like coffee and chafing-dish eggs. A banner—*WELCOME NEIGHBORS*—hung just right for TV. Evie tugged the videographer one step left. "We can show community," she murmured, "not endorsement."

Ashford took the podium in navy suit, white blouse, thin gold chain —a look Evie could spot in any future library portrait. She hit the stones in the river as rehearsed. Tradition. Family. Faith. The porch-light close landed exactly where Evie had placed it. Heads nodded. No prayer. No trespass.

Afterward, Ashford paused in Evie's doorway upstairs, backlit to a small halo. "You're writing again. How's it coming?"

"It lands," Evie said. "We're clean on legal. Tone's neighborly."

"We need sharper signal," Ashford replied. "Lean in, not out. The base needs to hear itself in me."

"They or you?" Evie asked—quiet enough not to count as insubordination.

Ashford's smile tucked in a millimeter. "Both."

By noon, volunteers streamed in with stacked postcards like offerings. A teen in a varsity jacket held the door for an older woman in orthopedic shoes and a hat with a tiny flag pinned neat as a stitch. "My granddaughter needs to see this," the woman told anyone willing to hear. Evie loved her instantly. Loving her didn't fix the words.

"Field wants a one-pager for church captains," Carmen said, reappearing. "Bulleted. Small enough to slide under a hymnal."

Evie wrote a letter to "friends in faith communities" that asked for "conversations about mercy and good work." She drained it of direct asks, salted it with neighbor words, and made it sound like air. She felt sick.

The county picnic offered heat, gravel, the bright mustard of summer. A butterfly-painted girl handed Ashford a balloon. Cameras snapped. The balloon bobbed above the candidate's head in every shot like punctuation you couldn't buy. A band sawed through "Rocky Top." Evie scribbled notes in the binder margin: *Thank food-bank volunteer by name. Hug the middle-school civics teacher; she's undecided. Avoid propane tanks in the photo line.*

"Family values," Ashford said into the microphone, and the crowd answered like it was a hymn.

Back at headquarters, the air-conditioner rattled bravely. "Focus group," Warren said. "Six o'clock. Faith close and kitchen-table tax line."

Behind the two-way mirror, ten strangers arranged themselves in metal chairs and confessed where they bought cereal and how often they went to church. The moderator played the breakfast clip.

A woman in a floral dress leaned forward, eyes shining. "She sounds like my pastor."

A man in a camo cap crossed his arms. "Don't like politicians talking church," he said. "But I like her voice." He didn't know it, but he liked Evie's.

A woman in her thirties, wedding ring catching the light, said softly, "I want my girls to see somebody like that win."

Then the moderator asked, "What does family values mean to you?"

Words tumbled out—respect, tradition, marriage, safety, responsibility. Too big to fit inside a sentence without warping.

The moderator tried a different clip—Ashford thanking a neighbor who'd organized a meal train for a chemo patient. No church words. Just a name, a casserole, a porch.

The camo-cap man nodded. "That. That's values."

Evie exhaled, a private confirmation she couldn't graph.

In the edit bay across the street—two decks, one small monitor, a sound board scarred with use—the producer cued up the thirty-second spot and settled the music bed under the voice like a porch step. Ashford's words poured through in the cadence Evie had arranged, sanded, sanded again. The producer swapped a close-up where Ashford's mouth made the shape of *mercy* for one where she looked more *order*. The change shifted the sentence's temperature by ten degrees.

"Reads strong," the producer said.

Evie nodded and tasted something metallic and old, like fear that remembered its own name. She scribbled the original sentence on a yellow sheet, slid it into a manila folder she'd labeled in thick marker— *Later*—and snapped the tab closed like a promise she meant to keep.

At dusk, the office emptied in a soft tide. She shut down the PS/2, collected the binder, and walked three blocks to her apartment, a one-bedroom with a view of a brick wall and a slice of honest sky. She poured a gin and tonic and sat on the floor because chairs belonged to work. The local news flickered: a house fire, a softball segment, then the breakfast cut, already spliced and broadcast. *Family values* landed again with practiced gravity.

The phone rang. She let it chirp three times before answering.

"Mags," she said, already hearing the steadiness.

"I saw Ashford," Maggie said—gentle, iron underneath. "She's leaning hard on family values. It feels... off. Is this the right path for you?"

Evie looked at the framed photo on her bookcase: her younger self on a Newspaper Guild picket line, rain gluing hair to her forehead, pen gripped like a flag. She could still hear the chant from that day, how other voices made hers louder.

"It's the game," she said, twisting the cord until it left a dent. "I write what wins."

"Is winning the point?" Maggie asked. "You shook things. Now it sounds like you're polishing them for the cameras."

The window went from nickel to blue-black.

"I don't know anymore," Evie said. "I used to chase truth like breaking news. Now, I've got talking points and a style guide. I'm good at it." The admission tasted like tin. "Maybe too good."

"Being good at something doesn't make it yours," Maggie said. "Or right."

They sat in a quiet that felt like standing at the edge of a pool at night, knowing the water would be colder than the air.

"I just want you happy," Maggie added. "I want you to be the woman who changed things, not the one who taught them how to stay the same."

Evie pressed her thumb into the old writer's bump the Royal had raised. "I don't know if she's still in me," she said. "But I know this—" She glanced at the TV where Ashford's face filled the screen in a spot that would air between church and roast chicken on Sunday. "I can't keep pretending it doesn't cost me."

"Then don't pretend," Maggie said. "Or write it down so you don't forget what it cost."

Evie opened a spiral notebook that mostly held grocery lists and phone numbers. The first page was blank. She wrote, small as a date:

What it took.

And beneath it: *What it took from me.*

She rested her palm on the binder like a hand on a piano lid and asked the question that had been coming all week: *When you lend your voice long enough, what's left when you want it back?*

She didn't have an answer. She opened the binder anyway.

27

THE BEATRICE YEAR

1997 • MAGGIE

The year family values turned into a campaign hymn and Evie's copy ran between church and Sunday chicken, Maggie pressed a Blockbuster case into the VCR and felt something old turn its head.

Saturday mornings the town woke slowly: sprinklers ticking, a radio somewhere soft with Whitney and weather. Maggie rinsed coffee cups in a sink that smelled faintly of lemon and daisies and stared at the case on the counter: *Much Ado About Nothing*. Her daughter had dropped it off the night before with a kiss and the line, "You'll love Emma Thompson —she's got your mouth."

Maggie laughed at that, then didn't. She slid the VHS into the player until it clicked. Sunlight smeared itself across the living room carpet. On screen, Messina bloomed: olive trees, wine, a woman whose wit carried like a bell. Something stirred under her ribs that hadn't moved in years.

The late news had been full of book clubs—Oprah's picks vanishing from shelves. Before that, hearings and arguments stuck to the wall-paper of the decade: Anita Hill's calm voice, a chorus of men leaning forward; the *Violence Against Women Act* said with protection like an oath; Oklahoma City; anniversaries of loss; headlines about the Internet as if it were a new ocean.

The world felt louder, closer. Her house was quieter now—children flown, a calendar with more white space than ink. Some nights, she listened to the dial-up bong of her son's computer like a distant ship.

She meant to fold laundry while the movie played. Instead, she sat cross-legged on the carpet with a towel in her lap and mouthed along to lines she hadn't touched since high school. When Beatrice said, "Kill Claudio," the towel slid to the floor. Maggie put a hand to her throat and felt the old path open—breath, voice, courage—like a road that had been there all along under summer vines. She sat very still, as if any sudden movement might scare the feeling away.

On Tuesday, the doorbell rang.

Henry Carmichael stood on the porch with a dog-eared script and a grin softened by time. The same crooked smile from senior year, when his Benedick had tripped over a prop barrel and made the audience love him more for it.

"Hi, Maggie," he said, shifting the script to his left hand the way he used to shift a basketball before passing. "Strange ask."

"I'm not promising anything," she replied automatically, stepping back to let the screen door sigh open. "Coffee?"

He shook his head. "I have exactly eleven minutes before I'm late to teach scene study to three teenagers who think *Rent* invented theater." His smile found its old mischief. "We're staging *Much Ado.* I'm direct-ing. We need a Beatrice who means it."

"I haven't acted in forty years," she said.

"Years aren't erasers." He didn't even blink. Just offered it as fact. "Just read one speech."

Her fingers found the page they'd always belonged to: words that tasted like flint and honey. "Is he not approved in the height a villain, that hath slandered, scorned, dishonoured my kinswoman? ... O that I were a man! I would eat his heart in the marketplace."

The room went very still.

"See?" Henry said, already backing down the steps. "Dangerous."

She stood in the doorway with the script like a telegram from a former life. After he left, she sat at the kitchen table and underlined: *O that I were a man.* The decade was full of voices about who gets believed, who is safe, which rooms belong to whom. The speech felt less like nostalgia and more like the thing itself—anger shaped into art and handed to a woman with pockets.

She didn't feel young. She felt accurate.

That night, she called Dot. "Tell me I'm not ridiculous."

"You're not ridiculous," Dot said. "You're breathing."

"And if I'm terrible?"

"Then you'll be terrible with friends in a dusty room that smells like hope. Go."

Rehearsals smelled like dust and optimism. The community theater's thermostat worked when it felt like it. Volunteers stapled programs while discussing the new mall. Someone's beeper kept chirping like a cricket that had learned manners. The stage manager, a pediatric nurse by day, taped spike marks along the floor and called five-minute breaks like a general who knew when teenagers needed sugar.

On the first night, the cast sat in a ragged semicircle for table read. Young Hero—fresh out of college—tucked a strand of hair behind her ear each time she said *my lord*; Claudio had a skateboard leaning against his chair; Dogberry was played by a retired mail carrier who announced, before page one, "I have always wanted to arrest someone."

Maggie's hands trembled on the first scene. By the end of Act I, she had her breath back and the rhythm like a river under her feet. She had forgotten how the work ordered your body: vowels round and set on air; breath dropped low; knees soft; eyes up and out. She warmed up in the wings with *red leather, yellow leather* tongue twister and—quietly, so as not to scare anyone—the first verse of the doxology.

At break, Henry leaned on the doorframe, watching her with the look she remembered from the wings in 1951. "You're still—"

"Don't say electric," she warned, smiling despite herself.

"—you," he finished. "Which is worse for my blood pressure."

She laughed, and something new and old twined in her chest.

Hope, maybe. Or memory standing up straighter.

She tucked rehearsals between real life: casseroles for a neighbor whose husband had started chemo; a midnight call from her son to explain email in a way that sounded like a magic trick; church gossip about whether the Internet would ruin or save the library. She practiced lines while unloading the dishwasher, while waiting for water to boil, while pinning sheets to the clothesline. She wrote tricky cues on index cards and taped them to the bathroom mirror. At night, she lay in bed and whispered into the dark: "Speak, cousin; or, if you cannot, stop his mouth with a kiss and let him not speak neither." The line made her blush again, the way it used to.

On the TV over meatloaf one night, the Branagh adaptation played again, and Maggie found herself saying Beatrice's lines with Emma Thompson, then shaking her head at how much she wanted to be inside that quickness again. When she turned off the set, she stood a long time in her quiet kitchen, palms flat on the counter, listening to the drone of the refrigerator and her own stubborn heart.

She didn't want to be younger. She wanted to be present.

"Try this," Henry said during blocking two weeks later, stepping toward her to set a mark. "When you say, 'Kill Claudio,' don't look at Benedick right away. Look at the audience. Let them feel it hit."

"Some of them won't like it," she said.

"Good," he said. "It's not a lullaby."

When June turned to July, he asked if she wanted to cut the scene down—some board members found it "harsh."

"It's supposed to be harsh," Maggie said, surprised by how steady her voice was. "Women live in it. This decade keeps proving why."

He lifted his hands in surrender. "As the director, I agree. As the man who has to face the board, I still agree. Keep it."

They kept it.

Tech week arrived with its usual tender cruelty. Lights cooked the stage; cues tangled; tempers frayed and mended with doughnuts. It still smelled like sawdust and optimism—now with a scorch of hot gels. The high schooler running sound whispered, awed, that the light board had more buttons than his father's new satellite dish. Maggie's feet ached in character shoes. She learned to pin her hair so it wouldn't come down when Hero fainted. Someone donated a box fan that roared like a small plane.

During fight call, the young man playing Claudio missed his partner's cue and grabbed a little too hard. "I'm so sorry," he said, mortified.

"It's all right," Maggie told him, flexing her wrist. "Let's make the hurt belong to the story, not the person. We try again." He nodded like a boy being handed a key.

At home, Maggie steamed her costume in the bathroom and watched wisps of heat lift like breath. She sewed a loose hem while talk radio argued about welfare reform, then turned the dial down and let the needle steady her. She wrote a postcard to Evie—*Beatrice is mouthy and righteous and she's saving me*—and never mailed it, unsure why.

Maybe because saying it out loud would make it real in ways she wasn't ready for yet.

Late August, Maggie was driving home from rehearsal with the windows down when the radio voice broke on the word *accident* on Route 83. She pulled into the grocery lot and watched people come and go with flowers like small flags. Grief could be private and public at once, she learned. She went home and ironed her costume even though it didn't need it. Pressing calmed her. The steam rose, a baptism of linen.

The day before opening, her daughter stopped by with peach scones and a look. "How's your boyfriend director?"

"Behaved," Maggie said, which was not precisely the question, nor precisely the answer.

"You happy?"

Maggie thought about the girl in the old yearbook, head tipped, eyes laughing; about the woman in the kitchen, hands in dishwater, counting grocery money and bedtime stories; about the quiet house that had learned her footsteps and the theater that was relearning her voice. "I feel... awake," she said finally.

"Good," her daughter said, relief unclenching her jaw. "Break a leg, Mom." On the way out she patted the VHS on the shelf. "Told you about Emma."

Opening night arrived on the cool edge of September. Backstage, someone softly sang "Seasons of Love"; someone else prayed into her hands. The pediatric-nurse stage manager taped a fresh list to the wall: *No food in costume. No gum. Find your light. Breathe.* Henry tied his tie in the warped mirror and winked. Maggie kept her eyes on her script as if it could steady the floor.

From the wings she watched the audience float in—church ladies in pastel sweater sets, high schoolers in hoodies with backpacks slung low, a row of town-council stalwarts, a girl in a flannel and scuffed combat boots, a couple holding hands the way people do when they've learned to be careful in public. The room carried all their weather, and she felt every change.

When the lights found her, the room narrowed into a kind of truth. The words were in her bones; the woman who spoke them was in her mouth. She caught Benedick listening, really listening, the way a person listens to rain that might turn to thunder. When she said, "Kill Claudio," she let her gaze go past Henry and into the house—past the front row where a man shifted uncomfortably, past the middle aisle where two teenage girls sat forward, eyes wide, past the exit sign that glowed like a cheap star. The line landed and didn't apologize.

At intermission, a woman Maggie knew from the bank found her by the drinking fountain. "I didn't like that part," she said, then softer, cheeks pink: "But I think I was supposed to hear it."

"Me too," Maggie said, which was true, and they smiled at each other, unexpected allies.

Act II ran with the quickness of a dream you get to keep. Dogberry brought the house down misusing words with authority. Hero rose from the ash of her shaming like morning itself. Benedick and Beatrice made their truce, stubborn and tender as two mules agreeing on a path. When the final dance began, Maggie let laughter lift up through her ribs and into her face. She had missed the way joy could be choreography.

After bows, someone handed her daisies and eucalyptus—her favorite, though she'd never said so aloud. The card was unsigned. She didn't need to ask.

"Welcome back," Henry murmured as he passed, careful not to touch her more than a second, respectful of the life around the play. "You were... you."

"Which is worse for your blood pressure," she said, and he grinned, and they both looked at the floor until they could look at each other without something spilling.

The applause faded, but something else didn't.

It wasn't the performance. It was the permission.

Permission that didn't evaporate when the lights cooled.

The run slid into routine—Thursday notes, Friday nerves, Saturday matinees where toddlers whispered loudly and grandfathers slept open-mouthed. People left small offerings at the stage door: a paper cone of zinnias, a postcard with *Sigh no more, ladies* scrawled in blue pen, a tin of lemon bars from the retired mail carrier who was now a star in the grocery store. On Sundays, Maggie napped with a heating pad wrapped around her lower back and woke to the damp imprint of daisies on her cheek from where she'd fallen asleep on the bouquet.

One evening, she found Dot and Evie in the second row like a benediction. Afterward, they met her by the mural of comedy and tragedy masks that had peeled into something more honest.

"Well?" Maggie asked, defensive and small and proud all at once.

Dot kissed her cheek. "You didn't act Beatrice. You were her."

Evie's eyes shone. "The line—'O that I were a man'—I heard it differently tonight. Not as a wish to be him, but as a refusal to be invisible. Thank you for that."

Maggie made a joke to keep from crying; they let her. Friends were good at the mercy of not pushing.

On closing night, the audience rose before the lights finished fading. The cast huddled in the greenroom afterward, faces de-painted, eyes bright. Henry gave a silly speech about borrowed swords and found courage. Maggie put her hand on the back of the plastic chair she'd used all summer, as if to thank it for holding her up. She took one last look from the wings at the empty set—the bench that had been love, the archway that had been a gate and a gallows—and let the room return to being a room.

At home, she hung her costume on the back of the closet door and stood a long time in the doorway, not ready to shut it. The house listened the way houses do. In the kitchen, she poured water over a tea bag and watched color bloom in her World's Okayest Mom mug. Then she carried it into the living room and pressed rewind just to hear the soft whirring, an old machine gathering itself, ready to begin again.

She had never really left. She'd only been waiting for the door to be unlocked from both sides.

In the weeks after, she said yes more readily: yes to reading poetry at the library, yes to helping the choir with vowels, yes to teaching the church youth a stage-combat workshop so they could slap their palms and not their friends' cheeks. She bought a secondhand tape recorder and made herself a little studio at the dining room table—tablecloth folded back, index cards in a cigar box, lamp angled like a small sun. When the house was particularly quiet, she'd press record and read Beatrice's lines into the dark, letting the words fill the room that had fed so many suppers and silences.

On a windy afternoon in October, the mail brought a note with a thin program folded around it. *You're in the board minutes,* Henry had scribbled, triumphant. *No cuts, for the record. P.S. They want to know if you'd consider Kate.* Maggie smiled at the old name of another stubborn woman—Kate Keller from *All My Sons*—and set the program under the magnet with the photograph of her children in Halloween costumes.

The fridge looked like a bulletin board for a life that kept finding new thumbtacks.

Later, when the evening news circled again to talking heads and polls, she turned the sound down and stood in the doorway of the living room, watching the light settle. She could almost hear the soft shuffle of a stagehand in the wings, the hush before an entrance. Her hands remembered where to place themselves—thumb on the spine of a script, fingers poised for the page turn.

Permission, she thought. And then: practice.

The two together felt a lot like a life.

28

LEGACY

2011 • BALTIMORE, MARYLAND • DOT

D ot's office was the last door at the end of the quiet wing, where the social sciences building forgot to echo. Students called it the history cul-de-sac, a place where hallways turned in on themselves and time did, too. She liked it that way. The brass plate on her door still read *D. CARTER*. The receptionist kept offering a new one that said *Professor*. Dot always said no. Her name was enough.

Inside, the room held the life she'd made: two bookcases bowed with paperbacks gone soft at the corners, a row of student theses with titles hand-lettered down the spines, a tin of peppermint tea, a leaning stack of yellow legal pads with the top sheet always half full of phrases she wasn't done with. She opened the narrow window to let November in —dry leaves, a far whistle from the train yard, the HVAC's faint hiss that never quite reached her end of the hall.

Her desk was the battered oak kind no one ordered anymore, its surface a quilt of scratches she'd long ago stopped noticing. Above it hung three frames: a pamphlet from the Atlanta sit-in training; a program from the March on Washington, where she met Clara, her once-love; and a photo of Dot at twenty-two, chin lifted, her arm threaded through strangers who had become kin in a single day. The straw hat sat low against the sun, shadowing her eyes. Looking at that girl, Dot always felt the same ache and the same private pride: *You were scared—and you went anyway.*

She adjusted her glasses and read the keynote again. A women's college in New England had invited her to deliver the fall convocation— old brick, bright leaves, a hall named for someone complicated. Seventy-six and still being called to the microphone. A miracle, yes. Also a responsibility.

Her pen hovered above the page, snagging on the same sentence she'd rewritten three times: *Legacy is—* She scratched it out again. On her screen, a new email subject line blinked: *assessment alignment guidance.* The memo cheerfully praised "measurable outcomes" and traveling rubrics. It read like furniture being pushed around a room. Dot exhaled, closed the email, tapped the desk twice the way she always did when choosing courage over annoyance, and rubbed the bridge of her nose.

A knock came, light and tentative.

"Professor Carter?"

She knew the voice by its cadence before she turned: cautious strength, like a clarinet finding its first clear note.

"Aaliyah?" Dot rose, glasses forgotten on the desk.

Aaliyah James filled the doorway—tall, warm brown skin, natural curls soft as a halo, eyes that still held more story than her age could explain. The same dimple, the same way of taking in the whole room at once, as if measuring where the light fell.

"It's been a while," Aaliyah said, and then they were already halfway into an embrace. Time folded to make room.

"Come in," Dot said, not pretending she wasn't blinking back tears. "Sit. Tell me how the world's treating you."

"It's trying me," Aaliyah laughed, sliding into the chair students had worn smooth over decades. "But I'm trying it right back."

"How long's it been?" Dot asked, lowering herself carefully. Her knees had their own weather now.

"Seventeen years," Aaliyah said. "But who's counting?"

"Apparently we are," Dot murmured, grinning.

They studied each other the way women do who've held versions of one another in their minds and wondered if those versions were still true. Aaliyah wore a teacher's lanyard looped through her bag; the laminated ID caught the light. Dot noticed a small tiredness at the edge of her smile and recognized it like kin.

"I'm teaching now," Aaliyah said. "High school history. Juniors and seniors. Title I—first-gen kids, jobs after school, families figuring out how to make one paycheck and a car with a prayer stretch. Predominantly Black and Brown. They're brilliant."

Dot's heart lifted. "Of course they are."

"And they're tested to death," Aaliyah added, dry but not bitter. "No Child Left Behind means we practice answering questions a machine can grade. Some days, it feels like they're measuring whether a child can fill in a circle fully between lunch and algebra."

"Mmm." Dot raised an eyebrow. "Circles can't hold what matters. But you were always good at teaching what matters anyway."

"I try. I sneak in what I can. Ida B. Wells inside the Reconstruction chapter. Audre Lorde with the poetry unit. We build a timeline on butcher paper that runs the room like a train. Every student adds one family story: a great-grandmother who cleaned offices at night, a dad who became a citizen in '02, a cousin who came back different from Iraq. During the last lockdown drill, Malik counted ceiling tiles to steady his breath. We added that moment to the timeline, too. They learn history isn't just something done to them."

Dot felt the familiar opening in her chest, the one that meant hope had pulled up a chair. "Tell me their names," she said.

"Malik, who can break down the Emancipation Proclamation like it owes him money," Aaliyah said, laughing. "Yesenia, who translates for her mother at every conference and writes diary entries from the Statue of Liberty's point of view. Ty, who swears he hates reading and then devours *Narrative of the Life of Frederick Douglass* when I 'accidentally' leave it on his desk. I could go on."

"Please do," Dot said softly. "Go on forever."

Aaliyah glanced at the frames. "I think about you whenever I plan a lesson. How you made history feel like something we could touch without permission. How you handed us your hat after the unit on the March and said, *Try it on if you want. Feel the sun.*"

Dot had forgotten that. The memory rose whole—students passing the hat hand to hand, trying not to bend the brim, giggling and then going a little still. "We weren't brave alone," she said, more to herself than to Aaliyah.

"You said that, too."

"Did I?" Dot smiled. "Sometimes I say a thing and don't know it's true until I hear it in somebody else's mouth."

"When I came to your class," Aaliyah said, leaning forward, elbows on her knees as if the truth were heavy and needed holding, "I was working nights at the diner. Falling asleep in chemistry. I thought smart belonged to other people. You wouldn't let me sit small. You looked at me, not past me. You said my questions were work worth doing."

"That's because they were," Dot said simply, throat tightening.

"I argued with Du Bois," Aaliyah said, laughing through a shine of tears.

"You did. *The Souls of Black Folk*. You said double consciousness was too tidy for a world that split you into pieces you didn't choose."

"And you told me to wrestle with it until I could stand up," Aaliyah said. "I still tell my kids that—'Wrestle, then stand.'"

Silence settled, comfortable as a church pew between hymns. Dot reached across and took Aaliyah's hand. Brown on brown, both mapped with years.

"I keep a little journal," Aaliyah confessed after a moment, suddenly shy. "Lines I hope my students say about me when I'm old. Most of them are things I once said about you."

"Oh, child," Dot whispered, blinking fast.

"Sometimes, I wonder if I'm doing enough," Aaliyah said. "My freshmen were born into fear. Lockdown drills are normal to them. I stand there counting heads and think about your stories of standing in doorways so other girls could enter. I don't have your march. I have hall passes and school-board meetings. It feels so small."

"It's not small," Dot said, fierce as she'd ever been. "It's the work."

Aaliyah nodded, relieved and not. "I wanted you to know you're the reason I'm in those rooms."

"You found your own door," Dot said. "I just made sure you saw it was open."

When Aaliyah stood to go, she lingered at the threshold. "This room," she said, sweeping her gaze over the shelves, the frames, the hat. "This is where I became myself."

"Thank you for coming back to tell me," Dot said. "We don't always get to hear the last verse of the song."

After the door clicked shut, the office felt both more full and more spacious, like something had been returned and something released. Dot sat awhile, letting the moment finish speaking. Then she turned to the keynote, and the pages were different in her hands—lighter, truer. She slid the old draft into a folder marked *keep* and pulled a fresh legal pad close. Her pen hovered, trembled, steadied.

Keynote Draft — Women's College, 2011

"Joan Didion wrote, 'We tell ourselves stories in order to live.' I've learned we also tell them to decide how to live together—what we carry, what we set down, and what we build when the blueprints are missing.

When I was your age, I learned to count my fear and keep walking. I marched because no one else could use my feet. I sat at counters that didn't want me. People told me I was too much—too loud, too angry. Sometimes, they were right. Anger was my tool, not my home. I wasn't there to burn the house down; I was there to light the way in.

A former student visited me this week. Aaliyah. Years ago, she worked nights, held up a family, and tried to take up as little space as possible. She argued with Du Bois and made me rethink tidy words. Today, she teaches high-school history. She stays late to translate a land-lord's letter. She tucks Ida B. Wells into the unit plan. She runs a time-line around her classroom and asks her students to add their kin.

She told me, 'You saw me.'

That's the assignment. Not to fix. Not to save. To see.

Legacy isn't a statue. It's a hand held out, a door left open, a voice used in a room that prefers your silence—and then passed on to someone else.

The decade ahead will ask a lot: speak precisely, listen past your certainty, vote, show up, forgive wisely, rest without quitting. Carry grief, but don't let it calcify. Keep faith with communities asked to be patient for generations.

You don't have to do it alone. Name the women who've kept you. Write their names in your margins. Become a name in someone else's. When a door opens, put your foot in the jamb. Hold it wide. Call out. Persist.

We're not here to rehearse the past. We're here to respect it, learn from it, and write an ending it couldn't imagine.

Sisters, the pen is in your hand. So is the light."

Dot set the pen down and read the draft aloud, testing cadence, listening for a place where the breath snagged. It didn't. The words stood up straight. She dated the page, slid it into her leather portfolio, and turned back to her email.

A note from the college waited at the top of the inbox—travel confirmed, a student escort assigned, permission to record.

Dot smiled, warmth moving through her like a remembered song. She reached for the hat on the shelf and touched the brim with two fingers, feeling the old straw give under her hand.

She shut off the lamp and locked the office, patting the door the way a person pats a faithful dog. The hallway held its end-of-day hush. On the cork board near the elevator, flyers overlapped: *Voter registration. Food pantry hours. A teach-in on the Iraq War, moved to the student union "due to fire code."* A photocopied poem: *we're each other's harvest / we're each other's business.* Someone had highlighted the lines.

Outside, campus put on its evening, dusky gold melting to blue. A student on a skateboard coasted while texting; another wheeled a cello case; three women in scrubs compared schedules and laughed like survivors. Dot breathed in the faint coal-smoke smell the city got when it turned cold. Somewhere, a church bell counted six.

She paused at the top of the steps and looked back through the glass at the corridor, at the last door on the quiet wing that had been a door for so many, including the woman who'd just walked through it to show her what legacy looks like when it comes home.

Then Dot set the hat on her head for the feel of it, tucked the portfolio under her arm, and stepped off the cul-de-sac and back into the through-line.

29

ACT TWO

PRESENT • MANCHESTER
MEADOWS • MAGGIE

Maggie had been folding the same sweater for the third time when the knock came, a quick double tap too eager to belong to a nurse.

Dot and Evie stood shoulder to shoulder in the hall, grinning like girls who'd cut class and gotten away with it.

"Mags, grab your sweater," Dot said. "You've got an audition."

"A what now?"

Evie waved a glossy flyer. *"Manchester Meadows Presents: A Night on Broadway!* Outside performers, glitzy costumes, and"—she tapped the line as if she'd written it—"special appearances from our very own residents."

"And who better than you?" Dot added. "You were born to be on stage."

Maggie reached for the flyer, then set it down as though it might spook. "It's been years."

"So?" Evie said. "Write the lines on your hand. Your timing hasn't expired yet."

Dot leaned in, conspiratorial. "Do the speech. That speech."

"'Kill Claudio?'" Maggie asked, half-laughing.

Evie pressed a palm to her heart. "You gave me chills before I even knew what half the words meant."

Maggie pulled her battered *Arden Shakespeare* from the shelf. The spine sighed. She began, voice a little rusty, then sure. "Is he not approved in the height a villain ...?"

Evie blinked back water. Dot's smile went wide and wicked. "We're putting your name down."

"Fine," Maggie said, closing the book with a soft thump. "Let's give them a show."

The Audition

The recreation room tried its best to look official. A sign-in sheet on a card table. A paper cup of pencils that had already lost their erasers. Kris had taped a sheet of printer paper to the door: *AUDITIONS* → with an arrow that pointed exactly nowhere and somehow still got everyone where they needed to go.

Luis handled sound because he trusted machines and they trusted him back. "This is Constance," he said, patting the lone standing mic. "She only misbehaves when she's ignored."

Doris swept in first, a red hat feathered enough to frighten small birds. "My Red Hat days aren't over," she announced. She sang the chorus of *Hello, Dolly!* with more brio than breath and bowed to such applause she bowed again just to keep it.

A retired math teacher recited the *Preamble* as if it were a patter song, brisk and exact. Two sisters attempted *Tonight* and argued, mid-harmony, about whether the alto part was "the low one or the right one." The man who slept through bingo woke to tap out eight astonishing bars using his walker, the tennis balls at the feet squeaking like shoes from another decade.

Maggie waited near the piano, palms cupped around a cup of water. She could already feel the speech lifting inside her like breath that had been waiting for a ribcage.

"Whenever you're ready, Ms. Maggie," Kris said, gentle as a prompter in the wings.

Maggie stepped forward. Breath in, ribs wide—Henry's note from a lifetime ago. She let the opening settle.

"Is he not approved in the height a villain, that hath slandered, scorned, dishonoured my kinswoman ...?"

Luis forgot to blink. Evie's fountain pen—the one that wrote like memory—stopped halfway down the audition form. Dot made exactly one note: *CAST.*

When Maggie reached "O that I were a man!" a sneeze detonated in the second row.

"Sorry!" Marlene waved a tissue. "My allergies think this is Shakespeare in the Park."

Laughter let the room exhale. Maggie smiled into it, the way a pilot smiles at a crosswind and keeps the plane steady, and landed the last line clean.

Dot tapped her clipboard. "You'll do."

Maggie put her hand over her heart and bowed to the folding chairs. "Lucky for you I'm free Thursdays."

Building a Stage Out of Tuesday

The recreation room transformed the way hope transforms a weekday— slowly, then all at once. Folding chairs became an amphitheater. A strip of painter's tape declared a stage. The baby grand wore a feather boa until the pianist shooed it off with dignity.

Dot arrived with a lawn chair labeled *QUEEN* in duct tape and established a director's corner. Evie appointed herself stage manager, acquired a clipboard, and lost the pen twice before warm-ups. She cupped her hands and called, with official flourish, "Work lights to porch!"

No one knew what that meant, but it sounded like welcome.

Residents ambled in carrying keepsakes: a handbag no one would put down, a teddy bear older than the building, a pair of tap shoes meant for a different decade. Doris took up residence stage-left and set her red hat on the piano like a leading lady catching her breath.

"Vocal warm-ups," Maggie called, clapping. No one noticed.

Evie tried again. "If you can hear me, clap once."

A handful of claps. A couple of people startled awake.

"Good," Dot said. "We're a precision machine."

Rehearsals became the week's pulse. The man from bingo tapped his soft-shoe to *Singin' in the Rain,* the walker now a partner instead of a prop. The sisters found a see-saw of harmony on *Tonight,* missing every third step and nailing the part that mattered—the way they looked at each other on the last note.

Dot created a costume boutique from donated silk scarves and something that might once have been a magician's cape. Evie labeled everything with tape and hope; when her wrists ached, she flexed, the dull throb coming and going like weather, and she kept going.

Between scenes, Maggie coached breath. "Fill from here," she said, pressing a hand to her ribs. "Wit rides on air." She didn't add that sorrow does too—but she felt it, watching residents steady themselves and, rehearsal by rehearsal, stand taller inside their own lives.

One afternoon, she found Leah—quiet, new to the building—staring at a lyric sheet from *The Sound of Music* as if the notes might bite.

"Stage fright isn't a stage," Maggie said, settling beside her. "It's a room. We can leave it."

"I croaked," Leah whispered. "Like a frog."

"Frogs have range," Maggie said. "Try this." She placed Leah's hand on her own back, just at the ribs. "Breathe with me. In for four, out for six."

They breathed until the paper stopped rustling. Leah tried the line again; the note rounded out, surprised by itself.

"There she is," Maggie said, and Leah smiled the small smile of a person who'd just found her keys.

Later, Maggie caught Dot watching her with that long professor's look—the one that weighed both the lesson and the teacher.

"Don't start," Maggie said.

"Wouldn't dream of it," Dot replied, which was a lie and a blessing.

Dress Rehearsal (Which Is to Say: Chaos)

The first dress rehearsal was a gentle calamity. The boa shed, the painter's tape curled at one corner like a tongue, and Constance emitted a staticky tsk-tsk every time anyone said *Broadway,* as if to warn against hubris.

Evie's clipboard became the town crier. "Places in five! Places in three! Places ... where are my places?" She pressed two gel packs to her wrists between cues and called out entrances with that newsroom cadence she'd kept even when newsrooms stopped having bells.

Maggie had taken refuge in a folding chair near the wings, rubbing the ache in her hands. Kris floated past like a practical angel—refilling water cups, wrapping Marlene's sneezy shoulders in a cardigan that didn't match and therefore read costume. Then she sidled up to Maggie with a bowl of warm water and a rolled towel.

"Ten minutes in heat, then cool wrap," she said. "Doctor's orders. And the doctor is you, circa 1997."

Maggie laughed. "Bossy."

"Efficient," Kris said, and winked.

Dot's directions were soft but surgical. "Find the light, not the lampshade." "Pause until you can hear the hush." "Doris, the hat is perfect. The hat is also not a blocking choice—your feet still have to move."

They ran the sequence again. This time, it held like a breath that decided to stay.

At the end, Evie stood center tape with the program mock-up. "Final order. Two-minute blackout between numbers, unless Doris is still bowing."

"I *do* bow slowly," Doris admitted.

"We honor your process," Dot said.

They laughed, and the laugh felt like luck.

Then, like all good rehearsals, it ended not with applause but with gathering—a folding of scarves, a quieting of nerves, a shared breath before the real thing.

Costumes were draped over chair backs, water cups emptied, Constance unplugged with something like dignity. One by one, they filtered toward the hall, voices softening, footsteps gentling as though not to disturb the spell they'd made.

Maggie lingered a moment longer, rubbing the warmth back into her hands, feeling anticipation move from tremor to steadiness.

Tomorrow, the lights would be brighter.

Tomorrow, the seats would be full.

Tomorrow was opening night.

30

CENTER STAGE

PRESENT • MANCHESTER MEADOWS, PENNSYLVANIA • MAGGIE

Morning found Maggie sitting on the edge of her bed, the index card on her mirror catching a slant of early light: *Permission, then practice.*

She said it under her breath, steady as scales before warm-up. The thrum in her ribs—the one rehearsal had woken—hadn't faded overnight. It hadn't dulled. It waited with her.

On her way to breakfast, she passed the activity room and saw the painter's tape still holding its shape on the floor—faithful as a bookmark, as if saving her place.

They were ready.

By evening, Manchester Meadows no longer looked like a nursing home; it looked like a place that fully expected magic.

The lobby brimmed with foot traffic—wheelchairs moving like polite bees, walkers clicking in time with nervous heels. Balloons—gold, silver, and one determined purple—bumped the crown molding and squeaked their excitement. Paper stars winked from every wall. Someone had rolled out a hallway runner from the linen closet and secured its corners with blue painter's tape so it wouldn't curl. It wasn't a red carpet, exactly, but when the light hit just right, it blushed as if it knew its role.

Maggie stood just inside the transformed activity room, tonight's theater, letting the noise wash over her. Lemon polish, hairspray, and the faint, comforting tang of menthol on knees blended into one determined perfume. Folded chairs rose in cheerful rows all the way back to the vending machine, where latecomers hovered clutching small cups of ginger ale, already whispering their favorites.

Family, staff, neighbors from the church two blocks over—and what appeared to be three generations of one very enthusiastic clan wearing matching T-shirts that read **WE 💜 GRANDMA D**—filled the room with expectation.

Laura from Activities wore a headset that wasn't actually connected to anything...but the hope on her face could've powered the soundboard on its own.

"Let's give them a show!" she sang out.

Behind a stage-left divider—technically the same queen-size bedsheet tacked to the wall with optimistic thumbtacks—Dot was retying Marlene's scarf for the fourth time as if steadiness could be woven. Evie, stage manager by declaration, fluffed Maggie's hair with solemn concentration, then rolled her wrists and fastened the slim braces she'd started wearing since dress rehearsal.

"You're luminous," Evie said.

"Luminous is good," Dot added. "Luminous says, 'I know my lines and I can still smuggle a cheesecake into a matinee.' And as always, find the light, not the lampshade."

Maggie laughed, but under the laugh a flock of birds lifted in her chest. It wasn't fear of forgetting or tripping or missing the tape mark someone had kindly labeled M on the linoleum. It was the tremor that comes before a door opens—an old door, one you've walked through before and thought you'd locked behind you. It was the tremor of being seen, fully, again.

She peeked through a gap in the bedsheet. Rows of faces waited, talking softly, the way people talk in a sanctuary before the music begins. That hush before joy felt holy. Being ready to receive felt like its own kind of generosity.

"Places," Evie whispered, which meant please don't wander off and also I love you. Then, with a grin only the three of them would catch, "Work lights to porch."

Overture: The Good Acts

The Harmony Hills Quartet—four retired music teachers in white pants, striped vests, and bow ties—opened with doo-wop *Under the Boardwalk,* finding a collective sway in the room, hips remembering things minds had filed away. By the last verse, a grandma in the third row had laced her fingers with her husband's and conducted the final chord with one satisfied flick.

Miss Rachel's Tiny Tappers tumbled on next, all bangs and bravery, sequined vests scattering light like they'd been dipped in sunshine. Their timing was chaos, their commitment absolute. When one little girl pirouetted directly into a folding chair, the audience gasped; she curt-sied, flashed double thumbs-up, and won the night's first standing ovation from the row of cousins near the vending machine.

A community theater trio did *Sit Down, You're Rockin' the Boat* with a laundry-basket canoe and the kind of confidence that comes from knowing the joke will land if you commit to it.

Then the ukulele group in matching sequined vests took their stools and, against every expectation, delivered a haunting instrumental *Memory,* pivoted to a strummed *Defying Gravity* that somehow caught the lift without leaving the ground, and finished with *She'll Be Comin' 'Round the Mountain,* featuring six kazoos and audience clapping that turned the room into a hoedown. It shouldn't have worked. It did. Joy, it turns out, is immune to logic.

Backstage, Dot dabbed the corners of her eyes with a tissue. "Kazoo modulation," she sniffed. "A lost art."

"Please don't say modulation to Harold," Evie said. "He's about to rhyme gun eight different ways, and that's already a lot."

The Residents Take the Stage

Laura stepped into the light, headset gleaming like a star. "And now," she announced, "talent from right here at Manchester Meadows!"

The clapping was proud, neighborly. A teenage grandson who'd worn a tie even though no one asked let out a tentative "woo!" that made his grandmother dab her eyes with a tissue.

Harold led off, squaring his shoulders, and launched into *I Am the Very Model of a Modern Major-General,* words flying like popcorn. At "vegetable, animal, and mineral," his dentures attempted a jailbreak, caught on a heroic intake of breath, and returned to duty. The room cheered him like a conquering hero.

Next, the Glee Bees—Edna, Ruth, and Bea—sweet in pastel cardigans, sang *My Favorite Things.* Edna's kazoo solo arrived with grave dignity, as though every great orchestra had simply been missing this exact tone. By the end of the verse on "brown paper packages," a toddler in the aisle was conducting with a glow stick. Somewhere, Nikita the night nurse filmed the whole thing for the staff group chat with captions of hearts.

Maggie felt the shift in the room before she stepped onto the tape. Not silence, exactly, but attention knitting itself tighter. Evie settled her hands on Maggie's shoulders for one steadying second. Dot squeezed her fingers, then let go like a blessing. The crimson shawl warmed like courage. The sleep-toned boom of the old baby grand quieted. The bedsheet swayed once, like a curtain nodding ready.

Maggie stepped into the light.

No props. No flourish. Just a woman and the words that had once lit a fuse in her that she'd been told, kindly, to hide.

She breathed.

"Is he not approved in the height a villain," she began, and it was as if a map unfolded inside her chest. The path—the one she'd walked at eighteen, the one she'd shown her kids from the third row, the one she'd dreamed of during long nights beside a sleeping husband—was right where she'd left it. Her voice warmed as it moved, the old rhythm finding her, Beatrice riding up through the bones to borrow her mouth.

"O God, that I were a man! I would eat his heart in the marketplace!"

Someone in the second row startled, then leaned forward, eyes bright. The Harmony Hills Quartet's phones dropped, screens forgotten. Even Doris, resplendent in her Red Hat regalia, lowered her feathered crown and listened with her whole face.

Maggie crossed the small stage with the surety of someone who'd been told once that anger didn't belong to her and had decided otherwise. She didn't shout. She didn't need to. She let the space do the work. She let breath carry wit, let fury sit beside love the way it does in a real kitchen, a real marriage, a real life. She felt Evie's attention steadying her, Dot's fierce pride like a spot of heat. Somewhere near the vending machine, a grandson stopped scrolling. Somewhere in memory, daisies breathed.

The last line landed. The room held.

It's a holy thing, the silence that honors. For two beats, the quiet was a cup, full to its rim.

Then the cup spilled—applause that wasn't about manners, but recognition. Not *we enjoyed that,* but *we saw you.* A whistle from the back. Dot's victorious whoop. Evie's hand at her mouth, eyes shining. Laura's headset bobbing like a buoy on a bright sea.

"Encore!" someone yelled.

Maggie dipped her head. Not the sweeping bow of a girl chasing reviews, but the small, grateful hinge of a woman whose life had been full and complicated and whose center had just, for three blessed minutes, come into perfect focus. There was no need for an encore. She had said what she came to say.

Backstage, Evie pressed a cold ginger ale into her palm. "Breathe," she whispered, laughing and crying in the same breath. Dot fanned her with the program as though oxygen were something you could gift.

"You didn't just perform," Dot said. "You testified." She leaned close, voice a thread only the three of them could hear. "And remember, we weren't brave alone."

Later That Night

The common room softly fizzed with afterglow—programs folded and refolded, cookies disappearing at a rate that made Laura revise her spreadsheet for next year. People replayed their favorite bits: the toddler conductor, the kazoo cadenza, Harold's miraculous dental save. Staff in scrubs loitered longer than their shifts required. Someone had draped the feather boa across the baby grand like a diva asleep after curtain call.

Maggie sank into an armchair between Dot and Evie. The crimson shawl still held stage warmth. Her cheeks ached from smiling in a way that had nothing to do with posing and everything to do with release.

"Well?" Dot said, nudging. "Feels good?"

"It felt like..." Maggie searched for the word and found the right one waiting like a coat on its peg. "Like stepping back into myself."

"To second acts," Evie declared, raising her plastic cup.

"And third. And fourth," Dot added, clinking. "We're not counting anymore. We're measuring."

Maggie laughed. "Then measure this—I'm not done yet."

At the front desk, a small envelope waited, no return address. Inside, a card with a single word in a familiar cramped hand and a crooked smiley: *Electric.* A turquoise smudge marked one corner—probably from Evie's fountain pen, which had a talent for touching anything she passed across a counter.

Evie slid the pen from behind her ear and, on the corner of the program, wrote a line before she could talk herself out of it: *This time, it's mine.* She tucked the program into her bag like a promise to herself —quiet, but beginning.

The Morning After

Applause was noisy; pride was a quiet warmth under the skin. In the dining hall, forks chimed against plates, and the coffee tasted a degree braver than usual. Every few minutes, someone touched Maggie's elbow or leaned in to murmur, "You were marvelous," or "Gave me goose-bumps, you did," or simply, "Thank you." Her eggs went cold and she didn't mind.

Dot and Evie approached carrying coffee like crown jewels.

"Behold," Dot said, "the woman who made Harold ask if he could go again—after *you* this time."

Evie slid into the chair. "He said your speech deserved a better opening act than him."

Maggie shook her head, smiling. "Oh, Harold."

"Also," Evie added, "you've been requested."

"Requested?"

Dot produced a flyer the color of valentine candy, sparkly stickers clinging to the corners like confetti that refused to go home. *Manchester Meadows Spring Fling—Community Encore!* it read. *With special guest: our very own Maggie Mae.*

Maggie blinked. "You're kidding."

"Laura says you brought the house down," Evie said. "She's inviting the library, the community center, and whoever runs that Facebook group for the neighborhood. You, my dear, are our thespian-in-residence."

"I haven't acted in forty years," Maggie protested automatically, the way you protest a compliment you secretly want.

Dot waved this away. "Years are seasoning. You're perfectly spiced."

Maggie looked around at the familiar faces, the ordinary brightness of morning, the bulletin board announcing chair yoga and Wednesday bingo and—new—*Broadway Night Photos Coming Soon!* Home. Not a stage, not an auditorium, but a place that kept showing up for her. Her chest lifted in that tender way that meant the answer had already arrived.

"I think I'll do it," she said. "But perhaps with a second scene. Something lighter after all that heart-eating. We can't have Harold fainting."

"They'd faint happy," Evie replied, and they all laughed.

Later That Day — Reprise

The activity room still smelled faintly of powder and lemon. The painter's tape remained on the floor like footprints from a dance you wanted to learn. Someone had pinned blurry stills from last night to the bulletin board—Doris mid-belter's arm, Harold mid-rhyme, Maggie mid-fury, her mouth a determined line. Underneath, a bold scrawl in thick marker: *STARRING MAGGIE MAE* with three stars.

Residents trickled in as Laura clicked her pen and clapped her hands. "We're doing another one," she announced, joyful and matter-of-fact. "Shorter program, broader audience, double the snacks. If you performed last night, or if you didn't and wish you had, today's your sign."

A murmur rose, the sound of people deciding to say yes.

"Maggie," Laura said, turning to her with the kind of smile that promises partnership, not pressure, "would you consider Beatrice again?"

"I would," Maggie said. Her fingers curled as if around an invisible script. "And I'd like to workshop a second piece, if that's all right."

The cheer that went up included at least two table thumps and one jubilant kazoo.

Dot leaned close. "Feather boa?"

"Rhinestone compression socks," Evie countered. "Function and sparkle."

"I'm a practical woman," Maggie said, laughing. "We'll start with support stockings and see where the muse leads."

She looked around the room—the chairs angled into brave semicircles, the baby grand waiting, the bedsheet curtain folded back like a soft wing. Last week had been a balm, yes. But it was also a beginning.

You didn't have to leave home to step onto a stage. Sometimes, the stage came to meet you, and your friends held the curtain and your courage, and your body, older, honest, learned a new way to carry its own quiet music.

Maggie slid her shawl from her shoulders and set it over the piano bench where the light caught the red and warmed it to ember. She rested her palm on the cool wood, felt the instrument's patient hush, and smiled.

"From the top?" she asked.

"From the top," Dot agreed, claiming the chair with QUEEN duct taped on the back like a title bestowed. "And remember, find the light, not the lampshade."

Evie raised her clipboard and found her pen. "Places, people," she called, voice steady and bright. "We've got an encore to build."

Maggie took her mark on the painter's tape. Breath in. Breath out. The door she thought she'd locked years ago stood open, generous as a stage.

She stepped through.

After the crowd drifted home, quiet took the halls like a soft stage.

Evie paused at the window where her breath made a small cloud and traced a V without thinking.

The first flakes found the light and kept falling.

"Lean with it," she said—words that opened a door she'd been carrying since the winter of 1945.

31

LEAN WITH IT

JANUARY 1945 • MANCHESTER, PENNSYLVANIA

S he'd said it once, to no one and everyone: lean with it.

The hill behind Cooper Street rose like a question, steep and shining, the kind of winter-white that made your eyes water. Evie dug the toes of her boots into the packed snow and hauled her new sled up by the rope, mittens squeaking against waxed wood. The runners flashed like silver fish when the sun found them. She'd rubbed paraffin from her mother's canning shelf along the blades that morning until her arms ached and the metal sang.

"Last one up's a rotten egg!" Dot called, already halfway to the top, braids thumping the back of her coat like excited punctuation.

Maggie came after, scarf ends flapping. "I'm not an egg," she puffed, slipping two steps and laughing anyway. "I'm a lady."

Evie paused to breathe the view, the row of porches snug against the cold, coal-stove smoke writing gray lines across the pale sky. Windows wore stars: blue for service, gold for the boys who wouldn't return. Mrs. Taylor's gold star hung quiet as a folded hand. War lived in town like steam in the kitchen—present even when you couldn't see it—but up here the air felt freer, carried by pine and chimney and the faint iron tang of snow.

Her father had finished the sled on Christmas Eve, sanding in the garage with the door propped a hand's width open, cold pooling around his ankles. He'd carved her initials along the side and varnished the red slats until they glowed. When he pulled it from behind the tree, he whistled, surprised at his own work.

"You'll fly now, kiddo," he'd said, tapping the runners. "Mind the curve at the bottom. Lean with it."

Lean with it, she kept hearing. *Lean.*

At the top, Dot planted her boots wide and pointed her sled downhill like a general over a battle map. "Once around the oak and under the clothesline. And nobody hit Mr. Han's trash cans—he's saving his tin can tops for the scrap drive."

"We should be saving our noses," Maggie muttered, rubbing hers, already pink as a radish.

They worked out a system—Dot first, then Evie, then Maggie—so the grooves stayed true. Evie tested the rope, the way a rider checks reins. The runners trembled with eagerness beneath her palms.

She dropped to her knees on the slats, the wood cold and good under her. For one breath, she thought of nothing but speed. Then she shoved off.

The world rushed. Wind stitched tears into the corners of her eyes. The sled tucked into the channels the boys cut yesterday and simply flew. Houses blurred; Mrs. Taylor's porch light winked like a kind eye. Dot whooped, a bright ribbon of sound unspooling behind her. Maggie shrieked, then laughed over it. Evie leaned into the first curve, fear and joy meeting and becoming the same breath.

Halfway down, a gust shouldered her toward the cans. She remembered the tap of her father's finger and tipped her weight—hips, shoulders, chin—until the runners hissed a new line and slid the danger clean. The relief tasted like winter apples.

At the bottom she dragged a heel to brake, too late, caught Maggie broadside, and the two of them tumbled into a heap of wool and squeals, snow puffing up like thrown flour. Dot arrived a second later and flopped on top, all three girls barking laughter so loud it startled a crow from the oak.

"Your scarf ate my mouth," Maggie said into Dot's sleeve.

"My elbow's married to someone's rib," Dot reported.

"Mine," Evie said cheerfully. "He's a good husband."

They sprawled until the cold nipped through the fun like a polite reminder. Above them, the sky held the faintest ache of blue, the color of ocean maps in the school atlas and far places those blue stars made too real.

"Again?" Dot asked, snow crystals glittering on her lashes.

"Again," Evie said, and they were off, climbing, sliding, losing one mitten and finding it tucked like a shy rabbit beside the oak.

On the third run, Dot overshot the curve and toppled, legs in the air like a fallen colt. She popped up grinning. "Leaning's an art," she declared. "Watch and learn." Maggie nodded solemnly, then practiced the shift of weight at the top as if curtsying to the hill before she set off. Evie loved them for the way they tried—Dot with swagger, Maggie with care—both of them brave in their different languages.

By noon, Maggie's mother came with a thermos and buttered bread in wax paper. "Eat," she ordered, a queen bestowing crusts. "And mind yourselves around Mr. Han's cans. He's collecting every tin for the war effort."

Maggie swallowed and wiped her mouth with the back of her glove. "We steered clear. Mostly."

"Almost doesn't count," her mother replied, but she tugged a wool hat tighter over Maggie's ears, cupped Dot's cheek with a mitten, and tucked Evie's scarf just so—the way mothers do, like they're threading you back to the earth.

They ate sitting on their sleds like queens on traveling thrones, heels dug into ice, talking about nothing and everything: who might jump the creek come spring, how Mr. Han's radio read the news at night like prayer, whether rationing would end soon so you could buy sugar without counting points. A ration book lay open on Evie's kitchen table at home; the Victory Garden slept under a crimped quilt of snow.

Mrs. Taylor stepped onto her porch for a minute, arms wrapped around herself. She didn't wave, only watched the hill and the three girls on it until the tightness in her shoulders softened. Evie pretended not to see—and, in not-seeing, saw everything.

"Think the war'll be over by my birthday?" Evie asked, not expecting an answer.

Dot bumped her boot to boot. "We'll sled on your birthday anyway," she said. "Even if it's July. We'll find a hill somewhere."

"I'll make lemon ice," Maggie promised solemnly, which made them laugh because—what lemon.

They ran until their hair stuck damp to their foreheads and the wax wore soft on the runners. They ran until the sun slid behind the church steeple and the slope turned blue-shadowed and serious. For the final race Dot shouted, "Winner gets the good cup at Evie's!"—the enamel mug with the satisfying chip that made cocoa taste better—and Evie leaned so hard into the curve she felt the sled sing beneath her. She didn't win. Maggie did, by a glove's length, and Dot accused her of bribery.

Inside Evie's kitchen, the air smelled of simmer and sweet. Her mother stirred cocoa in a dented pot, a strip of saved orange peel bobbing like a lucky boat. "Boot tray," she called. "Boots, then liners, then socks. Dry them by the register or we'll all be smelling wet wool till Easter."

Evie's father came in from the garage, frozen air riding in with him like a polite dog. "How's she running?"

"Like a dream," Evie said. "She whistles on the curve."

He set three mugs on the table, the chipped enamel one last. "For the champion," he said, sliding it to Maggie, who blushed and promised to maybe consider sharing.

They stood around the table, mittens spread like sleeping birds, steam making ghosts of their faces. The radio in the front room murmured battalions and towns in a careful voice; outside, a cough cut the cold air and vanished, the way winter carries small sounds farther than it should. For half a minute everyone went quiet. Then Evie's mother set down cinnamon toast with a flourish. "Hot and sweet in this house," she said, and that felt like permission to be ten again.

Before the girls left, they pressed their hands to the front window glass and looked out at Cooper Street. Porch lights bloomed one by one like small, stubborn stars. Mrs. Taylor's was the first to come on. Dot traced a V in the fog—victory small and private and theirs.

"We weren't brave alone," one of them said. Later, none of them could remember who.

They stepped back into the crisp blue dark, the grade resting now, holding their tracks like proof.

Present Day • Manchester Meadows

The storm began like a rumor you almost didn't hear: a few soft flakes, a wind testing the building's edge. By lunch, the rumor had teeth. Snow slanted across the windows in fast, fine lines, and the pines along the fence bowed as if to let something bigger pass. Someone from Maintenance shook salt like a blessing over the front steps. The generator thumped once in the basement and settled, satisfied.

Evie watched from her chair by the radiator, hands wrapped around a mug the soft beige of aged pages. She liked how snow stitched the world quiet, how walkway, lawn, and road became one white sheet. She leaned her head against the glass for the clean cold of it and felt the ache tucked behind her eyes ease a degree.

"Storm warning till midnight," Linda from the nurses' station announced, poking her head in as if weather were a guest. "Please stay inside. Bingo in the lounge. Tomato soup at 4."

Dot hovered near the window, tracking the angle like a navigator reading current. "It's knitting," she said. "Give it an hour and it'll be a wall."

Maggie smiled at their reflection in the glass—three faces, three winters, the same patience. "Then we'll be sensible," she said. "I brought tea."

They were sensible. They were good. They were also women who hadn't lost the habit of slipping the leash when the world turned interesting.

After soup and news and the soft hour when the building breathed itself down toward evening, Dot went to help Doris with her crossword and Maggie to hunt for the good hand lotion. Evie closed her eyes just for a minute, the way you promise a child you'll be right back.

When she opened them, the window was a white square. The radiator ticked. The sound made a memory cross the room and sit in her lap like a cat.

Paraffin on the runners, kiddo.

Lean with it.

She stood slowly, testing the usual treacheries—dizziness, mischief in the knees. She found only the kind pull of an old invitation. She tucked the blanket around the chair as if it might get lonely, slid her feet into slippers that looked like shoes, and walked into the hall.

Manchester Meadows was a maze she knew by heart: left at the fern, right at the painting of the little boat, past the bulletin board with the flier that curled at the corner no matter how much tape she pressed down. The laundry room yawned, quiet but lemon-bright. At the back entrance, the electric lock chirped; the door sighed open six inches to admit a delivery cart, a rubber wedge holding it for a breath. Snow breathed against her face, cool and familiar. She eased through before it latched.

Outside, air made a quick clean noise in her chest. The storm took her and tested its teeth. The world had become a blank and, on that blank, the hill drew itself—there, past the arbor, beyond the gazebo, a little dip where the land remembered a curve. Evie walked toward it, slippers darkening, nightgown fluttering at her calves. Snow gathered on her lashes and didn't melt.

Inside, Maggie capped the lotion, uncapped it, then frowned at the clock because the minutes felt like they'd jumped a track. "Evie?" she called from the doorway, too softly at first and then louder, knowing even as she asked. The blanket folded like a person in a hurry. The window a white wall.

The intercom clicked. "Weather alert. Staff, please check common areas. Evie is away from her room. Begin internal search and secure all exterior doors."

"Not internal," Maggie said, already moving. "She's after the snow."

Dot met her at the corner, eyes telling the same story. "Protocol says wait for Security."

"We don't have protocol for Evie in this weather," Maggie said, buttoning her coat. "We go."

Dot exhaled once, then flipped to action. "Fine. Out and back. You take the arbor and gazebo. I'll sweep the shed and treeline. Call every ten paces."

Linda thrust blankets into their arms and grabbed a radio. "I'm with you. Keep me in sight. Code Snowbird." The small joke steadied everyone's hands.

The first breath of the storm hit as the door opened—a slap and a blessing. Snow moved sideways, then up, then—trick of wind—seemed to fall from ground to sky.

"Evie!" Dot called, cupping her hands like summer. The wind took half, tossed the rest back broken.

They moved as a unit. Call. Scan. Touchpoint.

"Evie, honey!" Maggie called, slipping into the voice she once used for feverish kids. Scan: hedge, gazebo, trees. Touchpoint: the bench—brushed clean by a gloved hand? No—just wind.

The wind put its shoulder into them. Maggie's left knee argued and then, loyal as ever, obeyed. Dot counted fours under her breath, one, two, three, breathe, the way she used to crossing police lines. Linda paced the path parallel, eyes combing, radio at her mouth. "South path clear... moving to the stand of pines." A trail of slipper prints appeared and disappeared, each one half-filled and shining like shallow cups.

At the edge of the trees, the air softened, tired of bullying. For a moment, the world grew visible. Maggie blinked snow freckles from her lashes and felt Dot's hand close around her sleeve.

"There," Dot said.

A figure stood in the white, slim as a thought, hair unpinned by the wind, nightgown fluttering like an old flag. She faced slightly away, head lifted the way you lift it when you're sure you heard your name from far off. Snow pearled along her collarbone. Her fingers were waxy-cold at her sides; a small tremor worked at her jaw.

"Evie," Dot called, two syllables bearing the weight of years.

Evie turned. Her eyes were clear and far at once, a trick that had lately broken Maggie's heart sideways. For one quick, naughty second she looked ten. Then she looked exactly as she was—beloved, bewildered, alive in the storm.

"I was looking for the hill," she said, surprised, as if she'd meant to think it, not say it. "Where we used to sled."

"We see it," Maggie said, slowing the way you approach a brave bird with bread in your palm. "It's here."

Dot stepped to Evie's other side and lifted a blanket around her shoulders. In the white, the red glowed like a porch light. Maggie unwound her own scarf and wrapped it, not too tight, beneath Evie's chin. "There," she said, voice practical to hide the shake. "Now, we lean together."

"It's so quiet," Evie whispered.

"It's the good kind," Maggie said. "Lean with us now."

They began together, Dot's arm a brace, Maggie's hand an anchor. The wind rose again, annoyed, then lowered its chin and harried someone else.

Halfway back, Evie said, soft as breath, "Mrs. Taylor's porch light. It came on first."

"It did," Maggie said. "Told us where the curve was."

"We leaned with it," Evie murmured. "My dad said."

"He did," Dot said. "Lean with it."

By the door a small crowd gathered, faces pinked by cold and kindness. Inside, heat felt like walking into someone's hug. Wool steamed. Glasses fogged. The lobby smelled of lemon cleaner and soup and wet coats. The head nurse didn't bark, just meant it. "Medical. Warm and check."

They didn't argue. They were women who understood protocol because they'd written many of the ones that mattered.

In the exam room, Evie let care do what care does. Warm blankets from the cabinet, soft and steady as a lullaby. Socks that were more like hugs. A thermometer that beeped too cheerfully for the occasion. Fingers gentle against her wrist, counting. A doctor with eyes kind enough to make you forgive his youth.

"Cold stress," he said. "Vitals are good. Fluids, warmth. We'll observe overnight."

Observe. The word sat, took off its hat, and stayed. Maggie wanted to bargain—we watched her for years; she watched us back—but only nodded and took Evie's hand when there was room.

Laura reappeared with the Activities cart and, as if the day had been waiting for the rhyme, set down cocoa in an enamel mug. Steam curled up like tidy handwriting.

"I saw us," Evie said at last, eyes on the middle distance where memory lives. "Cooper Street. The hill. The star in Mrs. Taylor's window. The sled you made, Daddy—"

Maggie's voice was soft as cotton. "He made it for you, Evie."

Evie nodded, untroubled. "Right. My father made it." She turned to Dot. "You were so fast. You always were."

"I'm fast at paperwork now," Dot said, managing a smile. "Less glamorous."

Maggie tightened their hands together so the warmth made a small, determined triangle. "We were there," she said. "We're here."

After the checks and the wires and the cocoa to the last undisciplined sip, the doctor said they could stay. "One visitor," he began, then saw the way Dot and Maggie hovered at Evie's sides and relented with a small smile. "You're fine. Just keep her calm."

Dot settled in first, telling Evie about the student who'd come back after years to say thank you, and about the hat she'd wear to a speech because legacy sometimes needed a prop. Evie listened with her eyes closed, smiling where Dot's voice warmed.

Then Maggie picked up the thread—Henry, a script, a speech the board wanted softened and wasn't. Evie laughed, low, like something remembered in the bones.

"Keep it harsh," Evie murmured. "Women live in that weather."

"Always," Maggie said, tucking the blanket straighter as if punctuation mattered.

When the nurses dimmed the lights to a gentler blue and the beeping things agreed to sing more quietly, Dot and Maggie stood to go.

"Do you want anything?" Dot asked. "Your little notebook?"

Evie considered. The storm had worked some ache loose; it had left the sweet tiredness that follows a good cry or a long laugh. "Bring it," she said. "I have a line."

"What line?" Maggie asked, liking to catch them before they ran.

Evie looked at them both, steady. "Lean with it."

By morning, the storm had done its old work—erasing and remaking. Plows carved new edges on the world; the sky wore a washed linen blue. From Evie's window the lawn looked like a simple page with one small, remembered rise near the arbor—hardly a hill at all until someone leaned.

Dot arrived with a notebook and a pen that wrote dark. Maggie brought cinnamon toast wrapped in a napkin that still smelled faintly of the kitchen. They stood together at the glass. Dot traced a V on the fog, and Maggie pressed her palm beside it, a quiet second signature.

"Title?" Dot asked, opening the notebook.

Evie, warm now and properly bossy, said, "Chapter thirty-one. 'Lean With It.'"

Linda, passing by with the breakfast cart, slid an enamel mug onto the tray beside Evie. "For the champion," she said.

Maggie squeezed Dot's wrist, just loud enough to be heard. "We're not brave alone." And in the soft morning after, it felt less like a reminder and more like a vow.

32

A CANDLE FOR EACH YEAR

PRESENT DAY • MANCHESTER
MEADOWS • MAGGIE

The quiet before birthdays had its own hush. It pooled in Maggie's room—the warm rise of the radiator, the faint citrus the housekeeper favored, the soft rasp of a linen handkerchief under her thumb. The handkerchief had been a gift from her mother on Maggie's wedding day, its initials and date stitched neat and small. It had outlived tears, summer colds, and Sunday purses. She liked the feel of it now, a small square of continuity.

On the wall, a life in frames: a picnic blanket so green it looked painted, two girls in sundresses with blue popsicle tongues, a man's hand at her waist as they laughed on the porch the year the hydrangeas went wild. The glass had dulled, but the moments hadn't. They lived bright behind the glaze.

Sometimes, on mornings like this, she wondered what other frames might have joined them—Wendy's arm around a husband who stayed, a child on Cindy's hip. Wendy's marriage had blown through like weather, Cindy never found someone who fit, and the grandchildren she once imagined were stories she kept quietly to herself. Life had unfolded differently than she pictured—and still, looking at her girls now, she felt nothing but fullness.

She wore the rose cardigan Wendy gave her at Christmas. You

should wear your children's gifts until the softness learns your shape. Pearls rested cool at her throat—the armor she once used to look put together when nothing else was. She checked the clock. Any minute now.

A knock. Then the sound she loved best.

"Happy birthday, Mom!" Cindy sing-songed, stepping in with daisies and eucalyptus wrapped in brown paper. Wendy followed with a lemon cake in a white box and a bottle of sparkling cider that chimed gently against her ring.

Maggie stood, which still surprised them. "If it isn't my girls," she said, as if the thought alone had kept her awake. "I must be dreaming."

"You wish." Wendy kissed her cheeks, cold-faced from outside. "We would've rented sled dogs if we had to."

Cindy cracked the curtains a hand's width and set the flowers where the light could find them. "We didn't drop everything," she said, arranging the greens. "We planned it. Months."

"Only for you," Wendy added. "Though next year I'm lobbying for a beach party."

"At my age?" Maggie laughed. "I'm not going anywhere that isn't down the hall."

The smile on Cindy's face faltered, and the real conversation slipped in. She perched on the chair arm and coaxed a loose thread back into the cardigan. "Mom... the place near us has a new memory wing. Big rooms. A garden with raised beds. We could—"

"I know," Maggie said gently. "I know you're looking out for me."

"You'd be closer," Cindy tried. "Easier for us to come on weeknights."

"Home is a muscle," Maggie said, covering her daughter's hand. "When I look out that window, I can feel every tree, every brick. The halls know my footsteps. Your father... this is where we raised you. I'm stitched to this town."

Wendy, who could spit the truth and make it taste sweet, nodded. "Stubborn," she said, affection braided through. "But I get it."

"I just want more time," Cindy whispered, shimmer starting in her eyes.

"You have me now," Maggie said, cupping her cheek. "And I have you. That's the only time that behaves."

Cindy exhaled and smiled. "Nathan will call later from the hospital," she said, brightening. "Break room willing."

"Good man," Maggie said, pride warming her voice. "I'll take his face on a screen and count it a blessing, same as a hug."

They gathered flowers, cake, and the contraband favors Wendy had smuggled in ("don't ask," she said) and walked to the common room, where birthdays at Manchester Meadows were done properly—with streamers, neighbors, and coffee strong enough to make even the quietest resident opinionated.

Pastel garlands looped the windows. A banner Wendy had trimmed by hand read *Happy 91st, Maggie!* A photo table beneath it slid from black-and-white into color as the years unspooled. Dot had claimed the chair by the glass, cardigan over cardigan, posture proud. Evie sat beside her, smaller than the butterfly brooch could explain, the pin catching light whenever she moved.

"Magpie," Dot said, smiling the smile that had anchored Maggie through storms. "Look at you."

"So many candles," Evie whispered, eyes on the cake with a bright-flecked alertness that looked ten. "We'll have to call the fire brigade."

"Don't tempt them," Dot murmured, and they all laughed.

Wendy fit nine candles, one for each decade, and pressed a shorter one just off-center. "And a spare," she said. "For luck or mischief."

"Make it a good wish," Cindy said, phone poised.

Before Maggie could answer, the lights dimmed and a tambourine jangled. A tiny parade burst in—Shirley in a feather boa, Harold in a determined blond wig, and two more residents with paper flowers pinned to their lapels. The Glee Bees were back. They sang the sunshine verse with gusto (Shirley thriving, Harold a chaotic Rose), then knocked out a two-minute *Golden Girls Gone Rogue*. The room bubbled.

Maggie dabbed at her eyes with the linen square and thought, not for the first time, that joy made the best noise.

"Your command performance," Dot said when the lights came back up, raising a paper cup. "To the woman who never did anything by halves."

Maggie found her daughters across the room, side by side the way siblings revert when home. "Even when you're not here every day," she told them softly, "I'm not alone."

"That's all we could hope for," Wendy said, pressing her temple to Maggie's for a breath.

Cindy struck a match. The sulfur bloom met the lemon icing and, together, made a scent that reached backward.

The room hushed. Flames steadied after their first brave flicker. The years laid themselves across Maggie's mind like a string of backyard lights—one for each summer party, each newborn cry, each Tuesday that ended up mattering.

She inhaled; the room said yes without speaking.

She blew.

Wax and sugar and daffodils scented the dim as the flames curled away. Smoke lifted in pale ribbons. And with that scent, the seam of her life opened kindly.

March 1947 • Manchester

Thaw and wood smoke. Twelve felt like a door you could finally reach the knob on. Her mother made lemon cake; her father wrapped a small square box and smiled like he'd trapped a star.

Inside was a gold locket, her initials etched in the tidy script he used on canning labels. She pressed the cool circle to her skin and felt it warm, her heartbeat telling it what to keep.

The war had ended but still knocked around town. Ration books slept in kitchen drawers because you never know. The radio spoke of Europe and doctrine—words that didn't belong in a seventh-grader's mouth. But birthdays outranked geopolitics.

Dot arrived first with a tin of molasses cookies, soft-centered and wise. "Old-lady cookies for your old-lady age," she teased.

Evie came next, cheeks wind-bright, clutching a parcel wrapped in newspaper. Paper dolls cut by careful hands, outfits shaded with colored pencils, a tiny dog with a red collar. "They're a little like us," she said, shy and proud. "I gave you the best dress."

They ate lemon cake on the porch and talked about movie stars and tap shoes and a new girl who swore she'd seen the Statue of Liberty up close. Hopscotch chalked the driveway; their heels clicked the rhythm of someday.

"I hope we still know each other when we're ancient," Maggie blurted, honest to the bone.

"Please," Dot said. "We'll live next door, yelling across the hedge about cats."

"And we'll tell ghost stories," Evie giggled, "and eat lemon cake every birthday."

They couldn't imagine ninety-one. They could imagine together. At twelve, that was the same thing.

Present Day

"Mom?" Wendy prompted softly, and Maggie came back to candles smoking politely, community coffee, and the way Dot's hand had found Evie's without making a production.

"No wish," Maggie said, smiling through it. "I already have it."

They cut the cake. Wendy passed plates with clockwork efficiency; Cindy refilled cups like a friendly bartender. Around them, dear ordinary stories rose and fell—great-grandchildren's new teeth, knee replacements, a night-shift nurse who'd written a poem once and wanted to know if anyone would read it.

When the party thinned to a gentle murmur, Maggie touched the blanket as if remembering something tucked away. "Cindy. Wendy." Her voice had the kind of quiet that makes a room lean in.

From a worn blue velvet pouch, she drew the locket. The initials were still crisp; the hinge gave the small sound she'd know anywhere. Two faces inside: porch-laugh Maggie in a cotton dress, and Maggie and their father mid-laugh, heads tilted toward each other like magnets remembering their work.

"I wore it when I married him, and when I met each of you," she said. "I wore it to funerals and to Sunday dinners and to the grocery store because some days you need to carry your people right at your heart."

She looked from Wendy to Cindy. "I always imagined you sharing it," she said. "Passing it back and forth the way you do everything else."

Wendy unclasped the chain and fastened it at Cindy's collarbone. "Your week," she said. "Mine next."

"I don't want it locked in a drawer," Maggie added. "Keep it where a hand can find it on hard mornings. It isn't valuable, except that it is."

Cindy laced their fingers together—hers, Wendy's, Maggie's—the locket warm between their palms. "Thank you for making a life we want to carry."

Cindy's phone buzzed. "Nathan," she said, already smiling.

He filled their corner of the screen—scrubs, hospital break room, hair trying and failing to be professional. Tired and bright, the way people look when they've been useful.

"Happy birthday, Grandma!" His good heart came through first.

"Look at you," Maggie said, hand to her chest. "Are they working you to the bone again?"

"I told them I needed five minutes for the most important woman in my life," he said, leaning closer as if he could bridge the last inch.

"I'm sorry I couldn't be there," he added.

"You're exactly where you should be," she said. "I only wanted your face, and I have it."

He swallowed. "I miss you. I wish I could hug you."

"You just did," she said, pressing her palm to her collarbone. "Right here."

They were quiet together then, the small good quiet that doesn't need tending. He promised to call after his shift; she told him to go save something worth saving. When the screen went dark, she kept looking a beat longer, as if the echo might make another picture.

"He's a good man," she said, handing the phone back. "Your father would've been impossibly proud."

Dot moved closer, lifting her paper cup. "To grandsons," she said. "And to women who remember to lean with it."

Across the room, Mrs. Han pressed a folded poem into Wendy's hand; Mr. Russo asked for two photos to mail to his sister. A birthday, and also a small town.

Later, when it was time to head back, Wendy slipped the blue velvet pouch into her cardigan pocket—"on loan," she promised.

At Maggie's door, late light slanted across the carpet the way it once slanted across High Street floorboards. Eucalyptus breathed a tired sweetness from the vase. The handkerchief lay white against the rose cardigan.

"Leave the lamp on," Maggie said when they fussed with the switch. "We've always kept one on."

Cindy kissed her forehead; Wendy pressed her cheek to Maggie's hair the way she had as a girl afraid of thunder. "Rest," Wendy said. "We'll come back after dinner to steal the last slice of cake."

"You will not," Maggie said, delighted that they would.

When the door clicked shut, she touched the place where the locket usually lay. Bare, for now. But the weight hadn't gone anywhere; it had simply shifted into other hands, other hearts, widening the circle exactly as it was meant to.

Out the window, the sky thought about rain and then changed its mind. In the dim, birthday flowers tiled the air with green and honey. Maggie closed her eyes and let the day replay: the tambourine, the candles, lemon on her tongue, faces arranged like lights on a cake— many, steady, close enough to warm.

That night, after the last goodnights, Maggie left the lamp on and smoothed the corner of the tablecloth beside the daisies. She looked at the porch-laugh photo and said, "Tomorrow," just to hear it hold.

She had asked Dot to bring her old laptop—the one with the curled *VOTE AS IF* sticker and the NAACP pin still catching on the zipper— to the common room. Maggie would pull the decade binders from her closet, along with the blue accordion file of Evie's clippings.

Tomorrow, they would meet there, let the fish tank glow, and begin —scanning, typing, setting things down one true line at a time. They would write it before anything had the chance to slip away.

With the plan breathing beside her, Maggie turned the lamp low and slept.

33

THE MEMOIR

PRESENT DAY • MANCHESTER MEADOWS

Dot hadn't opened her laptop in years. It had followed her from house to apartment to the nursing home, tucked into a nylon sleeve with a faded NAACP pin still clipped to the zipper, a traveling altar to a life she'd argued with and loved in equal measure. She wasn't sure why she'd packed it on moving day. Habit, maybe. Or hope.

Evie's laptop had blinked its last one morning, a polite little sigh before the screen went dark for good. Maggie said maybe it had earned its rest. So, when Dot's machine stuttered awake that evening, it felt right, like passing a torch between old friends.

Now it lay on the common-room table under the gentled evening lights, quiet but insistent. The sticker—VOTE AS IF—peeled at the edges, a small survivor from marches and meetings where Dot had once lent her voice. Her fingers hovered over the keys, knuckles a little swollen, tendons lifting like quiet rivers under her skin. The machine felt foreign, then familiar, like getting back on a bicycle after decades.

The day had slipped into its gentler half, all edges softened. Someone had dimmed the overheads; the fish tank glowed ocean-blue; the radiator pinged a slow rhythm. By the window, Evie dozed under a pieced quilt, lashes fluttering whenever a dream brushed by. Beside Dot,

Maggie set down a neat pile that had traveled with her through every decade: spiral notebooks labeled by year in her tidy block letters, a shoebox of index cards and church bulletins, envelopes fat with clippings and snapshots.

On the top spiral, a note in fountain-pen ink read: *ASK DOT — Billie Holiday song at The Lantern.*

Maggie tugged another box from under the table, a blue accordion file held together by a tired rubber band. She set it beside the spirals and thumbed the tabs. "These are Evie's," she said softly. "Pieces she never stopped writing. We should save every one. We should scan them, too."

Dot slipped the top page free—a column cut with pinking shears, the byline smudged where someone had traced it. For a moment, she didn't type; she read, letting Evie's cadence lift the room.

I used to think a lede had to be sharp enough to cut. Age taught me it only has to open—like a window you've been meaning to unstick. Let the air in first; the truths will follow.

"You ready?" Maggie asked, the way she had before report cards and mammograms and a hundred little thresholds. Gentle, but with a steady push.

Dot nodded, but her eyes lingered on the note—and memory, that quiet archivist, opened a drawer.

"You remember The Lantern," she murmured.

And just like that, the years loosened and folded back.

Spring of 1965. The kind of damp that made hems heavy and hair misbehave.

The Lantern sat halfway down Market Street, its yellow sign flickering the way streetlights did before storms. Inside, the air smelled of percolated coffee, wet wool, and the faint citrus of the dish soap the owner's wife preferred. Newspapers were stacked in leaning towers near the door—headlines about marches, Vietnam, the Voting Rights Act hearings—ink smudging fingers and futures.

Dot and Maggie had slipped in after a day that had taken more out of them than they meant to admit. Maggie had just come from helping her mother; Dot from a student meeting where she'd been told, kindly and not kindly, that "girls should let the boys handle the politics." Both were tired in the way only young women carrying two versions of themselves can be.

They slid into a corner booth—Maggie warming her hands around a white mug, Dot shaking the rain from her sleeves.

Someone at the counter fed a nickel into the jukebox. The first soft bars of Billie Holiday's *I'll Be Seeing You* drifted through the room—scratchy, imperfect, intimate. A song about holding on through distance, about remembering a person through ordinary things. It quieted the space the way a truth does when it knows it's been waiting its turn.

Maggie stared into her coffee, shoulders rounding under a weight she'd been pretending was a coat.

"Dot," she said, barely above the hiss of the radiator, "I don't think I can keep being the girl everyone thinks I am."

Dot felt the words inside her own chest—sharp, vulnerable, familiar.

She slipped her hand across the Formica table. "Then don't."

Maggie's eyes lifted, startled.

Dot softened her voice. "We'll figure it out. Together."

Maggie let out the smallest laugh, but her chin trembled with it. "I just— I want a life that feels like mine. Not borrowed. Not inherited."

Holiday's voice rose—the line about *'the park across the way'*—and something unclenched between them.

"You'll get it," Dot said. "And when you start losing your footing, I'll remind you."

Maggie nodded once, as if accepting a contract. Billie finished the song, and the neon sign flickered again. And for one fleeting moment both women believed the world might still widen enough to let them through.

Dot blinked the present back into place, throat thick.

"That night mattered," she said quietly. "It wasn't just a song. It was the first time you let me see the part of you that wanted more."

Maggie's smile was small, steady. "I left myself a note so you'd remember it right."

Dot pressed her thumb to the edge of the spiral, grounding herself.

"All right," she whispered. "Let's make sure she gets on the page—the girl from The Lantern who finally said what she wanted."

Dot nodded and clicked open a blank document. The screen cast a soft square of light across her face. The cursor blinked like a firefly.

Dot felt it then: permission, from her past and from the women beside her, to finally tell it true.

I was born in southcentral Pennsylvania, the only child in one of the few Black families in a small, mostly white town. It wasn't always easy. But I was lucky. I had Evie and Maggie. They didn't just stand beside me. They stood up with me. That made all the difference.

The first lines came careful, as if pried loose with a butter knife. Then the well unsealed—measured, deliberate, true.

She wrote the rules that lived in grocery aisles and church pews, how her mother said pride like a password, how her father's shoulders squared at payday when a foreman looked past him toward a man with fewer years and more pay. She wrote laughter too: sled tracks carving Cooper Street, hopscotch knees bruised in a constellation, grape popsicles turning tongues royal, secrets traded behind the church where the ground held summer heat till midnight.

She typed the South—her grandfather's Georgia stories, red clay under nails that never scrubbed clean; humidity like a second skin; hymn lines braided with the news; the first time a chant rose from her ribs and she recognized it as her own. She typed Clara's name, first love, great love. She typed it again, letting the letters hold their weight: the sit-ins and the training and the Ebenezer Baptist Church basement in Atlanta where they learned not to flinch when hatred practiced its aim; the courthouse steps, fingers laced, a quiet rebellion that still lived in her bones.

She paused. Across the room, Evie turned her face toward the rhythm of keys. Dot's throat tightened. What would Evie keep? What would memory set down because it had run out of hands?

She turned back to the screen.

I marched because I believed we could be better. I taught so the next generation would know where they came from and where they could go. I stayed because I had a story to tell, and no one else could tell it for me.

She wrote the classroom—the boy who slept through first period because he worked nights; the girl who needed someone to say *scientist* out loud; the day she scraped the textbook timeline off the wall and rebuilt it with names her students brought from their own kitchens. She wrote loss—the season she and Clara unspooled, grief growing like a second spine inside her, unbending and always present.

Then she wrote friendship.

Maggie, who didn't move when storms did, the anchor with the porch light. Evie, fierce and defiant even now, even in forgetting, the spark that made kindling catch. Their story had stretched across decades: war and joy, letters and lemon cake and hard winters. Sitting here, Dot understood that what lived in these pages wasn't just a memoir. It was a record. A map. A legacy.

The keys drew her toward the moment she knew who they were to one another—and why.

1947 • Manchester, Pennsylvania

Thirteen. Late afternoon. Air syrupy and slow. Dot walked down Maple Street past the cemetery, shoes whispering against pavement, carrying the tune that curled out of Jake's Store radio all morning—Billie Holiday's *I'll Look Around*, velvet and ache, the sound of a girl beginning to understand herself.

"Hey, girl! Don't you know you're on the wrong side of town?"

Voices. Boys. Three of them, sleeves rolled, the grease from the garage slicking their hair and their smirks.

Dot kept walking. She'd learned the rule: don't give trouble teeth.

A shadow slid in front of her. "I'm talkin' to you."

"I'm headed home." She pitched her voice flat and even, eyes on the crack where the sidewalk heaved around a tree root.

A hand snatched the paper sack from under her arm—bread for supper—and shook it like a prize. "What's in here? Little miss servant girl running errands?"

"Give it back," she said, reaching, palm open.

"What's it worth?"

The shove wasn't hard—playful, almost—but it was meant to humiliate. Her heel caught the raised seam of concrete; her shoulder pinched; laughter cracked the hot air.

Fear flashed. Fury followed, hotter. A thousand words crowded her tongue and none were safe to spend alone.

"Hey!"

The word cut the street in two. Dot's head snapped up.

Maggie barreled from the corner, red pigtails flying, face the color of late tomatoes. Right behind, small and bright and dangerous, came Evie.

"What do you think you're doing?" Maggie said, planting herself between Dot and the boys like a brick wall with a pulse.

The tall one smirked. "Look. Little white girls come to fetch their pet."

Evie didn't flinch. She stepped in and shoved him square in the chest with the heel of her hand, just enough to pop his balance. "Funny," she said, eyes like ice water, "you talk real big for somebody hiding behind two other idiots."

For a breath, nobody moved.

"She's not a pet," Evie said, voice level and clean. "She's our friend. You've got about five seconds to figure out what that means."

Dot moved to stand shoulder to shoulder. Maggie crossed her arms, chin up like every mother she'd ever seen say no to a salesman.

The boys shifted, confused by this math: three girls, no fear, a whole town watching from behind curtains you couldn't see.

"Whatever," the tall one muttered, hands up in boredom that didn't quite fit his face. He thrust the paper sack toward Dot. "Not worth it."

They slouched off, practicing how not to run.

Silence rushed back. Dot steadied the bread with both hands and let the adrenaline shake through her like a summer storm moving off. Relief loosened her knees; gratitude did the rest.

"I can't believe you said that," Maggie whispered, half-scold, half-wonder, fists still curled.

"I can't believe I hit him," Evie said, grinning. "Did you see his face?"

"That was the dumbest and bravest thing I've ever seen," Dot said, the laugh breaking free.

"You could've gotten hurt," Maggie added, softer now, pride threaded in.

Evie shrugged her hair aside. "Some things are worth the risk."

Dot looked at both of them and felt something slide into place, a key turning. "You stood up for me."

Evie took her hand and squeezed. "We stand up for each other. That's the deal, right?"

"Right," Dot said. And because the street felt like church, she meant it like a vow.

It wasn't easy, the three of them. Manchester liked neat categories; they weren't neat. A Black girl walking with two white girls turned heads, raised eyebrows, set whispers rolling like tumbleweeds. But in their little republic, skin didn't divide. It braided. It made them hold on tighter.

When Dot got home, her mother checked the loaf for crushed slices, then checked Dot for bruises she didn't name.

Dot cried then for the first time in front of them. Not from sadness, from gratitude. She understood they weren't just friends. They were her people. Sisters by choice. And whatever the world threw, they'd lean together into the curve.

Present Day

By the time Dot lifted her hands from the keyboard, the fish tank had gone dark and the hall nightlights had clicked on, casting small amber moons on the floor. Maggie read slowly from the fresh pages, mouth shaping Dot's sentences as if tasting them. She paused to add a date, a storefront, a teacher's name. They quilted memory, Dot laying down the center pieces, Maggie choosing the border and the binding.

Evie's eyes opened to slits. "Dot?" she whispered.

Dot swiveled. "I'm here, Evie."

"I remember us," Evie said, and the three words made the room pull its breath in. "Do you?"

Dot leaned close. "I remember everything."

Evie smiled, small and sure. "You told the stories. Made them real."

"You made them fun," Dot said, laughing softly. "I just wrote fast enough to keep up."

"Don't forget," Evie murmured. "They matter."

"I won't," Dot promised. "I'll carry them where I can't lose them."

What began as one long evening became a ritual. After supper, Maggie wheeled out her decade binders like beloved cookbooks: the marbled black for the sixties, green for the fifties, a sun-faded red for the seventies. A shoebox labeled *Receipts / Church bulletins / misc.* rattled with paperclips and memory.

Linda from the nurses' station arrived with tea and a battered flash drive, *EVIE_CLIPS* scrawled across the plastic in Sharpie. A volunteer from Activities taped a sign to the door—Quiet Hours for Greatness— because she liked to make everything sound bigger.

Dot spoke; Maggie organized. Sometimes Dot typed, sometimes Maggie did, her fingers moving with the practiced economy of a woman who had kept minutes for PTA and choir and grief groups, who had written dates in the margins so faithfully that decades later they still led you right back to the day. When Dot's voice went quiet, Maggie filled the silence with something she'd scribbled on the back of a grocery list in 1991: *ask Dot re: Ella Mae quote.*

On the desktop, Maggie built a folder: *Victory_Club_WORKING.* Inside it, subfolders by decade. She slipped scanned photos into place and named files the way future readers would thank her for: *1947_Bread_Bag_Incident, 1963_March_Hat, 1978_Clara_Letters.* She added a simple document called *Glossary_people_places* because she'd learned across a lifetime that clarity is a kindness.

Then she made a second folder, *EVIE_SOURCE,* and slid scans in one by one: *1979_Paris_Window, 1992_Ashford_Speech_Draft, Undated_The_Things_We_Carry_to_the_Polls.* Evie had always written like tomorrow might need proof.

Dot paused over a paragraph and tapped the screen. "Bracket that. [Find exact hymn line.] It'll be in the shoebox with the green rubber band."

Maggie typed the bracket and, in the header, added *DRAFT—bring 1968 notes tomorrow.* She didn't even flirt with the words *The End.* She never had. The habit of her life was *to be continued.*

On the fifth night, Maggie set a page down but kept her palm on it as if steadying a picture frame. "We should publish yours with Evie's," she said quietly. "Side by side. Her wonder, your fire. Together you tell the whole truth."

Dot stared, unnerved by how right it sounded. For years, she'd written to survive—a private practice, like prayer or physical therapy. "I never thought anyone would want to read about me."

"Then it's overdue," Evie said from the quilt, eyes closed, voice thin but steady. She lifted her hand toward them and left it there until Dot took it.

Dot opened a new document, the title line waiting. "*The Victory Club: Two Voices and a Lifelong Chorus,*" she read aloud, then added beneath it, *by Dot and Evie, with Maggie keeping us honest.*

"You know," Dot said, turning to her, "you've been writing this with me the whole time. Every margin note. Every date. This is your book, too."

"I just kept track," Maggie said, eyes bright.

"Exactly," Dot said. "You kept track when the world didn't."

From the quilt, Evie's voice drifted clear as a bell. "We weren't brave alone."

All three looked up. The line hung there like thread pulled through fabric, making the whole stronger.

Linda turned the desk lamp to its brightest setting and left them to their papers. Outside, night stacked neatly against the glass. Inside, the soft clack of keys began again—the sound of three lives being stitched into something that could be carried forward.

When they finally stopped, they left the lamp on, the way they always had. On the top spiral, the sticky note waited—*Tomorrow: 1968 / Start with the hat*—and the cursor on the screen blinked, patient and bright, keeping time until the next hour when they would lean back in and take up the thread again.

Outside, the first leaves loosened and skittered across the courtyard paths—telling the truth the way trees do when a season decides it's time to turn.

34

THE UNRAVELING

PRESENT DAY • MANCHESTER MEADOWS

The leaves had begun their quiet surrender, skimming rust and gold across the courtyard paths and settling in the corners of benches like half-forgotten letters. Autumn had always been Evie's favorite season. She called it the honest one, when the trees stop pretending and tell the truth.

This year, autumn felt like a thief. Victory_Club_WORKING still glowed on Dot's laptop, waiting on the common-room sideboard. Some evenings, Evie added a line; some evenings Maggie simply closed the lid and smoothed a sticky note that read *Tomorrow,* as if that small promise could hold the light in place.

It started as slips that passed for ordinary: glasses lost while hanging from the chain around her neck; a pause mid-sentence, as if a word had ducked behind a curtain and refused to come back out; a name that once arrived without knocking and now lingered on the porch. Once she called Maggie "Mama." Another day, she asked the young maintenance tech if he still planned to filibuster the fair housing bill, because in her mind, just for a moment, he was the long-dead senator she had once cornered in a lobby with nothing but a notepad, a pen, and the audacity of a woman who expected an answer.

Residents had dimmed before, newsroom lights turning off one by one, but when it was Evie, the quiet felt deeper. She'd never had children and never regretted it; her life had been crowded with other sons and daughters: stories she raised into the light, questions she nursed until they learned to stand, truths she refused to put down. Dot liked to say Evie arrived on Earth with a deadline and a byline. Beneath the edge that made officials sweat was a tenderness for the small ache in other people's lives. Evie listened so fiercely that even pauses gave themselves away.

Dot could still feel the weight of the first time Evie printed her words, a column blistering the school board for refusing to fund Black history curriculum. Dot had wavered, not for lack of conviction but because she knew what attention could cost. Evie had looked at her evenly.

"If you don't say it, Dot," she said, "they'll pretend it never happened."

And Maggie, gentle, grounding Maggie, had been there the whole way, the porch light that never blinked, reminding Evie to eat, to sleep, to wear her scarf when she chased a story in January. Maggie clipped every one of Evie's pieces, sliding them into albums the way other people tucked away baby shoes. It wasn't journalism to the three of them. It was testimony. Resistance. Memory with edges you could feel.

Now, the remembering unraveled.

Most mornings, Maggie knitted at Evie's side, slow, steady rows on a scarf she knew would never be worn but kept her hands from breaking while her heart did. Dot came with a thin stack of poems and a new pair of readers she insisted she didn't need. When Evie's restlessness rose, Dot read aloud until the rhythm of another person's lines made a shelter. Sometimes, she only named the first five words of the old villanelle about not going gentle; the sound alone could coax Evie back toward shore.

"She's still in there," Maggie said, not looking away. "Just drifting further out."

"Not all the way," Dot answered, determined and practical in the same breath. "Not yet."

Because there were hours, glorious, infuriating hours, when the fog sheared off and Evie walked back through, quick and precise. One night, she phoned Dot in a panic to ask if the ERA column had cleared copy.

"They'll bury it on page six if we don't hold the line," she said, sharp as a typewriter bell. Before Dot could answer, Evie added, almost laughing, "Ask better follow-ups. The first answer's just a handshake."

Another morning, she insisted Maggie find her typewriter because she had one last truth to tell before they tucked her in the classifieds. Maggie set her phone to record and placed it where Evie could see the red light. Evie dictated a paragraph about the difference between scandal and harm, stopped midstream, winked toward the mic, and said simply, "Deadline."

They saved the voice file in the working folder because that's what they did, Maggie and Dot, the archivists of a life. They kept notes the way they always had: names, dates, the edges of stories; labels on manila tabs; a fresh Post-it labeled *EVIE—press ethics, one last truth* anchored to Dot's laptop. Another sticky, underlined twice—*Archives: audio clip, byline wall, press soundtrack*—sat on top of a folder in her bag.

The staff learned Evie's weather. Jen from the nurses' station carried peppermint tea for the afternoons when Evie paced the hall looking for the city desk. Shirley from the Glee Bees hummed standards until Evie nodded yes to the piano that now lived only in her hands. Laura from Activities printed a few of Evie's columns and tacked them to the bulletin board beneath the calendar. Residents stopped to read and murmured *I remember that, soft as* prayer.

The courtyard became Evie's barometer. On good days, she pointed out the tight hoops of squirrel nests and gave them nicknames. On the other days, she stared past the maple toward something only she could see and asked, "What time do we put the paper to bed?" When the wind tossed leaves in little spirals, she said, pleased, "They're running with the story."

They tried music. They tried silence. They tried the newsroom sounds Dot found online: the clatter of typebars, the bell at the end of a line, the exhale of a press starting up. The audio made other residents roll their eyes. It made Evie settle. "There," she'd whisper, eyes closed. "Truth getting printed."

On a bright afternoon, Maggie wheeled her onto the patio. The maple shed its costume in perfect sequins. Evie reached for a leaf and missed twice before Dot folded one into her palm.

"The trees are telling the truth again," Evie said, satisfied. She turned the leaf over, traced the veins, then looked up so suddenly both women stilled.

"Don't let them flatten us into good intentions," she said, voice clean and startling as a bell. "We had opinions."

"We still do," Dot said.

"Write them down," Evie told them. "Don't wait for permission."

They were never sure what stuck and what slid away, so they wrote everything down. The notebook in Maggie's bag grew fat. She titled a fresh page *Evie says* and dated it.

That evening, confusion gathered in small cruelties. Evie called for an old editor, certain he was just down the hall, waiting on copy. She fussed at invisible margins and asked Dot to move the Graf Four about violence prevention because "burying it will cost someone something." Maggie smoothed the blanket and, when Evie's breath hitched, matched her own to it, steady, steady, while Dot read snippets from the old 1963 issue of *Life* with Evie's byline splitting a two-page spread. The caption's ink had long gone soft, but the words still burned.

"You were brilliant," Dot said. No need to pretend objectivity when love was the truth.

Evie's eyelids heavy, she managed the smallest shrug. "Deadline," she breathed. "Write fast. Fix slow."

On a day that smelled like rain, Evie mistook the elevator for court-house steps and the exit alarm for the chant of a crowd that wasn't there. Maggie and Dot moved with her, two flanks turning the hallway into a march route. When a nurse tried to usher them back, Dot said, "Give us five. She's crossing the bridge." The nurse nodded; she had learned their metaphors.

Later, they met with the doctor in a small office that felt gentler than anyone expected. No machines. No noble speeches. Just a calm explanation of comfort and choices. "We can keep chasing," he said, "or we can shape the days."

"Shape them," Maggie said, because she had shaped days all her life —family schedules and condolence meals and the quiet ways women hold a community upright. Dot squeezed her hand under the table.

"Comfort care," the doctor said. "Radio, soft light, familiar work."

They set a bedside radio to the station that still read the news at the top of the hour. They asked for a soft lamp and a notepad and a pencil that wouldn't skid. They made a list titled *Good Hours* and promised to meet Evie there as often as life allowed.

Sometimes, all three of them were whole again for a breath long enough to laugh. Once, Evie pointed at Shirley's feather boa hanging on the Activities coat tree and said, stern as ever, "Off the record." They laughed until the aide in the doorway laughed too, not knowing why.

One night, the top-of-the-hour chime sounded from the radio, then hushed itself, as if it knew. Evie's face, which had never learned to lie, grew very calm. She took a breath, then another. Then the pause between them widened, widened, and didn't close.

It was morning by the time the light climbed the wall. It came soft, like benediction. Dot rose and pressed her lips to Evie's forehead, the gesture automatic and ancient. Maggie set her palm on the back of Evie's hand and smoothed across the knuckles the way she had once soothed children from fever into sleep.

"She's gone," Maggie said, and the words didn't crash. They landed like pebbles in still water, circles widening long after the surface stilled.

Nurse Jen came and pressed their shoulders and did her quiet professional tasks with a reverence that made Dot want to bless her. Shirley stood in the doorway with her boa bunched like a bouquet and, for once, said nothing. Someone brought a small vase and put two maple leaves and a sprig of eucalyptus into it because beauty doesn't ask for permission. It just shows up.

There were forms to sign and phone calls to make and a pause to let tears do what tears do. But there was also this: Maggie pulled the working folder from her bag and set it on the nightstand. She added a fresh sticky to the top labeled *Evie—obituary (no euphemisms), celebration plan* and tapped the Archives note beneath. Dot uncapped her pen and, instead of a prayer, wrote the line Evie had offered them like a thesis: *Ask better follow-ups. The first answer's just a handshake.* Under it, she wrote the one that belonged to all three: *We weren't brave alone.*

They didn't speak of finishing. They spoke of carrying. Of albums kept like sacrament. Of a byline wall and a small exhibit in the library meeting room with the poor overhead lighting but the good, patient people. Of a reading where residents and staff would stand and lend their voices to Evie's, paragraphs passed hand to hand like bread.

In the common room the laptop waited, lid closed, sticky notes standing like little flags. Maggie opened it. The working folder blinked awake. She created a new file titled *For Evie — Not an Ending*. Dot typed the first line: *We weren't brave alone.* Then the second: *Start with the trees telling the truth.*

"What do we write next?" Maggie asked.

"The story of the woman who asked better questions," Dot said. "Then the story of the women who kept the lamp on."

"And tomorrow?" Maggie asked, because asking about tomorrow is how you live through today.

"Tomorrow we plan the reading," Dot said, steady now. "We start with the trees telling the truth."

They stood. Maggie slid a last sticky onto the top notebook labeled *SERVICE / STORIES—assign readers* and pressed the page down the way she always did, as if sealing an envelope for a dear friend. Dot turned back toward Room 219 and, without deciding to, spoke into the air.

"File to follow, Evie," she said. "We'll put it to bed."

And for the first time, they meant it without her—and because of her.

35

THE LAST LIGHT: THE SERVICE
PRESENT DAY • MANCHESTER MEADOWS

They slept an hour at most. By morning, the courtyard was rinsed in thin, faithful gold. From her chair by the window, Maggie watched the light find the zinnias first, then the bench, then the flagstones the groundskeeper had swept clean.

Outside, the trees held the last of their color, a rust and amber hush before winter. Inside her, something shifted and refused to settle: grief, yes, and a tender relief she didn't quite trust. Free, a part of her thought —free of confusion, free of the hunt for missing words. Relief didn't cancel ache.

Their lives had grown right up through each other like lilacs through a fence. Losing Evie felt less like something taken and more like a room inside herself going quiet.

Across from her, Dot sat tucked into the armchair, a stack balanced across her knees: the green spiral labeled '50s, the marbled '60s, a sun-faded red '70s, Linda's flash drive with the drawn-on smiley, and a manila envelope printed in Maggie's block letters: For Service / Readings & Photos. No finished manuscript. Not by design. What they had was a living archive—chapters, notes, Evie's voice file, margins full of arrows and questions.

The staff worked quietly around them: Shirley from the Glee Bees hung a small banner that read *For Evie* in the neat script she used for birthday posters, Linda set a lamp on the piano and clicked it to a warm low, and Laura pinned copies of Evie's columns to a corkboard and tucked eucalyptus around the edges because Maggie had said Evie liked the smell.

On the sideboard, Dot's laptop waited with *Victory_Club_-WORKING* open and a fresh sticky marked *Program / order* flagging the corner. Maggie carried in the Archives folder from last night—audio, byline wall, press soundtrack—and laid it beside the laptop.

Wendy and Cindy slipped in with a box of lemon bars, powdered sugar dusting their sleeves like first snow. Luis from maintenance wheeled in the old speaker he'd rescued from storage and introduced it as "Eleanor." He wiped the mic with a careful hand. "Candace still works," he said proudly, giving the cord a little tap. The sound that followed was clean, bright, and steady.

"She would've loved the fuss," Dot said, stroking a thumb across a framed beach photo of the three of them at fifteen. "Then she would've made us cut half of it for clarity."

"With cake," Maggie said.

"Always cake."

A soft knock. Mrs. Horn stepped in. "It's almost time," she said. "We'll start seating in ten."

"We're ready," Maggie answered.

The Service

The common room filled like a letters page: colleagues, neighbors, orderlies in scrubs, the night nurse in street clothes, a former city editor with a tie that remembered better days, residents with canes and gentle opinions, Wendy and Cindy on either side of their mother. Nathan had wanted to come, but his ER schedule couldn't be shifted. He'd sent flowers instead, yellow chrysanthemums with a note that read, *Ask better follow-ups.*

Kris, who had left the home a year earlier, slipped quietly into a chair near the front. She'd been the one who turned the courtyard into a beach day, and she couldn't imagine not being here.

At the front, a simple podium, flowers tucked into mason jars, a byline wall made of cork and string where columns fanned like a flock. Next to the podium, one candle. On the piano, the little lamp—the one that made any room look like a kind hand.

Linda welcomed them and, at Maggie's request, pressed play on thirty seconds of newsroom sound: type bars, a bell, the steady exhale of a press coming to life. The air changed.

Maggie rose first. Her heart wrestled her chest, but her steps were steady. She hadn't written a speech, only notes, and even those she tucked under her palm as if to keep them from misbehaving.

"Evie was one of the most remarkable women I've ever known," she said. "She was fierce and unapologetically honest. She asked better questions. When doors didn't open, she leaned with the hinge."

A small laugh moved through the room.

"But she wasn't just a journalist," Maggie added. "She was a keeper of us. She believed stories, truthfully told, keep people alive." She glanced at the byline wall and felt steadier. "I'll remember the laughter. The lemon bars she insisted were breakfast. The way she made everything feel possible—especially on days that weren't."

Maggie sat. Dot stood with the green spiral open and one of Evie's columns tucked inside like a pressed leaf.

"Evie always said the truth doesn't die. It just ages," Dot began. "This"—she lifted the column—"was the first time she printed my words. School board meeting. Curriculum fight. I was scared. She looked at me and said, 'If you don't say it, Dot, they'll pretend it never happened.' So I said it. She printed it. People argued. Good. Democracy made noise that day."

She set the column down and read a paragraph from *1963_-March_Hat*—pinning the hat in place before the march because "you can't make good trouble if you're fixing your hair." Laughter again, the kind that heals.

Linda spoke about "the city desk" Evie invented at the nurses' station every afternoon at three. A high-school teacher said Evie's columns had stocked her classroom library when budgets didn't. Shirley from the Glee Bees, boa modest for once, sang a verse of *I'll Be Seeing You* and didn't push the high note.

Then Kris stood. "I only worked here a few years," she said, hands clasped like she wasn't sure where to rest them. "But I'll never forget the afternoon we turned the courtyard into a beach for her. Towels for sand, lemonade for sea. She called it the best deadline she ever made."

Soft laughter rippled through the room.

"She taught me to listen better," Kris added. "Not just to what people said, but to what they meant. Every day since, I've tried to do that. She made this place feel like living, not waiting."

For the last reading, Maggie returned to the podium and opened the manila envelope. "From our working notes," she said, "filed under *Evie says.*" She read two lines:

"Ask better follow-ups. The first answer's just a handshake. Don't let them flatten us into good intentions. We had opinions."

"Amen," someone said softly.

Linda lit the candle. They stood quiet enough to hear the aquarium motor hum. The flame made a small bright circle; its light walked out across faces like ripples, circles widening long after the surface stilled. On the program, under *Song,* someone had typed *The Trees Tell the Truth,* their private joke now public, and Shirley led them in a low hum that sounded like wind through leaves.

The room didn't feel empty when it thinned. It felt well used.

36

NOT AN ENDING

PRESENT DAY • MANCHESTER MEADOWS

Days folded in on themselves the way they do after a funeral: quiet, then busy, then quiet again. Grief hung like a cardigan on the back of a chair—there when needed, too warm when not. Maggie and Dot did what they had always done when life got loud or blank: they met at the little table by the window and worked.

They didn't talk about finishing a book. They talked about continuing a record. Maggie unpacked the archive: notebooks by decade, stacks of notes, a nylon pouch of flash drives. She added a fresh sticky to the laptop's edge: *For Evie — Not an Ending.* Under it:

Byline wall → library exhibit

Community reading: assign paragraphs

Audio: press track

"Feels right," Maggie said, typing the day's to-dos into the working folder. She wore her rose cardigan. Cindy had the locket this week; she'd fasten it at breakfast, then called Wendy to report it had warmed by the second cup of coffee and felt like company settling in.

Dot opened a document titled *VC_outline*, then minimized it. "We start smaller," she said. "An essay. A selection. Let the story arrive in rooms before it arrives in bookstores."

Maggie nodded, relief easing her shoulders. "A reading at the library," she said. "Laura can wrangle chairs."

"And the weekly," Dot added. "A profile, not a eulogy. They can run the column reprint in the center spread."

They spread the notes and stitched them, same as they'd been doing for months: Evie's quotes, places to verify, Maggie's bracketed bread-crumbs—[check ration book in archives], [find hymn line]. When the ache swelled, they let it. When it ebbed, they worked.

Wendy called that afternoon—voice bright with purpose even from states away. "What about a scholarship?" she said. "Something small in her name for a student who asks better questions."

Dot's eyes warmed. "The Ask Better Questions Award," she said. "A line item in courage."

By Thursday afternoon, Laura appeared in the doorway, a clipboard tucked under her arm. "All right," she said, breathless with purpose. "I've contacted the library—they're thrilled to host a reading. I'll set up the fund page tonight, and a sign-up sheet for the event. And don't worry about equipment—Activities has a mic we can spare."

That afternoon, while Maggie drafted the library program (plain, exact), Dot stared at an open email window. Asking had never been her favorite verb. Evie had trained her out of pride more than once.

"I need a hand," she said.

"From whom?" Maggie asked.

"Ellen Navarro," Dot said, surprised by the name's certainty. "Senior-year seminar. Smart. Patient with other people's drafts. She's in publishing now—small press, big taste."

Maggie smiled. "Find her."

Dot wrote, deleting only twice:

Subject: A project that has your fingerprints on it, whether you know it or not

Dear Ellen,

It's been too long. I'm writing with something close to the bone. My oldest friends and I have been assembling a book—working title The Victory Club. It's about a friendship that spanned a lifetime, and the work, losses, and good trouble inside it.

We don't have a finished manuscript by design; we're keeping an

archive that breathes. Would you advise us on next steps (essay placement, proposal, excerpt)? If it's not your lane anymore, point me to someone you trust.

With affection and hope,

Dot (Professor Carter if your inbox still thinks in formality)

She hit send and expected to wait a week. Thirty-eight minutes later, the little bell dinged.

Subject: Re: A project that has your fingerprints on it

Professor Dot,

I remember everything—your class, your stories, the way you wrote dates like anchors. I'm so sorry about Evie; I used to read her column in the library after school.

I'd be honored to help. Start with three sample chapters plus an outline and a short note about the library reading. If you like, we can place an excerpt first to build the conversation.

I'll clear my Friday 3 p.m. for a call.

With respect,

Ellen

"She remembers," Dot said, more to herself than to Maggie.

"What does she suggest?"

"Exactly what we can do," Dot answered. "Not a book-shaped promise, but a path."

They printed Ellen's email and slid it into the manila folder labeled *External — Help.* Maggie added a sticky: *Friday 3 p.m. — phone room.* She also wrote, because it soothed her, *Lemon bars,* and underlined it twice.

As afternoon softened toward evening, the building took its breath. Residents drifted to dinner; a cart rattled past with soup bowls and spoons; somewhere down the hall a television argued with the weather. Maggie and Dot kept the table light on. They read the passage Evie had dictated—the one about scandal versus harm—and chose a paragraph to close the library program. On the back of the program, under *Call & Response,* they rehearsed:

Reader: Who kept the lamp on?

All: We weren't brave alone.

When they finally stood, Maggie tucked the recipe card into her cardigan pocket, as if remembrance needed choreography. At the doorway she paused at the laptop—the cursor blinking, steady as a porch light left on for someone expected home.

"Tomorrow," she said.

"Tomorrow," Dot echoed.

They left the lamp on. They always had.

EPILOGUE

FULL CIRCLE • MAGGIE

I click on the lamp, the same one Dot and I used at the window table, and the room gentles. I tap my phone and let thirty seconds of press-room clatter play into the quiet: the bell at the end of a line, the steady breath of a machine finding its work. When the sound fades, lemon and old paper lift from the notebook as I open it. Memory doesn't knock; it simply sits down.

A year has passed since the exhibit, the evening of cherry petals and borrowed light, the listening station and the crooked press passes, and six months since Dot slipped into sleep the way strong swimmers slip into water, without splash or fear. I read to her until her breathing softened, kissed her forehead, and left the lamp on. Morning found the room still and peaceful. Free, I thought, gratitude that didn't cancel ache.

The book followed, stitched from notebooks and margins, living and unfinished by design. The library keeps a waiting list tacked to the desk with a thumbtack that squeaks when you turn it. The Ask Better Questions Scholarship sent its first small check to a girl who interviewed her city council with a borrowed pen and a brave chin.

Their laughter lives in the common room anyhow—Evie's quick edge, Dot's warm thunder—caught in the eucalyptus jar and the stack of clippings on the shelf. On the table sits the hardcover (the good kind, with a ribbon) and beside it a letter addressed in round, careful printing I recognize at once: the little girl from opening night with the earnest question, *Have you been friends forever?*—who turned a school assignment into a bright, stubborn thing called *The Victory Diaries.*

With help from her teacher and her great-aunt Laura, Cassie made a site for stories from women who remember, told the way they want. The categories make me smile: *Ask Better Questions, Recipes & Resistance, We Weren't Brave Alone, Make the City Desk.* She's interviewed me three times now, arriving with a pencil sharpened to ambition and a list that always begins with *What did you wish you'd known?*

I unfold the newest letter.

Dear Ms. Maggie,

I read where Ms. Evie says "don't wait for permission." I asked my principal if I can run a lunchtime Victory Diaries and she said yes (I think she would have even if I forgot to ask).

Also, my Nana has a ration book. We're going to write about it.

Love, Cassie

P.S. Is it true you fixed a dress with safety pins and still went to the dance? Because that sounds brave and kind of awesome.

I laugh, then feel the warmth behind it, gratitude not grief. The thread hasn't broken. It has simply passed hands. I picture Cassie at a library table with a lamp and a list, passing lemon cookies on napkins, a little city desk blooming at the edge of sixth grade.

Later, walking the hall, I pause at the framed clipping the staff mounted: *Three Residents Tell the Truth.* Someone has tucked a pressed cherry blossom under the corner of the glass. The pink has held.

In the activity room, the air is dust-sweet, pages whispering in their shelves. I sit and open the notebook that was once Evie's. Many pages are gone now, torn out, scanned, given away to be held in other hands. A few remain. Blank. Patient as a shoreline.

I touch the locket at my throat, on loan from Cindy this week; Wendy will wear it next. The schedule comforts me, the way recipes and appointment cards always have, continuity disguised as paper. Outside the window, the maple lifts its young leaves. The trees tell the truth, Evie would say.

Today they say: keep going.

I set my pen to the first clean line. Not for myself. For the next girl who might wonder how to be brave in a world that prefers you quiet. I print the date in my neat block letters, dates are anchors, and write:

We weren't brave alone.

I keep going about lending out a locket and a recipe card, about asking the better question, about how sometimes the kindest thing is to leave (space reserved for future notes). I write until the light thins and the lamp's circle grows cozier, until the copy bell on my phone chimes the end of a line and reminds me to breathe.

On my way back to my room, I stop at the cork board where notices gather like neighbors. I pin a small card in my tidy hand:

Community Story Hour — Tuesday at 3

A table, a lamp, a list.

Bring a name, a date, and something you remember.

At my door, I reach for the switch and don't. I leave the lamp on. I always have.

"The truth shapes us," Evie wrote once, ink steady on a page now under glass. "Even when we forget it, it remembers us."

Because three women dared to remember and kept the light steady, truth has new hands. And somewhere across town, a girl opens her notebook and begins. She doesn't wait for permission.

We weren't brave alone.

The light keeps its promise.

AUTHOR'S NOTE

Dear Reader,

Thank you for bringing *The Victory Club* into your life. I imagine a small circle of lamplight, a cup cooling beside you, maybe a cherry petal still clinging to your sleeve. That's where this story began for me—a table, a lamp, a list, and three girls who grew into women determined to keep the truth alive.

When I first met Evie, Dot, and Maggie, they were sketches at the edge of hearing. Writing pulled them into the chair beside me: Evie, quick as the bell at the end of a line; Dot, steady and brave, always asking the better question; and Maggie, the keeper of notes and hearts alike. I didn't expect to love them like this. Even off the page, I could still hear them—wisecracks, courage, and comfort braided together.

They taught me more than any outline could: that friendship is a kind of infrastructure. That small, faithful acts—labeling a photo, saving a recipe card, leaving the lamp on—are how we honor who we love. And that stories, told truthfully, don't end. They keep working in us.

While writing this book, I thought often about my own circle—the friends who have carried me through laughter and loss, and the ones I've had to say goodbye to far too soon. I wrote through grief, and somewhere along the way, it softened into gratitude. The act of remembering became its own kind of prayer. Every scene, every detail, felt like a way of keeping someone's light from going out.

Their love lives quietly in these pages, and maybe in the pages you've just turned. *The Victory Club* became a love letter—to friendship that endures, to family that shapes us, and to the small, ordinary kindnesses that keep us stitched to one another.

I'm grateful to the real-world keepers of memory who inspired this book's heartbeat: librarians and archivists who make rooms where history can breathe, caregivers who turn a counter into a city desk at three o'clock, elders who share names, dates, smells, and songs, and readers like you who show up and listen.

If this story moved you, I hope you'll pass the light. Start your own Victory Club. It doesn't need a banner. It only needs a table, a lamp, and a list. Ask someone you love for one detail—a name, a year, what the kitchen smelled like on a good day. Ask better follow-ups. The first answer's just a handshake. Write it down. Say it aloud at dinner. We weren't brave alone, and we don't remember alone either.

Thank you for making room for Evie, Dot, and Maggie—for their laughter, their grit, and their grace. And thank you for reminding me that stories don't just preserve the past—they keep love alive. I'll be carrying them forward. I hope you will, too.

Keep the lamp on.

With love,

Buffy Andrews

APPENDIX A — BOOK CLUB QUESTIONS

1. **The Power of Friendship:** Evie, Dot, and Maggie share an extraordinary bond that lasts through decades of change. What qualities in their friendship made it so enduring? How did their individual personalities contribute to their dynamic?

2. **Historical Context:** The novel spans several decades, touching on significant events like the Civil Rights Movement, wartime struggles, and personal challenges. How does the historical backdrop influence the characters' lives and decisions? In what ways do these historical moments shape who they become?

3. **The Role of Memory:** Memory plays a significant role in the novel, especially in relation to Evie's memory loss. How do the characters navigate their pasts, and how do their memories shape their present lives? Do you think the act of remembering is empowering or limiting for them?

4. **Character Development:** Maggie, Dot, and Evie evolve in different ways throughout the story. Which character do you relate to the most, and why? Did any of the characters surprise you with their choices or actions?

5. **The Legacy of The Victory Club:** The exhibit that Maggie and Dot create is a tribute to their friendship and shared history. What do you think the exhibit represents in terms of preserving their legacies? Why is it important for their story to be shared with the next generation?

6. **Grief and Loss:** The novel delves deeply into themes of grief, particularly after Evie's passing. How do Maggie and Dot cope with the loss of their dear friend? How does their grief influence their actions in the latter part of the book?

7. **The Intersection of Generations:** Maggie, Dot, and Evie's lives span across multiple generations. What role do the younger characters, like Laura's niece, play in passing on their legacy? What does the novel say about the importance of intergenerational connections?

8. **The Ending:** The epilogue presents a sense of continuity for the characters, even after their lives are over. What did you think of the ending? How does it reflect the themes of resilience and the power of memory?

9. **Cultural and Social Change:** How do the characters navigate the shifting cultural and social landscape of their times, particularly when it comes to women's roles in society? How do they adapt, resist, or embrace change?

10. **Themes of Courage and Resilience:** What does the book suggest about courage—both big and small? How do the characters demonstrate resilience in the face of personal and historical challenges?

11. **The Title's Significance:** *The Victory Club* refers to the lifelong friendship and the shared experiences of Evie, Dot, and Maggie. How does the title reflect the themes of victory, both personal and collective, in the story?

12. **Friendship vs. Romance:** While there are elements of love and romance in the story, the central theme is the bond between these three women. How do you think the book explores the idea of friendship as the most important relationship in a person's life? Why might this be significant?

13. **Personal Reflections:** If you could sit down with any of the characters—Evie, Dot, or Maggie—what would you ask them? What advice do you think they would offer based on their experiences?

APPENDIX B — EVIE
ON TRUTH & LIFE

.

Pulled from Maggie's spiral and Evie's notebook.

- Ask better follow-ups. The first answer's just a handshake.
- Truth ages, but it doesn't die.
- Know the difference between scandal and harm.
- Let the air in first; the truths will follow.
- Burying it will cost someone something.
- Don't let them flatten us into good intentions. We had opinions.
- Write them down. Don't wait for permission.
- You can't make good trouble if you're fixing your hair.
- Listen—that's truth getting printed.
- The trees tell the truth.
- Don't let them forget us.
- We weren't brave alone.
- Lean with it.
- We learned courage in groups.
- Don't skip the parts that cost.

APPENDIX C — DOT'S PLAYLIST
THE SOUND OF TRUTH & TIME

A period-true set pulled from Dot's classroom turntable and the Sunday-morning kitchen radio, sequenced to follow the moods that shaped her life: protest, persistence, joy, loss, reunion, hope.

I. Morning / Resolve
1. "Lovely Day" — Bill Withers (1977)
2. "People Get Ready" — The Impressions (1965)
3. "Ain't No Mountain High Enough" — Diana Ross (1970)

II. Work / Classroom Hours
4. "Respect Yourself" — The Staple Singers (1971)
5. "I Wish" — Stevie Wonder (1976)
6. "Lean on Me" — Bill Withers (1972)

III. March / Movement

7. "Say It Loud – I'm Black and I'm Proud" — James Brown (1968)

8. "Inner City Blues (Make Me Wanna Holler)" — Marvin Gaye (1971)

9. "You Got to Be Ready for Love (If You Wanna Be Mine)" — The Chi-Lites (1972)

IV. Evening / Home

10. "Midnight Train to Georgia" — Gladys Knight & the Pips (1973)

11. "Let's Stay Together" — Al Green (1972)

12. "Best of My Love" — The Emotions (1977)

V. Reflection / Remembrance

13. "Someday We'll All Be Free" — Donny Hathaway (1973)

14. "Give Me Just a Little More Time" — Chairmen of the Board (1970)

15. "What's Going On" — Marvin Gaye (1971)

VI. Closing / Hope

16. "I'm Every Woman" — Chaka Khan (1978)

17. "Lovely Day (Reprise)" — Bill Withers (needle lifted, hum of the room remaining)

When asked what these songs had in common, Dot smiled and said, "They all tell the truth, just in four-four time."

The needle lifts.
The lamp stays on.

APPENDIX D — BOOK-CLUB RECIPES
FROM MAGGIE'S CARD FILE

Picked for make-ahead ease, easy transport, and scenes in the book.

Suggested Menu: Lemon Bars • Tea-Sandwich Trio • Citrus Iced Tea • Popcorn Mix • Molasses Cookies

Shopping List (Core):

Lemons (6 to 8), butter, flour, three sugars (granulated, powdered, brown), 1 dozen eggs, cream cheese, mayonnaise or yogurt, cucumber, dill, rotisserie chicken or chickpeas, curry powder, capers, sandwich bread (plus a gluten-free loaf if needed), black tea, oranges, popcorn, pretzels, nuts or seeds, dried cherries, milk or plant milk, cocoa powder, chocolate (optional).

Mrs. Thompson's Lemon Bars
Pan: 9 × 13 in. *Serves:* 16–24
Crust

- 2 cups all-purpose flour
- ½ cup powdered sugar
- ¼ teaspoon salt
- 1 cup cold unsalted butter, diced

Filling

- 1 ½ cups granulated sugar
- ¼ cup flour
- 4 large eggs
- ¾ cup fresh lemon juice
- Zest of 2 lemons
- Pinch of salt

To finish
Powdered sugar, for dusting

1. Heat oven to 350°F. Line pan with parchment, leaving an overhang.
2. Pulse or cut crust ingredients together until sandy. Press into pan. Bake 18–20 minutes, until pale golden.
3. Whisk filling until smooth. Pour over hot crust. Bake 18–22 minutes, until just set with a slight jiggle.
4. Cool completely, chill 1 hour, and dust with powdered sugar.

Make-ahead: Bake a day ahead and chill.
Tip: Cut small; offer a pinch of flaky salt for "grown-up" bites.
Pan note: Glass pans brown slowly (bake at 325°F); metal pans brown best.
Gluten-free: Use a 1:1 GF blend and add ¼ teaspoon xanthan gum if needed.

Dot & Mrs. Carter's Soft Molasses Cookies
Makes: about 30

- ¾ cup granulated sugar
- ¾ cup packed brown sugar
- ¾ cup unsalted butter, softened
- 1 large egg
- ½ cup unsulphured molasses
- 3 cups all-purpose flour
- 2 teaspoons baking soda
- 1 teaspoon ground cinnamon
- 1 teaspoon ground ginger
- ¼ teaspoon ground cloves
- ½ teaspoon salt
- Extra sugar for rolling

1. Cream sugars and butter until fluffy. Beat in egg and molasses.
2. Whisk dry ingredients; mix into wet just until combined. Chill 30–60 minutes.
3. Scoop 1-tablespoon balls, roll in sugar, place on lined sheet 2 inches apart.
4. Bake at 350°F for 8–10 minutes, until puffed and cracked on top. Cool on sheets 5 minutes; transfer to racks.

Variation: Add 1–2 teaspoons orange zest.
Storage: Airtight up to 3 days; they stay soft.

Press-Room Citrus Iced Tea
Makes 2 quarts

- 8 black tea bags
- 8 cups water
- ¼ to ½ cup sugar, to taste
- 1 strip orange peel (about 3 inches)
- 2 lemons, thinly sliced

- Fresh mint (optional)

1. Bring 4 cups water to a boil; steep tea 5 minutes. Remove bags.
2. Stir in sugar and orange peel. Add 4 cups cold water. Chill.
3. Serve over ice with lemon and mint.

Winter swap: See Press-Room Cocoa with Orange Peel.

Press-Room Cocoa with Orange Peel (Hot)
Serves 4 to 6 mugs

- 4 cups milk (or oat/almond milk)
- ¼ cup unsweetened cocoa powder
- ¼ cup sugar (or to taste)
- 4 ounces semisweet chocolate, chopped (optional)
- 1 strip fresh orange peel (about 3 inches)
- Pinch of salt
- ½ teaspoon vanilla extract

Whisk cocoa, sugar, and salt with a splash of milk to make a smooth paste. Add remaining milk, orange peel, and chocolate; warm gently, whisking, until steamy. Remove peel and stir in vanilla.

Tea-Sandwich Trio (One Filling, Three Ways)
Makes about 36 triangles
Base Mix

- 8 ounces cream cheese (or plant-based)
- 2 tablespoons mayonnaise or plain yogurt
- 1 tablespoon lemon juice
- Salt and pepper

Bread
18 slices thin white or wheat bread, crusts removed (gluten-free works).

Divide the base mix into three bowls:

1. ***Cucumber-Dill:*** ½ cup diced cucumber (patted dry) + 2 tablespoons chopped dill.
2. ***Curried Chicken or Chickpea:*** 1 cup shredded chicken or smashed chickpeas + 1 teaspoon curry powder + 2 tablespoons golden raisins.
3. ***Egg & Capers:*** 3 hard-boiled eggs, chopped + 1 tablespoon capers + pinch paprika.

Spread thinly, sandwich, press, trim crusts, and cut each into four triangles. Cover with a damp towel and chill up to 6 hours.

Ration-Book Popcorn Mix (Sweet-Salty)
Makes 12 cups

- 10 cups air-popped popcorn
- 1 cup mini pretzels
- ½ cup toasted nuts or seeds
- ½ cup dried cherries

Sweet Coating

- 3 tablespoons melted butter or coconut oil
- 2 tablespoons sugar
- 1 teaspoon cinnamon
- ½ teaspoon salt

Toss dry ingredients, drizzle with coating, and toss again.

Savory Variation: Mix 3 tablespoons melted butter with 1 teaspoon smoked paprika and ½ teaspoon salt; toss and sprinkle with ⅓ cup Parmesan while warm.

Lemon Posset Cups (No Bake)
Serves 8

- 2 cups heavy cream
- ¾ cup sugar
- Pinch of salt
- ⅓ cup fresh lemon juice
- Zest of 1 lemon

1. Bring cream, sugar, and salt to a gentle simmer for 3 minutes.
2. Remove from heat; stir in lemon juice and zest. Strain.
3. Pour into 8 small cups and chill at least 4 hours. Top with crushed shortbread or berries.

"Tomato Soup at Four" Shooters (Thermos-Friendly)
Makes about 20 small cups

- 2 tablespoons olive oil or butter
- 1 small onion, chopped
- 1 garlic clove, sliced
- 1 can (28 ounces) crushed tomatoes
- 2 cups vegetable or chicken broth
- ½ teaspoon sugar
- Salt and pepper
- ½ cup cream or coconut milk
- Fresh basil (handful) or a pinch dried

Sauté onion in oil 5–7 minutes; add garlic 30 seconds. Stir in tomatoes, broth, and sugar; simmer 10 minutes. Blend if desired. Stir in cream and basil; season. Keep warm in a thermos.

Garnish: Grilled-cheese "croutons" (cubed and toasted sandwich).

Hosting Notes for The Victory Club Party
Make-Ahead

- Lemon bars and cookies: Bake 1 day ahead.
- Posset: Chill 24–48 hours ahead.
- Tea sandwiches: Assemble morning of; keep covered with a damp towel.
- Popcorn: Mix same day for best crunch.
- Soup, cocoa, or tea: Keep warm in thermoses or a slow cooker.

Scaling for 10–14 Guests

- Lemon bars: 1 pan = about 24 small squares.
- Cookies: 1 batch = 30 (consider 1½ × batch).
- Tea sandwiches: As written = 36 triangles.
- Posset: 8 servings — double for a crowd.
- Soup shooters: 16–24 small pours.
- Drinks: Plan 8–10 ounces per person across options.

Enjoy — and save a lemon bar for the archivist in the room.

APPENDIX E — HOW TO HOST
A VICTORY CLUB NIGHT

A table. A lamp. A list. That's all you need to begin.

This gathering isn't about perfection. It's about presence, the kind of evening where the lights are soft, the stories spill, and someone remembers the smell of their grandmother's kitchen for the first time in years.

You don't need to call it a book club. Call it a *Victory Club Night* — a celebration of memory, friendship, and truth told out loud.

Setting the Scene

- **Start with the table.** Cover it with a cloth that holds history — an old quilt, a flour-sack runner, a newspaper spread open to yesterday's good news.
- **Add a lamp.** Soft light works best. The kind that warms faces and makes the air feel like it's listening.
- **Include one thing that holds a story:** a ration book, a photograph, a press badge, a recipe card, a charm bracelet, a city map.

Optional décor:

- A bowl of lemons (for Maggie).
- A small vase of cherry blossoms (for Evie).
- A stack of pencils and paper slips marked *Ask Better Questions* (for Dot).
- Vintage-style library cards for guests to write on.

Opening the Night

Cue a song from *Dot's Playlist* (Appendix C) —

♫ "Lovely Day" or "People Get Ready" make a gentle welcome.

Then, invite guests to read one favorite passage from *The Victory Club* or one line from *Evie Says* (Appendix B).

Have a notebook open for shared quotes, laughter, or moments that landed softly.

Conversation Prompts

Each guest brings three things: a name, a date, and a detail they remember.

You can start simple:

- "Who kept the lamp on for you?"
- "What did you wish you'd known?"
- "What was something small that mattered?"
- Where were you when you learned what courage felt like?"

Let the stories wander. Don't rush them. Someone will mention lemon bars; someone else will remember a song.

The Menu

Choose a few favorites from *Maggie's Recipe Box* (Appendix C):

- Lemon Bars — bright as memory.
- Tea Sandwich Trio — one filling for every kind of day.
- Ration-Book Popcorn Mix — sweet-salty truth in a bowl.
- Press-Room Citrus Iced Tea — for warmer months.

- Cocoa with Orange Peel — when the air needs comfort.

Arrange everything buffet-style with recipe cards clipped to each dish. Label the table: *Press Room Potluck.*

Activities & Keepsakes

- **Make a Memory Wall:** Pin names and moments to a corkboard or hang them from twine with clothespins.
- **Create "The Next Issue":** Have guests write short lines beginning with *"We were not brave alone when..."* Collect them into a folder labeled *Community Edition.*
- **Send guests home** with a printed bookmark or card that reads:

Keep the lamp on. Ask better questions. Tell the truth kindly.

Optional keepsake favors:

- Mini LED tealight labeled *Keep the light steady.*
- A lemon-shaped tag with *"For the archivist in the room."*
- A small envelope of seeds — *Memory blooms where you tend it.*

To Close the Night

Turn down the lights. Play *"Someday We'll All Be Free"* or *"Best of My Love."*

Have one person read the final line from *The Victory Club*:
We weren't brave alone.

Then lift your glasses — cocoa, tea, lemonade, whatever's in them — and say together:
The needle lifts. The lamp stays on.

THANK YOU FOR READING

If *The Victory Club* found its way into your heart, I'd truly love to hear from you.

You can reach me at *Buffyandrews@gmail.com* — just put "The Victory Club" in the subject line so I know it's you.

I don't love asking for reviews (it feels a little like interrupting someone mid-story), but they matter more than most people realize. Reviews and word-of-mouth are how books like this get found—how Evie, Dot, and Maggie's legacy reaches the readers who might need their courage, their humor, or their hope.

If you have a moment to leave a few words wherever you bought the book, it would mean more than I can say. You'd be helping keep their lamp lit for others.

You're welcome to visit **www.authorbuffyandrews.com** to explore more of my books, sign up for updates, or share your own Victory Club story. I treasure every message.

Thank you for reading—and for remembering that we are never brave alone.

With gratitude,
Buffy

ABOUT THE AUTHOR

Buffy Andrews is an award-winning journalist, author, and storyteller whose work celebrates the power of memory, compassion, and human connection.

For more than three decades, she chronicled real lives as a reporter, columnist, and editor—writing memoirs, obituaries, and features that preserved the voices of ordinary people with extraordinary stories. Those years spent honoring others' histories shaped her deep belief that storytelling is an act of remembrance—and that what we save, saves us in return.

She is the author of more than twenty novels across genres, including contemporary women's fiction, historical narratives, and speculative literary works. Her writing blends lyrical prose with emotional truth, exploring the threads that link people across generations.

When she isn't writing, Buffy can be found in her craft studio creating mixed-media art from found materials, or traveling the world in search of beauty, history, and stories that connect us all. Above all, she cherishes time with her family, who remain the heart of every story she tells.

She believes stories are how we keep one another alive—and that every life is worth writing down.